VOW

OF

REVENGE

BY P. RAYNE

VOW
OF
REVENGE

THE MAFIA ACADEMY

P. RAYNE

AVON

An Imprint of HarperCollins*Publishers*

VOW OF REVENGE. Copyright © 2023 by Piper Rayne. All rights reserved. Bonus epilogue copyright © 2023 by Piper Rayne. Printed in the United States of America. No part of this book may be used or reproduced in any manner whatsoever without written permission except in the case of brief quotations embodied in critical articles and reviews. For information, address HarperCollins Publishers, 195 Broadway, New York, NY 10007.

HarperCollins books may be purchased for educational, business, or sales promotional use. For information, please email the Special Markets Department at SPsales@harpercollins.com.

Originally published as *Vow of Revenge* in the United States in 2023 by Piper Rayne Incorporated. Bonus epilogue originally published online in 2023.

FIRST AVON TRADE EDITION PUBLISHED 2024.

Interior text design by Diahann Sturge-Campbell

Interior art © Oleksandr/Stock.Adobe.com

Library of Congress Cataloging-in-Publication Data has been applied for.

ISBN 978-0-06-341240-8

24 25 26 27 28 LBC 5 4 3 2 1

To all the women who won't get on their knees
for any man . . . unless he's your equal.

AUTHOR'S NOTE

This book contains references to content that may be upsetting to some readers. Trigger warnings include alcohol, attempted murder, murder, profanity, sexually explicit scenes, stalking, physical violence, and gun violence. Reader discretion is advised.

PLAYLIST

Here's a list of songs that inspired us while we were writing *Vow of Revenge*.

Blood in the Cut – K. Flay
Tear You Apart – She Wants Revenge
Ghosts – The Acid
A Forest – The Cure
High Enough – K. Flay
World in My Eyes – Depeche Mode
Closer – Nine Inch Nails
Fascination Street – The Cure
The Hand That Feeds – Nine Inch Nails
Red Right Hand – Nick Cave & The Bad Seeds
The Killing Moon – Echo & the Bunnymen
Liability – Lorde
when the party's over – Billie Eilish
Love Song – The Cure

SICURO ACADEMY — ITALIAN CRIME FAMILIES

Northeast Territory

Specializes in running weapons
Marcelo Costa
(head of the Costa crime family)

Southeast Territory

Specializes in counterfeit rings and embezzlement schemes
Antonio La Rosa
(next in line to run the La Rosa crime family)

Southwest Territory

Specializes in drug trafficking and money laundering
Dante Accardi
(next in line to run the Accardi crime family)

Northwest Territory

Specializes in securities fraud and cyber-warfare
Gabriele Vitale
(next in line to run the Vitale crime family)

VOW
OF
REVENGE

CHAPTER ONE
MIRABELLA

Nothing ruins a perfect day like your dead fiancé showing up in the middle of your first college class.

I don't pay attention when someone knocks on the door, but when all my classmates gasp, my curiosity piques and I look up from my papers toward the open classroom door. My jaw falls open and I do a double take, blinking. Marcelo Costa stands in the doorway—alive.

Marcelo Costa, the man who was to be the head of the Costa crime family.

Marcelo Costa, the man my father arranged for me to marry.

Marcelo Costa, the man who was buried three months ago.

A little toddler tantrum voice screams in my head, "Damn it to hell, he's going to ruin everything."

"Can I help you?" Professor Edwards tilts her head down to look at Marcelo from above the rim of her glasses.

"Marcelo Costa. Late transfer." He breaks the distance with his usual confident air and hands her a note.

I swear all the girls track his movements, each one growing a little wetter between her thighs. There's no denying Marcelo Costa is the most stunning specimen most will ever see in person.

I'm reeling from shock when he turns and meets my gaze. Until his stupid cocky smirk spreads across his face, replacing my shock with annoyance.

Sofia whips her head in my direction. "What the hell is he doing here?"

The horrified expression on my best friend's face probably matches mine. She knows exactly what this means for me.

Marcelo's resurrection threatens my very presence at the Sicuro Academy. Before he was "killed," I was expected to marry him and be the dutiful Mafia wife. Stay at home, pop out a few kids—crossing my fingers they're boys—while he went out and did whatever or whoever he wished.

Fuck that.

I'm more than a piece of arm candy at church on Sundays and holidays. I have just as much to offer the family business as any of the guys sitting in this classroom.

Sicuro Academy was a boys-only school until five years ago, but even now that girls are allowed to attend, we still need the permission of our fathers or husbands to do so. Basically, the patriarchy decides if we're allowed to make more of ourselves than being a wife or mother.

And during the little get-together in which our families made our betrothal official last spring, Marcelo made it very clear—he wants a good little wife at home.

Heaven forbid that we learn how to launder money or win in a street fight or hack computers and make bombs like the guys do when they're here. Why would we want the opportunity to move up the ranks like the guys when we're not even in the ranks to begin with? It's infuriating.

"Take a seat," Professor Edwards says.

Marcelo scans the classroom, ignoring the only empty seat. Instead, he walks down the aisle and stops at the desk beside me.

"Get out," he demands of the guy sitting there.

I've only been on campus for a few days, so I don't know the guy's name, but from his bright-red hair, I'd bet he's part of the Irish Mafia.

The guy stares Marcelo down, presumably deciding whether Marcelo is worth taking on. If he asked any of us from the East Coast, we'd tell him hell no. Marcelo Costa is one mean motherfucker, and though he might not be able to make the guy pay right now, here in this classroom or even on this campus, he'd figure out a way in due time.

Irish Boy seems to figure this out too, because he scurries to pack up his things and moves to the empty desk a few rows over.

Marcelo slides into the empty seat and looks at me, his dark eyes intense. "Ciao, fidanzata."

He's lucky the Sicuro Academy is considered neutral ground, otherwise I'd likely leap over this desk and strangle him to death.

Everyone else in class turns their attention back to Professor Edwards when they see us in a stare-off. No one wants to be on Marcelo's bad side. But I don't care. His existence almost ruined my life once. I won't let it happen again.

* * *

CLASS DRAGS ON, Marcelo's eyes on me the majority of the time. When class is over, I stand, rushing to collect my things and get the hell out of here.

Today was supposed to be fun and exciting. My first day of classes and a fresh start toward the future I'm building for myself. Now, the black hole that is the future my father and fiancé want for me is sucking me back in.

Sofia waits for me, and as I'm about to walk out with her, Marcelo grips my wrist.

"Everyone out." His eyes remain on me. He doesn't even double-check that everyone followed his order because he knows they did.

Stronzo.

I yank my wrist from his grip. "I thought you were dead." I hike my backpack higher on my shoulder.

"Aw . . ." He steps closer and tucks a strand of my long, dark hair behind my ear. "Did you mourn me, dolcezza?"

Marcelo is so close, it's almost unnerving how good-looking he is. His hair is the same length as the hair of his beard, both shaved close. And his intense dark eyes are encased by long eyelashes most women would kill for. He's tall with wide shoulders and lean muscle covers his body. He has on the school uniform—gray dress pants with a white button-down and a tie that matches my skirt of red, white, and green plaid. Of course, he's not wearing the suit jacket because he has to do something to buck the system. If I'm really honest, being this close to him affects me in the complete opposite way that an enemy should. I have to remind myself he wants to trap me in a life I don't want.

"I'm serious, Marcelo. Everyone thought . . ."

He tilts his head, studying me. "Not everyone."

I scowl at him. "What does that mean?"

"My nonno knew I was alive."

I sputter for a moment. But his grandfather attended the funeral. He talked to me and told me what a shame it was that Marcelo died so young because we would have made beautiful babies and that our union would have solidified the bond between the Costas and the La Rosas.

Marcelo's family controls the Northeast part of the United States, while the La Rosas control the Southeast portion of the country. While his family's expertise is in running weapons, my family specializes in counterfeit rings and embezzlement schemes. Uniting the two families would fulfill our fathers' desire for more power and Marcelo's family's need for more ports down the coastline to run their weapons, giving my father a piece of the profits in return.

"I don't understand." My hand squeezes the backpack strap. "Is your father really dead?"

Supposedly, a car bomb killed Marcelo and his father, Sam Costa.

His mouth presses into a thin line and he nods. "He's dead."

"I'm sorry." And I honestly mean my condolences, even though I hate the man and the future role he sees me in. But losing my father would crush me, not to mention Marcelo is only twenty-one. Is he ready to take over as head of the family?

He shrugs and stares at me for another unnerving beat. I fidget under his scrutiny.

"Were you even in the car when it exploded?" My gaze runs up and down his fit body. People saw him near the car, but they didn't see him escape. Shouldn't he have burn marks? "You don't look any different."

Again, his mouth thins. "No. We can talk about all that later."

"When? When the car arrives to take me home? You can forget it, Marcelo. I won't leave the academy." My voice grows louder as I think about the bags I unpacked last week and imagine them packed and put in some limo with him in the back seat.

He chuckles, and it's entirely patronizing. As if it's cute that I think I have any agency over my own life.

He looks around the room and back at me. "For now, you can stay. It's not safe for either of us out there until I figure out who killed my father. We were able to figure out that the bomb was detonated using a computer program, but I don't know who set the bomb or who wrote the program."

"Too bad they didn't do a better job."

His eyes dance with enjoyment, as if it's humorous that I wish him dead. "I'm going to enjoy getting to know you better, amore. Since we're classmates *and* dorm mates now."

I mask my reaction when I really want to knee him in the balls.

The Roma House is coed, but males and females have separate floors. Have to preserve all the girls' virtue somehow, right? If Marcelo thinks he'll be slipping into my room after dark, I'll be introducing him to my knee for sure.

Under any other circumstances, I would welcome a man like Marcelo into my bed—hot, powerful, and knows his way around a woman's pussy. But the fact that he thinks he has a right to be there?

No way.

"Sorry. Consider this our official breakup. I'm not marrying you."

He looks nonplussed by my words, running his pointer finger slowly down my cheek. "And what would your father think of that?"

I open my mouth to berate him, but the classroom door whips open.

Marcelo flips his head in anger, and I'm reminded he is still a man to be feared. But his expression quickly changes. The smile softens his hard features as if he's just a regular college student— easygoing and affable and not poised to be the head of a major crime family.

I follow his vision. Sure as hell, his cousin Giovanni and Marcelo's best friends, Nicolo and Andrea, rush into the room. Based on the way their mouths hang ajar, they're just as surprised as I am he's here in the flesh.

I push past the three guys hugging and pumping fists with Marcelo.

"Fidanzata?" Marcelo calls when I've almost cleared the doorway.

I stop and look over, the word fiancée causing me to inwardly scream. All four sets of eyes are on me. "What?"

"We'll pick this back up tonight."

I roll my eyes and walk out the door. But I can't run forever. He knows where to find me.

CHAPTER TWO
MARCELO

"What the fuck?" Giovanni shoves my chest with both hands, his initial smile on seeing me wiped clean from his face.

Andrea's eyes shoot wide open. Their joy and relief at finding out I wasn't blown up didn't last nearly as long as I'd hoped. I knew after the surprise wore off, they'd be pissed I allowed them to think I was dead for three months.

"Sorry," Giovanni immediately spits out when I stare at him. I'll give him this one transgression given the circumstances. He might be my cousin, but nobody touches me like that. "I'm just so . . . fuck, man. We thought you were dead."

Nicolo and Andrea nod.

"We need details," Andrea says.

They're not getting any. Nicolo and Andrea are my two best friends, but that doesn't mean I trust them. Especially now, after someone set out to kill the head and next in line of the Costa crime family. They succeeded with my father, but I refuse to give anyone another chance at me. Revenge is my only concern now. I may have lost a lot of respect for my father over the past few years, but no one wipes out a member of my family without paying for it.

The new students file in with a new professor, who instructs us to get to our next class.

"Fill us in later," Nicolo says, and he and Andrea jog down the hall while Giovanni and I casually walk to our next class.

"Since when are they teacher's pet?" I ask my cousin.

The only reason all four of us graduated high school was because of our name. We held the record for ditch days, but the principal was too scared of our dads to discipline us. Plus, he probably wanted us out of the high school anyway.

He grins. "You missed orientation, but you'll learn that lateness isn't allowed here. Too many absences and you're kicked out."

I laugh.

Giovanni stops and nods. "I'm dead serious. Your—*our* name doesn't mean anything here."

I doubt that very much, but then again, I never planned on coming to this pathetic school where we pretend we're in kindergarten and play safe. I still feel naked without my guns and knives. Especially when I see the other Mafias' and politicians' kids here.

The Sicuro Academy was founded three decades ago by the Italian Mafia after a series of bloodbaths over territory. Huge numbers of up-and-coming Mob men were wiped out. The heads of the families had the brilliant idea to found a school on what would be considered neutral territory—a small plot of land nestled in the middle of the country in Vitale territory but accepted as a law unto its own.

Four Italian crime families run the United States. My family, the Costas, run the Northeast, while Mirabella's father and his family, the La Rosas, run the Southeast. The Vitales have control of the Southwest and the Accardis the Northwest. And here at the Sicuro Academy, they can all send their children when they are eighteen without having to worry that we'll blow each other's heads off since there's a zero-violence policy—and no weapons allowed unless we're in fight class.

Eventually, the board let in other Mob families like the Irish and the Russians, even cartel members. Then they really went low and let in politicians' kids because it made financial sense to do so. Everyone's astronomical tuition to attend pads the pockets of the

four founding families, so it made sense to let in our enemies—
giving us the ability to know who was up-and-coming in their ranks.

"So? Are you going to tell me?" Giovanni asks, pulling me from
my thoughts.

"What?" I walk out of the building, even though my second class
starts right now on the second floor. We'll see how much weight my
family name carries here.

"How the hell you're alive and why I'm finding out with every
other fucking person?"

The anger in his voice doesn't surprise me. Of course, he's hurt.
He's like my brother. After his mom and dad died in a car accident
where another car pushed theirs off a bridge, my family took him
in because that's what family does.

I scour the immediate area as we jog down the stairs. "Where
can we talk?"

He nods to the right and I follow him away from the building.
Even trusting Giovanni is hard right now. He has his reasons why he
might want me dead too. Nonno told me to be skeptical of everyone—
including Giovanni. Without a gun or a knife on me, I only have my
bare hands to kill a man. Which has never been a problem.

Giovanni leads us to the metal rod fence that traps us in this
Harry Potter–like school—except they're training us to be crim-
inals, not hone our magic. Hell, I'm enrolled in a knife fighting
class. That's got to be a joke.

"This is about the farthest we can get on this side of campus.
Watch for any guards who might pass us."

The main part of the campus, where the school and all the boarding houses are located, is surrounded by metal fencing, but beyond
that are hundreds of acres of rolling landscape, barren except for
grass and the odd tree. No one can see the campus, let alone have
any idea what goes on here from the main country road that leads
here.

Giovanni pulls out a pack of cigarettes and lights up, blowing smoke out the side of his mouth. "So, how'd you escape death?"

"I'm a lucky bastard, I guess." I pause before telling my story, changing a few things here and there so Giovanni doesn't know the entire truth. "My dad summoned me to his yacht anchored in New York. Supposedly we were gonna talk about my upcoming wedding to Mirabella and binding our family with the La Rosas. It was late, I was annoyed, and he made me wait while he finished fucking his whore. He came out dressed in his silk robe tied below his protruding stomach."

Giovanni chuckles, but the image in my head disgusts me. I never understood how my father could walk around as if he was Mr. Olympia. If people didn't fear for their lives around him and he didn't have so much money and power, he'd just be an overweight, middle-aged man.

"Silve, his latest piece, strutted out five minutes later wearing her own silk robe."

She was just like the rest—a gold-digging whore who'd suck my father's cock for a chance to be on his arm. But I don't think Silve realized how things are done in our family.

I had a mother sitting in the mansion she shared with my father. And after he was done with Silve, he would go home to my mom. Always. And forever. Divorce isn't an option in our family. It messes with business and loyalties, so there's always an understanding. My mom probably knew my dad was there that night. At the very least, she knew he was fucking someone else—and quite frankly, she probably preferred it that way.

"Silve? She came to your father's funeral," Giovanni says, blowing smoke out of his mouth.

"She was the gutsiest of them all. That's for sure." We continue walking the path. "Anyway, he got a call. Answered it and I heard him say we'll be there in ten, then he disappeared back into the yacht."

I think back to what happened next, as I've done a thousand times before. Wondering if there's something I've missed, some clue as to who was responsible.

Silve sat across from me and opened her legs to give me a glimpse of her shaved pussy. "So, Marcelo, I heard you're marrying that La Rosa girl."

I never understood why Silve was around us so much. My father was letting his guard down around her, thinking she was a stupid whore who knew nothing. It was shameless how lazy he'd become.

I nodded. "I am."

"She's very beautiful." Her robe opened and the swell of her tits was visible.

Gesù Cristo. Did she think I'd share her with my father?

"She is." I stood and downed the rest of my scotch.

"Well, you know where to come when she's not in the mood." She leaned across the table, picked up a grape, and slowly sucked it into her mouth.

Thankfully, my father came out then, saving me from putting his whore in her place. He bent and kissed her cheek, but she tugged him down, pressing her lips to his, sticking her tongue down his throat while her eyes remained on me. My dad slid his hand into her robe, squeezed her tit, and she moaned, took his hand, and guided it down between her legs.

My dad growled. "Stay wet for when I get back. I'm going to fuck you until dawn." He allowed her to stand with the robe completely open now.

I turned my back, not interested in seeing any more of this bullshit.

"Marcelo, turn around," my father dictated. "You're not a child anymore."

I slowly turned and he stood behind Silve, his hands on her tits before sliding down to between her thighs. She had an amazing body, but it did nothing for me.

"Anytime you want to borrow Silve, you have my permission."

Silve smiled and pushed out her tits, whining that she didn't want him to leave. He gave her one last kiss and she rubbed his cock over his pants, making sure he was hard when he left. "I'll be waiting to suck this cock dry."

My dad groaned and stepped back. "Damn, woman, what you do to me." He looked up at me. "She's insatiable and can take it rough. How did I get so blessed in this life?" He smacked my back, and I followed him up the ramp, our guards trailing behind us.

I had no idea why my father was offering me Silve, but I believe a small piece of him knew I resented him for the other women, and he wanted me to sink down to his level to ease his own guilt.

"And?" Giovanni needs more.

I realize I've gone off on a tangent with the whole Silve thing, but it disgusted me—offering me his sloppy seconds of a whore while my mom was at home alone. He was the asshole of the century. I've never understood why married men who have the perfect woman at home dig some puttana out of the trenches to give their time and attention to.

"We got into the car and drove to a warehouse I wasn't familiar with. I questioned my dad about it, but he wouldn't say much. We walked in, and although my dad didn't have his hand on his gun, my hand was on mine. It felt like a trap. We wound down the hallways and I heard some shouting that got louder the farther we went. When we stepped into the room, hundreds of people were there, swarming around a makeshift circle. He'd brought me to an underground fight."

"Remember when you wanted to fight at sixteen?" Giovanni laughs.

"The training made me faster." I pull the cigarette from his fingers, take a pull, then flick it at him.

He dodges it then pats my shoulder. "That it did, brother."

"My dad leads me to the guy who's obviously in charge of these events—his guard has the money, and he's screaming out rules and talking to the guys fighting before they start. After one guy was beaten to a bloody pulp but still standing, the fight was called, and we were ushered into a back room. My dad introduced me to the guy and informed him that I'd be the one in charge now."

Giovanni laughs. "Bet he liked that."

"We both looked at him like he was crazy. I wasn't going into underground fighting again. The guy was pissed, but he must've owed my father a shit ton of money. The idiot lost it, and my dad's guards held him back while my dad kicked the shit outa him. He couldn't fight back because his arms were held behind his back."

"That's not a fun way to fight." Giovanni snickers.

I couldn't agree with him more. But my dad didn't just like pussy, he very often was one. "Agreed. Anyway, by the time we left, my dad's white button-down shirt was covered in blood. Thankfully, I wore black."

I always wore black because I wasn't a fucking idiot. You never knew when you might have to get another man's blood on you.

"We left, and when we got close to making it outside, a mob of people swarmed out of the place. A brawl had broken out, and yeah, we were armed, but we had no idea what these people had and there were only four of us there—two guards, my dad, and me. Besides, who knew if there were any undercover cops in the crowd? That idiot running the place didn't exactly have the tightest security. I couldn't go dropping bodies. My dad's guards rushed him to the car while I fought, eventually making it close to the car—then it blew up."

"Fuck." He pushes his hand through his hair and his light-blue eyes widen.

"My dad and his driver were inside, along with his two guards. I fled the minute the screams started and chaos broke out. I didn't know if someone wanted me or him dead or both, so I went to

Nonno's. He insisted I keep the fact that I was alive a secret until we knew who was responsible. 'The time for retribution will come,' he said."

We arrive back where we began our walk. I have no idea how in hell I'm not gonna feel like a caged rat in this place. I'm not used to the word no.

I notice Mirabella sitting at a table by the trees, talking with Sofia. Silve was right, she is beautiful—but she's a pain in the ass.

"And what will you do with her?" Giovanni lights another cigarette and nods in my fiancée's direction.

"Marry her, of course."

He shakes his head. "Why can't you ever take the easy route?"

"Because I'm a Costa, that's why. The arrangement was set. If I go back on it now, it will only show weakness and deny us what we gain from the marriage."

I begin the walk over to my fiancée, who has her back to me, Giovanni still at my side. It's about time we figure out this shit between us. But I'm interrupted by a teacher walking toward me, waving a slip. Her small heels don't allow her to reach me as fast as she's trying.

My lips quirk up in a smirk.

"Are you Marcelo Costa?" She crosses her arms. She's about five-two with dark hair that's pulled back, wisps of gray on the sides, and must weigh next to nothing. She pushes up her glasses on her nose.

I could crush her as easily as stepping on an ant. "That would be me."

"You missed my class, Mr. Costa. Therefore, you're on dish duty tonight." She hands me a slip and turns on her small heel.

"Did you know that punishments are domestic tasks here? Don't forget to use Dawn so you don't have dishpan hands." Giovanni walks off with a laugh.

The bastard knows the rules because while I was studying under my father for two years after Nonno got kidney disease, Giovanni's been living in a bubble here.

My eyes catch Mirabella's as she looks over her shoulder at me. Hers are cold and distant. Either the woman has been trained to hide her fear, or she's not afraid of me.

Well, she'll be afraid of me when I'm done with her.

CHAPTER THREE

MIRABELLA

What a shit day. All anyone talked about was how Marcelo wasn't actually dead.

This was supposed to be one of the best days of my life, not the most depressing. Somehow, today is even worse than the night my dad told me I would wed into the Costa family. Maybe because then I thought I would figure a way out. But the man just resurrected himself from death. How can I compete with that?

Marcelo has a reputation—cold, cruel, vicious, and a ladies' man—but none of that bothers me as much as if I marry him, my fate is sealed and I'm destined to be another Mafia wife who deliberately turns a blind eye to the kind of man her husband really is.

No part of me wants that life for myself and I refuse to accept it.

Attending Sicuro Academy was supposed to be my foot in the door, my first step toward being able to participate in the world I grew up in. The men in my world might think women are only useful as the Madonna or the whore, but we have a lot more to offer.

I want to be in the mix as much as my older brother, Antonio, is afforded. And why shouldn't I be? I'm smart, capable, and cunning, though no one knows quite how much because when I popped out without a penis, they shoved me in a category. I'm done being relegated to the shadows only to be pulled off the shelf for Sunday dinners, weddings, and christenings.

The women in our world, especially my generation, have fought for and earned the right to attend the Sicuro Academy for years. Finally, women are allowed to attend, and I got a blessed late admission because my fiancé had been murdered. Even then, my parents only agreed to allow me to attend if Sofia came with me. I'd hoped that by attending, I'd be able to prove my worth to my father and he'd give up the idea of an arranged marriage for me, seeing me as having more to offer than a strategic marriage. But now that Marcelo's very much alive, he can send me home to wait until he finishes here and there isn't anything I can do about it.

My stomach rumbles like the beginning of a thunderstorm as my last class ends.

I step out of the building and onto the winding path that works its way across campus to the dorms. Trees line the pathway and the leaves rustle as they sway in the breeze.

When I pass a few girls with green, orange, and white plaid in their pleated school uniform skirts, I look away. We may all live on campus together, but we stick to our own and barely tolerate the other factions.

It's about a ten-minute walk to the Roma building, but the fresh air does me good. Each faction has its own building since mixing the Italians, Irish, Russians, and cartel members is a recipe for disaster—even in a place where no weapons are allowed and no violence is the absolute law. The founding fathers of Sicuro arranged it that way because although we're allowed to play with one another here, as soon as we leave, we'll be gunning for each other's territory and will kill to claim it.

The walk lets me clear my head and consider how I'm going to handle Marcelo's reappearance. I wonder if my father already heard the news. We don't have access to the outside world here. Our personal cell phones and computers are confiscated the moment we step onto campus, and in return, we're given cell phones that will only allow us to text or call other people on campus. We each get one outside call a week, on Sundays. Even the internet is locked down. We can use it in the computer lab, but it's like living in some regime state where they control your access to information. Basically, we can only see what the administration allows.

The old-world charm of the stone-and-ivy-covered building belies the modern interior of the Roma House. When I showed up a week ago to move in, I was surprised at just how modern the inside was. Though knowing the net worth of all the students who attend here, perhaps it shouldn't be that much of a surprise. Tuition and donations have obviously gone a long way in keeping up with a changing society over the decades.

My phone buzzes in my pocket as I approach the tall, arched doors that lead inside. I pull the phone from my bag to find a text from Sofia.

> **SOFIA:** Stopping at Café Ambrosia on my way back. You want anything?

Every dorm room has dual occupancy, and Sofia and I share a room.

> **ME:** Sure, grab me a Biscotti Frappuccino?

> **SOFIA:** Will do.

I shove my phone back in my bag and head into the building, making my way to the elevator. As I'm crossing the lounge, I spot a familiar face. He's sitting on one of the chairs and talking to one of the other house residents. My ex-boyfriend's eyes light up when he sees me, and he ends his conversation quickly and walks over to me.

Lorenzo Bruni and I dated until shortly after it was arranged that I marry Marcelo. More accurately, we sneaked around behind our parents' backs for a year.

Everyone knew I would be promised to someone. I'd seen it happen to other girls in our world over the years. We're simply a bargaining chip for rich and powerful men. I was never permitted to date anyone so as not to soil my reputation or my body. The purer I was, the more I would be worth after all.

What a load of shit.

So when Lorenzo flirted with me last fall when he was home for a long weekend from the academy and made it clear he was interested, I saw him as my one shot to do something rebellious and something that I had full control over. And so every long weekend, Christmas, or Easter break, I'd see him in secret. I'd considered taking up with him again when I found out I'd be able to attend school here this year, but I wasn't sure if I wanted to. It's not like I was madly in love with him when we were sneaking around, but he was a nice distraction.

"Hey, can we talk?" he says when he reaches me.

I glance around for anyone from the Costa Mafia family, but don't see anyone. "I can't talk right now. I'll text you when I can sneak away."

He frowns, the lines carving deep into his forehead. "I heard Marcelo crawled back up from the grave."

I start toward the elevator again and he walks alongside me.

"I told you I can't talk right now," I whisper.

"Just tell me what this means for us."

I reach the elevator and stab the up button. "I don't even know what it means for me, Lorenzo. Let me at least figure that part out before I have to make you feel better about it."

The elevator door dings and opens, revealing an empty box. I step in, and when I turn around, I realize if there's anyone who has taken this turn of events as hard as me, it's Lorenzo.

"I promise I'll text you and we can meet, okay? But it might be a few days before I get sorted."

His lips are still pointing downward, but he nods as the doors slide closed.

"Fuck!" I shout as the elevator rises to the fifth floor. Marcelo's appearance is messing with my life and he's been back for less than twelve hours.

The elevator dings, the doors slide open, and I'm hit in the chest with a football.

"Merda, my bad," the guy closest to me says.

What are guys even doing on our floor anyway?

The other guy playing catch grins and saunters down the hall toward me. Him, I know. Dante Accardi. Next in line to the throne in the Southwest part of the country.

I pick up the football that landed at my feet and toss it to the first guy, then rub my chest. Because that fucking hurt.

"I can kiss it better, Mira," Dante says with a healthy dose of innuendo.

"An apology would be nice enough." I cross my arms.

He chuckles but of course doesn't give one.

The elevator dings behind me, but I pay it no mind because whomever it is can walk around me. There's no way I'm backing down against this prick.

Clearly Dante can tell, and he says, "You'd have to beg, and while you're on your knees, there's something else you can do while you're down there."

My eyes narrow. It's been made very clear that not every guy is excited that women were let into their little boys' club five years ago, and the ones who don't seem to mind only appear to want one thing from us. As if they granted us admission so that we could be their little playthings.

I open my mouth to give a rebuttal, but before I can, Dante's mouth drops open and I hear *his* voice behind me.

"I hope I didn't just hear you suggest that my fiancée drop to her knees and suck your cock, stronzo?" The barely contained rage in Marcelo's voice rings in my ears.

Being in the presence of the man who represents the loss of my freedom is almost worth it to witness the look on Dante's face. He's clearly the one person who hasn't heard the news that Marcelo is still alive.

"The only man she falls to her knees for is me." He clasps the back of my neck, but I wrench away from him.

"Fuck you."

Marcelo smirks. "Try not to be so impatient, dolcezza. All in good time."

I growl, clench my fists, and stomp down the hall, shoulder pushing my way past Dante. Let these two assholes work it out. I don't care if they beat each other to death. They'd both be doing me a favor.

I unlock my door and enter my room, angrily tossing my bag on my bed.

The room is bigger than most dorm rooms I've seen on TV and in movies. And we have our own private bathroom, which is a bonus, even if there's still a urinal in there.

I flop down on one of our two armchairs, frustrated beyond belief, unable to believe how much my life has changed in the span of hours. Everything I thought was within reach is now being snatched away from me.

A heavy knock on the door sounds and I ignore it, knowing exactly who it is. It sounds again and again, and I continue to ignore it. Less than a minute after the pounding stops, the door whips open and slams against the wall.

I stare at Marcelo, dwarfing the open doorway. The bastard picked the lock.

"What do you want?"

He steps in and slams the door. "I have something of yours."

I scoff. "You don't have anything I want, I can assure you." I stand to hold my own with him.

His dark eyes take me in from head to foot, and I fight not to squirm under his perusal. "You'll take it just the same." He breaches the distance until he's in front of me, standing with his hand out.

My forehead wrinkles and I look at his open palm. Nestled almost delicately in his big, brutal hand is my five-carat cushion-cut engagement ring.

"You're out of your mind if you think I'm wearing that." I cross my arms and walk to the other side of the room, away from him and his admittedly alluring scent. I don't know what kind of cologne he's wearing, but it's divine, which is a word I refuse to associate with this man.

He follows me until my back is pressed against the wall. "You mistake me, principessa. I'm not asking." The glint in his eyes dares me to refuse him.

Challenge accepted.

"You say that like I care."

Without warning, his hand locks around my neck, squeezing gently. Not enough to hurt me, but enough to make it clear that he could if he wanted to.

I stare him straight in his dark eyes.

The corner of his mouth tips up at my refusal to be cowed. "Careful, I find I like it when you fight back." He strokes his thumb up and down my jugular and my traitorous nipples tighten.

What is wrong with me?

"Go to hell." I pucker my lips and spit right in his face.

A flash of rage sears his face, and he wipes off my saliva with the back of his hand. "That's the one and only time I'll allow you to disrespect me. Consider it an engagement gift. The next time, I'll put you over my knee and spank you like an insolent child."

Why does that image make my core ache?

"Oh." He arches an eyebrow and gently brushes his knuckles over my hard nipples poking through my white button-down shirt. "Principessa likes that."

I suck in a breath.

My door opens, but I can't see since Marcelo is so much bigger than me. He obstructs my view.

"Oh shit," Sofia says.

Marcelo's dark gaze locks with mine before his free hand goes to my left one and slides his ring onto my finger. The hand wrapped around my neck twitches when he does. "If I find you without it, I'll superglue it to your finger."

Tears well in my eyes as what feels like a brand around my finger burns. But I won't let the tears fall. "You're an asshole."

He drops his hand from my neck and chuckles. "I'm *your* asshole. Don't forget who you belong to."

He turns and stalks out of the room.

The entire time I watch him go, I vow that I will never belong to anyone but myself, no matter what I have to do to make it happen.

CHAPTER FOUR
MARCELO

Six o'clock, a stampede of students hustle down the hall toward the elevators. I glance out of my room, unsure what the hell is going on. Some impatient students push open the steel doors to the stairs, not wanting to wait.

"Dinner." Giovanni nods to me as he walks past.

I have my own room because of who I am. Apparently, all guys who are next in line to be in charge also have their own rooms. Giovanni tried to move in with me, but I threw him and his shit out. I'm still figuring out how to get a king bed delivered here.

I shut my door and lock it, stepping in line with Giovanni.

He nods to the scrawny guy next to him. "This is my roommate, Domenico Accardi."

"Dante's little brother?" I ask, appraising him. The poor kid doesn't stand a chance. I could break him over my knee like a twig. He must be a freshman.

"Yeah," he says, barely above a whisper.

"Your brother got lucky—I almost beat his ass today." My molars grind together when I think of what he said to my fiancée.

Giovanni quirks an eyebrow. "I can only assume . . ."

"He said some fucked-up shit to Mirabella."

Domenico groans. "You should kill him. I'd consider it a favor."

Huh. Maybe I underestimated this kid.

Giovanni and I laugh, although mine dies shortly because it's not lost on me that one of my own could be trying to get rid of me. Is it a family member who wants to be next in line?

My uncle Joey has always been power hungry. He got our club raided when he was being too liberal around a girl, talking on his phone to my father while thinking she was just getting dressed to leave. Amateur mistake. Nonno sent him away for a month after that one. Maybe Joey is seeking revenge.

"You're thinking pretty hard over there," Giovanni whispers as we walk through the courtyard.

The other groups file out of their designated dorms. The Irish, the Russians, the goddamn cartel. I can't help looking them up and down while they all whisper and check me out.

I never wanted to come here. Why would I? To become friends with my enemy? I get why the Sicuro Academy was built, but it's not for everyone in our industry. Not the ones who are up in the ranks, bound to take over. I happen to be one of them, but Nonno and I agree I need to be here to gather intel about who acted against my father and me.

"We all eat together?" I ask.

Giovanni nods. "They're all about inclusion."

When we reach the doors of the dining hall, some cartel members stop in front of us, lining the doorway shoulder to shoulder, blocking our way.

"Juan Carlos, what the hell do you think you're doing?" Giovanni asks.

I cross my arms and stare them down.

"I just wanted to welcome our new student to the academy." He steps closer to me, and I peer down at him. "Just a little warning now that you're head of your family. Stay out of our business."

"I have no interest in your business." I try to remain calm, but I'm growing impatient and anxious to fight someone, if only for the fact I'm stuck here under someone else's rules.

"I just want to make sure since your father didn't."

I step closer, pushing my chest toward him. "That sounds a lot like a threat. Did you kill my father?"

He laughs and all of his men step forward as if looking for a fight. I cock my arm back, ready to flatten him, but Giovanni grabs it and lowers it, eyeing someone in the doorway.

"Gentlemen, is there a problem?" The chancellor, a man in his midfifties with sandy-colored hair, comes out and purposely walks between us and the cartel members.

A ring of "No, sirs" sounds around us and again, I'm struck by how unbelievable this place is.

"Good. Now go eat."

The cartel guys go into the dining hall and I move to a spot under a tree, motioning Giovanni and Domenico over.

"How are there not any fights here?"

Giovanni laughs. "It's in the paperwork we signed. You'll get kicked out. They have a three-strike system . . . did you not read it?"

I shake my head. "Nonno said there was no choice. I needed to be here, so I just signed it. But those assholes are asking for it."

"You have to keep your cool, Marcelo. I'm telling you, the chancellor doesn't mess around." Giovanni's face says it all. There isn't much leeway here and I better remember that so I can stay here long enough to find out who planned my murder.

I catch sight of Mirabella walking into the dining hall with her friend Sofia. Her short plaid skirt shows off her long legs that, at some point, will be wrapped around my waist. Her brother is a few steps back. I met him the day my father and Mirabella's father decided on our arranged marriage.

Antonio is in the same position I was in before my father died. Next in line and already in charge of a lot of the facets of his family's companies and crew. Our eyes catch and he detours away from his sister over to where Giovanni is lecturing me about taking the rules here seriously because they aren't afraid to enforce them. When did he become such a pussy?

"Costa." Antonio puts out his hand, a few of his guys huddled around him.

I take the hand he's offering. "Hey, Antonio. Good to see you."

"Thought you were dead." Always a straight shooter, Antonio. Our hands release and he shoves his in the pockets of his pants.

The guys behind him say nothing to me—nor should they. Giovanni isn't putting his hand out to Antonio either.

"So did your sister, though she seems the most upset to find out her fiancé is alive and well."

He matches my scowl. "Well, she should be grateful. I'll talk to her—"

"No need, Antonio. She's mine now, so I'm sure we'll see eye to eye soon." I grin wickedly.

"Well, should she be a problem, just let me know."

I nod. "I will."

We shake hands again and he heads toward the dining hall.

"He's on the third floor of our dorm if you need him in the future," Giovanni says.

"I can handle my fiancée. I don't need her big brother dealing with it on my behalf. She'll come to heel."

I don't mention how I enjoy the fight Mirabella puts up—it'll make it that much better when I break her. I've never wanted to marry a woman who just says yes and cows to me all the time. I do, however, want a wife who wants to be with me and wasn't over the moon when she found out I was murdered, but there's an attraction between Mirabella and me, and that's a starting point. Even if Mirabella wants to fight it. We have a spark that most arranged marriages don't have. Her body yearns for me, and I love watching her fight herself to keep her hands off me.

"If you say so." Giovanni clasps me on the shoulder. "Have fun doing the dishes."

Just as he says that the woman from earlier, who's standing at the doors with her arms crossed, spots me. "Mr. Costa, I figured I should make sure you report to the kitchen." She turns on her librarian-type shoes, expecting me to follow.

Giovanni laughs, heading toward the tables.

There's no way I'll do the dishes. Once the woman—who I discover is Professor Gardner—leaves to have dinner with the faculty, I find the first kid from the Costa crime family whose dad is low in the ranks and tell him to do my job.

I head into the dining hall and see that the Costa crime family sits in the far-right corner. Giovanni is there with Nicolo and Andrea, among others. I scour the rest of the area, finding Mirabella with Sofia and that Lorenzo Bruni piece of shit. My jaw clenches and I storm across the room.

Her back is to me, and the table of my friends spots me first, each elbowing one another to watch the show I'm about to give. I slide into a chair to Mirabella's left, right before someone else does.

"That's my spot," the girl says.

"Not tonight."

"Where will I sit then?" she whines.

I raise my hand for her to leave.

Mirabella finally picks up her head from her salad and sees me. "What are you doing?" She looks behind me at where the girl is still standing. "Angelica sits there."

"You sit with the Costas."

She laughs. "Um . . . no."

"Okay then." I slide out my chair and pat my lap. "Put your sweet ass in my lap, Angelica." My eyes remain on Mirabella.

Her face reddens and she's trying really hard to act as though it won't bother her to see another woman on my lap.

"Okay then." The girl steps forward.

"Angelica," Sofia whispers.

"What? I have to eat." Angelica shrugs.

"Mr. Costa." Chancellor Thompson approaches the table with the kid I told to wash the dishes at his side. "Did you tell Mario to wash the dishes for you?"

I groan.

"Come with me." He crooks his finger.

"I don't wash dishes." I stand from the chair and Angelica quickly sits, but Mirabella scoots her chair closer to Sofia.

"I've been wanting to have a word with you, so perhaps this is the perfect opportunity. I figure we'll have to reacquaint you with rules, let alone the rules of Sicuro Academy." He turns on his heels and walks out a side door, clearly expecting me to follow.

I want to tell him to fuck off, but Nonno's words repeat in my head. "Do not make a spectacle of yourself and do not get yourself kicked out. We know the danger is coming from there and either one of us or both of us could be killed if we don't find the person responsible. The killer is at Sicuro Academy as far as we know."

Giovanni stands, but I shoo him back down with my hand and follow the chancellor. The only sound in the halls is the click of our shoes on the hardwood.

He unlocks his office and signals toward the couch. "Please sit, Mr. Costa."

"You do know that anyone here worth their position in their family could pick that lock." I sit on the green leather sofa and put one leg up to rest on my ankle.

He grabs a file folder and joins me, sitting in the matching green chair to my right. "Which would be why I keep nothing of value in here." He waves the manila folder. "This is your file with all the paperwork your grandfather filled out. I understand you lost your father recently and that we're fortunate to have you here too, but that's no excuse to disrespect how things are done around here."

"I can't be the first one not to do my punishment."

He shakes his head. "Usually, your type will just use the threat of violence to get weaker students to do your bidding, but most of those men are no longer welcome here. As you know, if we didn't strictly adhere to our rules at this academy, chaos and mass murder would ensue. So, if you don't want to do dishes, don't skip class."

"It's a stupid chore to give someone of my stature. I've never washed a dish in my life."

He inhales deeply. "Exactly. I'm sure you think it's beneath you, but it is to entice you to follow the rules, Mr. Costa."

I say nothing.

"I knew you were going to be a problem. I told the board as much. I denied your admittance because you're already at the top of your food chain and with your youth, you think you're above it all. Now I doubt this will do any good, but this is strike one. Two more and you're out."

I scoff. "You tried to deny me entrance?"

"Yes, and the board overruled me only because of who you are. They were scared of your grandfather. But I am not. When I took this job, I promised the board I would not take bribes and I would not be soft on certain families. That every student would be treated equally. However, since you missed the orientation because you arrived on campus late, I'll let it slide this one time. That said, the strike on your record still counts. Am I clear?"

"Fuck you" is on the tip of my tongue, but I nod. "Clear. May I go?"

He nods and I stand, walking to the door. "This can be easy, or it can be hard, Mr. Costa. It's your decision. Maybe revisit the handbook of rules to make sure you don't break any others."

My hand is on the doorknob and I don't turn around. "Some people aren't made to follow rules, chancellor." I open the door and shut it behind me.

God, I cannot wait to get the fuck out of this place. I'll do his dishes, but only until I find the bastard I'm looking for. In the meantime, I need to remember what I've learned and use the men under me here to do my dirty work.

My hand digs into my slacks pocket and I pull out the small piece of plastic with the sticker that reads The Property of Sicuro Academy. It's half-burnt, but when one of our soldiers brought it to me, it finally gave us a lead. The killer is within these gates.

I step outside and find Mirabella heading back toward Roma House with Sofia. As strong as the urge is to go over there and put her in her place, I refrain. I'll deal with her and her insolence later.

CHAPTER FIVE
MIRABELLA

I smooth my hands over my stomach and turn to see my profile in the mirror. I'm wearing tight-fitting black jeans and a black scoop-neck body suit that does a great job of showing off the decent amount of cleavage I have. My dark hair hangs past my shoulders in waves and I have on more makeup than I normally wear during the day.

"Are you almost ready?" Sofia asks from her bed. "I want to get there soon in case the party gets shut down."

After Marcelo left the dining hall—thank God—word spread about a party in the woods on the north end of the school. I'm assuming they didn't have these parties before—unless they were just sausage fests. Now that it's a coed campus, a lot more can happen, and I've never been more in the mood to blow off some steam.

Security is tight around here, so Sofia's right, we have no idea how quickly the party will get shut down.

With Marcelo Costa here, reality has come crashing down and I want to act like a typical college kid by partying and flirting with boys—something I've never been able to do, even outside of the Sicuro Academy gates.

"I'm ready. You look hot by the way."

Sofia preens and flips her straight brown hair over her shoulder with an exaggerated eyelid flutter. "I'll have the boys eating out of my hand."

"*We'll* have them eating out of *our* hands."

She hooks her arm around mine and we head toward the door of our room. "You better hope your fiancé doesn't show up then."

"Do not call him my fiancé."

We reach the elevator and press the down button. No one else is in the hall, which is a bit of a rarity. I guess they're all already at the party.

"But he is, Mira." She looks at me, concern glistening in her deep-hazel eyes. "And I don't think he'll like it if you're all over some other guy."

The elevator doors open, and I step in with a shrug. "I don't care. He might as well figure out now that I'm not going quietly into this marriage. Maybe if he does, he'll think I'm more trouble than I'm worth and cut me loose to find himself some other demure Mafia princess who will be happy servicing him as he wishes."

"That's doubtful." She hits the button for the ground floor.

I jut my chin up a bit. "I like to think you make your own luck and I intend to sway this situation to my liking, no matter what it takes."

* * *

Twenty minutes later, after trekking across campus, we're about a mile from the Roma House and approaching the woods. From the bass, it's clear the party has started.

Sofia puts her arm through mine again, clinging to me as if a serial killer is about to jump out of the woods. I have no idea how big these woods are and I don't want to get lost in the middle of the night any more than she does, but hopefully, it will all be worth the risk.

Five minutes into the forest, we find ourselves at the edge of a clearing. For the first time since Marcelo's resurrection, a smile transforms my face. A generator runs a sound system at the far end, and they have some of those laser solar system projectors hooked up around the perimeter so that the trees are bathed in purple, pink, and blue images of galaxies. Above us, some drones fly around, projecting lasers that move with the beat of the music onto the crowd. People are dancing in the center of the clearing, and surrounding them is everyone else drinking out of their Solo cups.

"Oh my god, it's a keg party. C'mon!" I drag Sofia over to where the keg is set up, grab two empty cups from the pile, and fill them both before passing her one.

My first keg party—it feels like a rite of passage. Hell, it feels like such a *normal* thing to do that I'm probably more excited than I should be.

One thing about the Mafia and people who attend Sicuro Academy, they get shit done. They've learned bribes, intimidation, and hacking skills since they were young, and I have no doubt that's how the resources for this party made their way past the gates.

Sofia sips her beer and crinkles her nose. "Ugh. I hate beer."

It's not my favorite either, but I slug back a bunch, then scour the crowd. It's not just the Roma House residents here. There are students from the Dublin House and the Moskva House too, though each faction keeps to itself.

Eyeing my brother not too far from us, I grab Sofia's hand and pull her away from the keg area. "Over here. I don't want to talk to Antonio."

He talked to me at dinner about Marcelo and I shut him down. I'm not in the mood for a lecture. Antonio let me avoid the conversation earlier tonight, but I know that will only last so long. He's just as pigheaded as my father and sometimes he tries to act as though he is my father. Newsflash, he's not the head of the family—yet.

"He's not that bad," Sofia says once we're standing at the edge of the clearing again.

I roll my eyes and take another healthy sip. "Easy for you to say. He's not barking orders at you all day."

Something passes across her face, but I can't be sure what it is. I don't get a chance to ask her because Lorenzo pops up in front of us.

"Hey, Mira." He gives me the same smile that garnered my interest in the first place.

"Hey." I smile back while Sofia's head turns this way and that way as if I need a lookout or something.

Lorenzo reaches for my hand, and I let him make contact for a moment before I pull away.

"We need to talk," he says imploringly.

I find myself searching the immediate area. "I know. And we will. Just not here."

He leans in and speaks directly into my ear. "I know you miss me."

My eyes close briefly. Not because his words move me—at least, not in the way he's hoping they will. But because my time with him and picking things back up with him represents freedom of choice and agency within my own life.

"I promise we'll talk. Just not tonight. I want to have fun, okay?" I give him the same doe eyes I used to give to my dad when I was a little girl and wanted something. They worked when I was only asking for an extra serving of dessert or the latest and greatest toy, but once I was older and asking for things like freedom and not to be pushed into a marriage I didn't want, their charm apparently had been depleted.

But Lorenzo acquiesces, as I thought he would. "Fine. But don't leave me waiting too long or I'll come looking for you." He winks and disappears into the crowd.

"He can be intense sometimes," Sofia says.

"I can handle him." I toss back the rest of my beer and turn to her. "Finish yours and let's get a refill. We need to get this party started."

Sometime later, I'm feeling the effects of the beer when The Acid's "Ghost" blares through the speakers. Sofia and I turn to each other and scream. We're the only two I know who love The Acid. We grab one another's hand and make our way into the center of the clearing where everyone is dancing.

I raise my Solo cup in the air and move to the music, feeling as if I'm in a trance as I stare into the canopy of the trees with swirling images of colorful galaxies moving over them. In this moment, my body feels so alive, so free, and I'm going to chase and try to hold on to this feeling as long as I can.

When the beat really drops, a set of hands settle on my hips and the warmth of a body presses against my back. Looking over my shoulder, Lorenzo smiles. With a smile, I push back against him and his hard length hits me as we gyrate against each other.

My eyes drift closed, and I become one with the music, falling deeper and deeper into myself until Lorenzo's hand drifts across my stomach. A flutter between my thighs awakens my sexuality. His fingers tease the top of my pants, sliding in and out along the waist of my jeans. I lean back into his hold, one arm raised behind his head. His hot breath hits my neck and I close my eyes, and the only man in my head is Marcelo. My eyes snap open.

What the hell?

Lorenzo dips his mouth to my ear and whispers, "Come take a walk with me in the woods."

I grin, leaning into Sofia, who's also in her own world, singing at the top of her lungs. "I'll be back in a few minutes. You okay here alone?"

She nods.

I accept Lorenzo's hand and drag him through the crowd until we reach the edge of the clearing. From there, he leads us through the trees until we're twenty feet away from the party. He backs me against a large tree trunk, hands on my hips, and I wrap my arms around his neck, staring up at him.

He's an attractive guy with his swoop of dark hair on the top of his head and his chocolate eyes. He doesn't have the powerful intensity that Marcelo has and oh my god . . . *Stop thinking of Marcelo!*

Lorenzo's eyes glitter in a way that tells me he's pretty drunk. Maybe that's why the two of us are tempting Marcelo's wrath. Because there's no doubt that if he ever hears about this, much less sees us, one or both of us might be dead.

I don't want Lorenzo to risk himself, but zero violence is the school policy, and if Marcelo violates it, he'll be expelled. For whatever reason, I don't think he wants that, otherwise he wouldn't have gone with the chancellor so willingly tonight.

Fuck it. Marcelo needs to understand how opposed I am to this union between us and that I won't ever back down. I'll do whatever it takes to get out of this situation—even if it means shaming myself and my family so that he no longer wants me. And Marcelo can't act against Lorenzo without risking angering my father since Lorenzo's father is one of the capos in the La Rosa Mafia.

Lorenzo takes my left hand, fingering the diamond on my ring finger. "You're wearing his ring?"

"I have no choice." I hate the words coming from my mouth and hate even more that they're true. I have no doubt that Marcelo was serious when he said he'd superglue it to my finger. Until I can speak to my father on Sunday, I have to play along.

"Still, I hate seeing it. It makes me want to break his neck." His jaw flexes.

"You and me both."

But Lorenzo couldn't take Marcelo. He's not strong enough, not vengeful enough. Lorenzo doesn't have what it takes to be number one in the La Rosa family. I doubt he's ever even killed anybody.

His hand cups my cheek and he steps forward. "At least I know one thing . . ." Lorenzo's head dips.

My heart pounds because if I do this, if I fool around with Lorenzo now that Marcelo has claimed me again, it's an act of war against my future husband and the ultimate disrespect. I could very well be killed, thrown in a duffel bag, and tossed into some body of water, never to be found again.

"What's that?" I whisper.

"I'll always be the one who had you first."

I grin and chuckle, tilting my face up to his.

A twig snaps near us right before the warmth of Lorenzo's body is violently ripped away from me.

Marcelo stands with fists clenched at his sides, flanked by Giovanni. Nicolo and Andrea have Lorenzo in their hold. "You just wrote your death certificate, stronzo."

CHAPTER SIX
MARCELO

"Let him go," I say in an even voice.

"You sure?" Giovanni asks.

I nod.

Nicolo and Andrea release Lorenzo and he stumbles forward, attempting to catch his footing on all the forest debris littering the ground. I could easily kill him here with my bare hands.

I step forward. "Seems you think you can place your hands on what's mine and not suffer any consequences. You're either really stupid or really tough. So just how tough are you?"

Andrea scans the area, his concerned gaze shifting to Giovanni, as if my cousin could change my mind once it's set. "Fuck, there's no fighting here."

I look at my friend. "I don't give a shit." Then I set my eyes on Lorenzo. "Are you a pussy, Bruni?" I take another step closer to him. "A tattletale?"

His eyes are wide, and his chin shakes the slightest amount under the light filtering through the trees from the party. I swing back and cock my fist right into Lorenzo Bruni's gut. I might not be able to touch his pretty little face, but there are other parts of the body I can punish as long as he's even half a man and keeps his mouth shut.

"Come on. I'll give you one shot." I stand with my arms open. "Give it to me."

"Stop it, Marcelo," Mirabella says from behind me.

A sadistic laugh bubbles out of my throat. "Feeling protective of your lover, are you?"

I glance over my shoulder to see that she's standing with a defiant look, arms crossed, staring at Lorenzo, who's bent over and coughing.

I grab Lorenzo by his hair and give him another punch to the ribs, then tug him over to her, putting him face-to-face with her. "This is the type of man you want?"

She opens her mouth, but closes it without a word.

"Fuck, Mira," Lorenzo says, clearly insulted.

"You still haven't answered my question, Lorenzo." I push him away by the hair and he falls to the ground. I squat next to him. "Why do you think you're worthy to touch what's mine?"

"I'm not yours!" Mirabella screams.

"Look at your left hand," I say calmly, not bothering to look back at her. I stand and nudge Lorenzo with my boot. "So? Awfully quiet."

"This is so juvenile," she says from behind me.

I look at Nicolo and Andrea and nod. They each take one of her arms, escorting her away.

"You cannot push me around like some rag doll. Let me go!" She shimmies to get out of their hold, but she's wasting her energy. They're way too strong for her. "Marcelo, I swear if you don't call your goons off . . ."

I don't respond. My time to deal with her will come later.

"Now it's just me and you." I pick Lorenzo up by his shirt and set him on his feet. I straighten his shirt for him. "Let's remain on our feet like real men, shall we?" I brush debris off his shoulders.

His eyes narrow and I want to bait him to come after me just so I can beat him to a bloody pulp. But this isn't the place. With one strike against me already, I can only assume if I get caught fighting, it'll be an automatic expulsion.

"I'm going to make this real clear. Mirabella is mine. She's my fiancée and she will one day be my wife and mother of my children. The only cock she's going to suck is mine." I stop inches from his face, and he juts his chin up as if his heart isn't beating out of his chest.

It's almost insulting that Mirabella has chosen someone so weak.

Though he proves he has at least a little bit of gumption when he says, "It must really kill you that she'd do anything to get out of marrying you."

Giovanni steps forward, but I raise my hand. "Just wait until I fuck her. She'll be begging for me once she knows what my cock feels like snug inside of her." I wink and let his shirt go and step back. "You can go now. But if I see you even breathing in my fiancée's direction again, you'll have cement blocks for shoes."

He cocks his fist back and throws a punch. I step aside and he scrambles so fast he loses his footing, falling to the ground before he gets up and stares me down as if he could intimidate me. He opens his mouth and I calmly wait to see what he's about to say, but he shuts his mouth and walks away.

"He might've pissed himself." Giovanni slaps me on the back.

I'm not in a gloating mood. I still have to deal with Mirabella. It appears that she wants to make herself a real problem in my life.

We walk out of the woods to find Nicolo's hand still clamped around Mirabella's upper arm while his other hand swipes at a drone. Andrea is talking to her friend Sofia.

"What are you doing? Who is this?"

Nicolo glances back and swats again. "This drone won't leave us alone. Probably recording our conversations." The small black flying object gets right in front of my face.

"Who's is it?"

"Gabriele Vitali. He's known for all this computer shit." Giovanni jumps up, but it zooms higher.

It floats back down and rocks side to side in front of me. I throw a punch and the drone hits the ground. I stomp on it until all the fancy lights on it die.

"Feel better?" Giovanni asks.

"Much."

"What did you do to him?" Mirabella interrupts. There's real concern in her gaze and my blood runs like fire through my veins.

"Cut out his heart. It's back there if you still want it." I nod behind me.

She narrows her eyes. "You wouldn't."

I nod for Nicolo to let her go, but in exchange, I put my hand on her upper arm where his was. "We're going to walk back to the Roma House like an engaged couple."

She tries to wrestle herself free. "The hell we are. I came with Sofia."

Sofia cringes and looks between Mirabella and Andrea.

"Andrea, bring Sofia along."

"You know what I meant!" Her voice grows louder, and a few people glance over. As though I give a shit. "Ow, you're hurting me."

"If you want to go to a party, you go with me." I loosen my grip—slightly.

"*Ugh* . . . I'm so done with this." She turns to me and swings her arm out of my hold. "Why are you so desperate that you want to marry someone who doesn't even want you?"

"Mira," Sofia says softly from behind her.

The only thing I know about Sofia—other than that she's probably going to be the maid of honor at our wedding—is that she has the common sense to tell Mirabella when she's crossing a line she shouldn't. Then again, Sofia fears me. Mirabella is either pretending, or she honestly doesn't.

I laugh at my fiancée and grab her hand, leading her away from the party and our friends. Once we're secluded, I press her back up against a tree. "Do you think I can't fuck anyone in this place I want to? Hell, your friend Angelica would've begged to suck me off right there in the dining hall."

She tries to mask her indifference, but she can't. Her cheeks are red, and she diverts her gaze from me. "Spare me."

"It's not a threat, it's a fact."

She turns her gaze my way and her eyes lock with mine, but there's a challenge in them. Just as I expected there to be. "Then do it. I don't care!"

"Oh, principessa, you care." My finger glides down her arm before I take her wrist in my palm. I bring her hand to my cock that's half-hard now from the defiant blaze in her eyes. "I see it . . . you want this. You want me, and though you might not like what I represent and you might hate the fact you're a female brought up in a Mafia family, from the day you were born, you were groomed to love power, especially in your man. I am now in charge of the Costa family, and you know I'll do whatever it takes to stay at the top. That turns you on whether you admit it or not."

She shakes her head. "You can think whatever you want."

I keep her hand on my cock and lean in, knowing if I kiss her, she'll kiss me back. She tilts her head, and her tongue slides out of her mouth. She's so fucking easy to read.

"Time to kiss and make up," I whisper when our lips are millimeters apart. She has one free hand to slap me if she wishes, but she won't because she *wants* to kiss me. Just as I'm about to place my lips to hers, I draw back. "As soon as you use mouthwash and get that stronzo Lorenzo's breath out of your mouth."

Her fists clench and she yanks her wrist from my hand. "I hate you."

There's true venom in her voice. But somewhere under all that hatred is need and she can't hide it from me.

She stomps off in front of me and we eventually come into view of the Roma House. I escort her to the elevator and see her to her room.

Once we're outside it, she addresses me for the first time in fifteen minutes. "If you think you're getting a kiss, you're wrong."

"I told you I wouldn't kiss you until you wash Lorenzo off you. Now stay inside your room for the rest of the night and make my job easier, would you?"

She walks into her room and slams the door in my face.

I shake my head and adjust myself before walking to my room, where I text Andrea, Nicolo, and Giovanni to meet me first thing in the morning. It's about time we talk about more important things than my impending nuptials.

* * *

I've wasted more time than needed tracking and making sure Mirabella knows she's mine. During Sunday's call, Nonno will expect some answers, and if all I can tell him is that I hit the guy Mirabella was almost making out with in the woods, he'll be disappointed.

Giovanni comes in my room first and stays standing by the door because he's always more comfortable that way. Then Nicolo and Andrea join us, sitting on my desk and the ledge on the window.

"Okay, guys, I'm talking to Nonno on Sunday and I need to tell him we made some headway on who planted the bomb." I drop the piece of plastic our soldier found scattered in the debris around the vehicle. "This was found by the car, so right now, this is where we investigate. The killer made the bomb here at Sicuro Academy."

"I say Mirabella." Andrea raises his hand. "She has no respect for you. She should be on her knees to be arranged to marry a guy with your status." Andrea, always the kiss-ass.

"I'm not taking her off the list, but come on, I highly doubt it was her as much as she wants me dead. First, you two are going to find out where these stickers are sold and what they're adhered to."

Nicolo picks up the plastic and flips it over and over.

"Lorenzo Bruni is a real problem, but I think he's too much of a wimp to pull off the move, but no one is out of the realm of possibility," I continue. "He wants my fiancée, so that makes him a threat."

"Boss." Nicolo clears his throat and lifts his finger.

"We're not in fucking class, Nicolo. What?"

"I heard a rumor that Mirabella and Lorenzo were messing around before you two got arranged."

My teeth grind together when I think of the two of them "messing around" together, even if I wasn't in the picture yet. And who's to say it's over?

"He has reason to kill Marcelo, but why his dad? Plus, Lorenzo has nothing to gain. Antonio is next in line in the Southeast."

Giovanni pulls out a cigarette, but I eye him.

I'm not against smoking, but I'll be damned if he fills my dorm room with that shit.

He tucks it behind his ear.

"Unless my father was collateral damage." I shake my head. "To go after my father, the person has to have giant steel nuts. Lorenzo is weak."

"Maybe you were the collateral damage?" Nicolo asks. "And your father was the intended target?"

I shrug. "It's possible. I wasn't supposed to be there that night. My dad's request to have me at his yacht was last minute. But it doesn't change the fact that I need to figure out who it was."

"What about Antonio then?" Nicolo raises a brow.

"Maybe. So far, he's been more than accommodating, what with his sister being as difficult as she is." But my gut tells me it isn't my fiancée's brother. Still, I can't cross him off the list of people.

We sit in silence.

"Obviously, keep all this on the down-low. Whoever it is, we don't want them to think we're closing in on them." I stare out the window for a beat and watch the students file out of their dorms toward their first class of the day. "I can't be late to anything today, so let's meet here after dinner." I get up from my bed and grab my backpack. They all stand, but I stop them with my hand in the air. "Last thing, don't act on your own. When we find this fucker, you bring him to me. Am I clear?"

They all nod.

That's one thing about being in my position—I have no idea who is true to me or not. For once, I wish I could be comfortable in a room and not feel as though I have to be one step ahead in case someone wants me dead. At the same time, I can't imagine not having that tension filling me at all times. I guess that's the life of someone born into my family.

We all leave Roma House and I spot Mirabella up ahead on the path, looking as hot as always in her uniform. The way her skirt swooshes side to side has me licking my lips.

Like a good soldier, I do what I'm told and attend all my classes for the day. I'm even asked to demonstrate my knife skills in weaponry class tomorrow. It's what I'm known for. Well, that and the fact I've killed with my bare hands.

Just before dinner, my three friends come into my room. We were supposed to talk after dinner, but one of them must've found out something they didn't think could wait.

"What?"

Giovanni leans along the wall by the door. "Andrea overheard Dante Accardi bragging." He nods to Andrea to tell me himself.

"He was going on and on about how he doesn't understand what the big deal is about you. That Northeast has no more money than the rest of the territories. He said he sailed his yacht this summer and went down to Panama then back up north until he was outside New York City. Couldn't stop himself from going on and on about how his yacht was bigger than your father's."

My eyes narrow. "And he knows that how?"

"He said he was docked at the same marina as your dad the night he was killed. Said your dad's mistress screamed and carried on so much it woke everyone in the marina."

My fists clench. "He was there?"

They all nod. I don't believe in coincidences, but I need to figure out a motive. Why the hell would the Accardis, who run the southwest, want us dead unless they want to get further into the weapons market? No doubt all the drugs that pass the borders into their territory pad their coffers, but they could be getting greedy.

Don't be so naive, Marcelo. There's always motive in this profession.

CHAPTER SEVEN
MIRABELLA

It's bad enough that I spent my entire day feeling Marcelo's gaze on me during classes, but at dinner too?

The most infuriating part is the betrayal of my body. How it seems affected by his proximity. Well, that changes right now. Last night he was callous and insensitive with his comments regarding Lorenzo, but he wants to kiss me, I know it. And there's no chance I'll give him the satisfaction.

I didn't reach out to Lorenzo last night and he didn't attend any classes today. When I asked one of his friends, they just said he was sick, glanced at Marcelo on the other side of the room with fear, and ran out the door. Pussies.

Now it's dinner and I haven't escaped him. I'm bringing my food back to my table, purposely not looking at where Marcelo is standing near the entrance. But my willpower wanes and I take a quick peek. My fingers tighten on my tray because he's flirting with some girl. I don't know her, but she's from one of the Italian families, because her skirt has a red, green, and white plaid pattern.

She leans up against the wall, smiling at him like a Barbie doll while he hovers over her, hand against the wall to the left of her head. The girl laughs and brushes her fingers over the short hair on the top of his head with a giggle. *Moron.*

My hand itches to know how his short hair will feel under my palm. The hair on his head is the same length as his beard—cropped close—and only adds to his intense persona.

Marcelo smiles at her and laughs in a way he never will with me. The hot flash of a jealous rage fires through me, startling me to my core.

Finally, I reach my table. Thankfully, my back is to him.

Sofia leans in close and whispers, "He's just doing it to piss you off."

"It's not my business what he does." I pick up my fork and stab the lettuce in my salad.

"Then why do you look like you want to gouge out someone's eyes with that fork?" She quirks an eyebrow at me.

"Because he's annoying as hell. He's just trying to prove a point. I was about to mess around with Lorenzo last night and now he's trying to stick it to me. Well, he can go stick it in her for all I care. At least if she's giving it to him, he won't look to me for it."

Sofia laughs and picks up her fork.

"What?" I scowl at her.

"It wouldn't exactly be a hardship to find yourself in bed with him. There are far worse things."

My mouth drops open. "Sofia!" I've never heard Sofia say anything like that before.

She shrugs. "What? I may want to save myself for my own husband one day, but that doesn't mean I have no sex drive or know when a guy is hot as hell. And all Marcelo's intense energy? I'll bet it's fun when he dedicates all that energy into making you come."

I squeeze my legs together under the table from the image her words evoke. I point at her with my fork stuffed with salad. "Don't forget that he's the enemy."

"I won't. I'm just saying that if you're going to be forced to marry someone, it could be worse."

Always looking at things through rose-colored glasses.

"You're missing the point—I don't want to be forced to marry anyone." When I glance over my shoulder, Marcelo is gone and the girl he was talking to is nowhere in sight. I ignore the twinge in my belly at the thought that maybe they took off somewhere to fool around.

In the process of looking for Marcelo, I see my brother stomping toward our table. It looks as if he's pushed his hand through his dark wavy hair a hundred times and his cheeks are red. Great. I've managed to avoid him all day since he's in his third year here and we don't take the same classes, but my good fortune has run out.

"Antonio looks pissed." Sofia stabs her salad and puts her head down.

He comes to an abrupt stop beside me. "We need to talk."

"I'm eating." I face my salad, bringing my fork to my mouth, but it's ripped from my hand and Antonio tosses it against the wall.

Sofia flinches, but doesn't say anything.

"Get unbusy."

"What the hell?" I bolt up from my seat and stand on my tiptoes.

He wraps his large hand around my upper arm and leads me out of the dining hall.

Jesus, I am so sick of being dragged around like a rag doll by these damn men. But I don't fight back, knowing this confrontation is inevitable after what happened last night.

Antonio leads me outside and away from the entrance doors to the dining hall so no one will eavesdrop. When we reach far enough away, he drops my arm and whips around to face me.

"Lorenzo Bruni? What the fuck, Mira, you're an engaged woman." The veins in his neck stick out. Yeah, pissed isn't even the word to describe him.

"I've made it perfectly clear that I don't want to be forced to marry Marcelo, so in my head, I'm not engaged."

My brother growls and steps toward me. "Be that as it may, you have a duty to this family, and bringing shame to the La Rosa name won't get you out of it—you will marry Marcelo Costa."

I throw my hands in the air. "Why does no one care what I want for my life?"

He looks around and lowers his voice, still seething as he clenches his jaw. "Because it doesn't matter. You were born into this family and that means you have responsibilities and expectations. The merging of our families will be profitable for all of us."

"And I take the punishment for all of you to benefit. I hand over my life and free will. No big deal, right?" I press my finger into my chest.

Antonio clamps his hands on my shoulders. "I know you don't like this—you don't have to. But you do have to stop disrespecting Marcelo. You have no choice. You will marry him, Mira. You might as well try to get on his good side. You never know, maybe he'll let you have some of what you want."

I scoff. "Not likely." The man is intent on infuriating me. "How are you going to feel when a wife is chosen for you? Someone you don't love. Someone who helps the family."

He raises his chin and drops his hands. "I'll do what I have to for the benefit of this family—just like you're doing now."

I don't even bother arguing because he will, though as the man, he'll still be entitled to live the rest of his life outside his marriage however he wants. Which usually means affairs. Whereas if I get caught with another man, they'll cut off his dick.

"Play nice, Mira. If you don't, I'll have to intervene and tell Dad. Maybe insist he drag you back home to wait until Marcelo is ready for marriage."

I gasp. "You wouldn't!"

"Shh," he says.

I lower my voice again. "Antonio, you know what going here means to me."

He crosses his arms. "I'll be the head of this family someday, and that means I have to do what's best for *everyone* and that means you marrying Marcelo. He's the head of his family now. Think of what that means for you two."

I jab my brother in the chest with my finger. "For him, not me. I just get all of the ceremony and none of the power."

Antonio shakes his head. "Do what you need to do to deal with this, Mira, but fall in line. You won't like what happens if you don't." He turns and walks back toward the dining hall while I stand there with my fists clenched at my sides.

God, he's just as bad as my father and Marcelo.

I take a few minutes to gather myself before going back in and halfheartedly eating my dinner.

"Everything okay?" Sofia asks, glancing at my brother.

"Fine," I grumble.

I remain quiet through the rest of dinner. When everyone else decides to head to the commons to hang out, I feign tiredness from last night's party and head back to Roma House. I'm not in the mood to socialize. I'm also not in the mood to admit defeat, but a night of sulking in my bed sounds perfect.

There are only a few people sitting around the lounge as I walk toward the elevator, and I'm deep in thought as I punch the button to call the elevator. Antonio is right. I'm stuck in this engagement and marriage until I can figure a way out for myself. I thought I'd removed the collar and leash from around my throat, but reality is crueler than that. I shed it only briefly. I tasted freedom only to have it ripped away.

Even when I thought Marcelo was dead, I knew my dad would eventually find another match for me, but I thought I had time. And that learning everything I could here at the academy would help me prove to him that I'm more valuable than just being married off to the highest bidder. What in my nineteen years in the La Rosa family ever gave me the idea that I could refuse what's planned for me?

The elevator dings and I step into the empty box and hit the button for the fifth floor. I lean back against the far side and spot Marcelo running to get on with me.

"Oh, like hell." I stab the door-close button, but nothing happens. A few seconds later, they start to close, and I smirk at him as they slide together.

Just as I'm about to celebrate, his hand pops between them, and they slowly open for him, much like I imagine most women do.

"Today is not my day," I grumble as he steps in, grinning at me.

Another guy is about to step in, but when Marcelo barks, "Get the next one," the poor guy scurries out. How must it feel to be feared by everyone?

"How's my doting fiancée this evening?" he asks as the doors close.

"Peachy." I give him a saccharine smile. "Surprised to see you here. You must be pretty fast then? Not a lot of stamina? Or does getting her off not really coincide with what you want, so you leave her to finish herself?"

A deep chuckle rumbles from his chest. "I like you jealous."

"You wish." I cross my arms and jut out my hip. His gaze trails up my legs and my breath lodges in my throat.

He hits the button that stops the elevator. I'm sure he wants me to react, so I purposely lock my eyes with his. I'm not going to stand down.

"I saw you watching me from across the room." He steps closer, but I hold my ground. "You didn't like what you saw."

I scoff. "Let's remember who was jealous first. But if you want to play a game of who can make who more jealous, you should know I play to win."

Our eyes lock and I suck in a breath at the intensity of his glare.

He towers over me and places his hands on the elevator wall on either side of my hips. "That's one of the things I like about you."

I wish his words didn't affect me, but I can't help but wonder what else he likes about me. "Don't go getting soft on me now, big guy."

"You already know how hard I am, dolcezza. Got a firsthand grip on it the other night."

My eyes glance down on their own and I grit my teeth. "Careful, keep talking like that and the knife might slip out of my hand tomorrow in weaponry class. I have a feeling it just might head in your direction."

His face screws up. "You won't have your hands on any knives."

Something about the way he says it tells me he's not saying it as part of our game. "What are you talking about?" My hands drop to my sides.

He grins. I'm not going to like whatever he has to say. "Women aren't permitted to take weaponry class. You guys will be stuck in a class more suited to you while the men train with knives and guns—as if it's anything new to us."

I search his face but don't see anything that indicates he's not telling the truth. "Bullshit. Who told you that?"

He laughs. "Giovanni. You really didn't know?" He shrugs. "Guess they thought it might offend all your delicate sensibilities."

"You're lying." Even I hear the desperation in my voice.

He studies me for a beat. "You really want to learn how to slice someone up? Where to shoot someone for a clean kill and where to shoot them to prolong their suffering?"

I don't answer. I can't. I'm too busy trying to keep the tears building in my eyes from falling. I will never show him my weakness.

I had such high hopes when I found out I would attend the Sicuro Academy, but it feels as though everything I hoped to gain by coming here is still so far out of my reach.

CHAPTER EIGHT
MARCELO

On the way to weaponry class the next day, all I can think of are the tears brimming in Mirabella's eyes last night. Crying usually annoys the fuck out of me—a baby crying and a grown-ass man crying get the same reaction out of me, even if I enjoy the grown-ass man's tears if I'm the one doing the torturing. But Mirabella's unshed tears felt like a knife to the chest. Even if she didn't allow one tear to fall.

Questions rattled me all night. Does she want to learn to use a knife to kill me? Her father? Her brother? For protection, and if so, from who? Why would any woman who's marrying a man like me, who will always protect and kill for her, want to learn to kill for herself?

"You're thinking too hard." Giovanni comes to my side.

I wouldn't mind a break from him. He's always hanging around before and after classes and grates on my nerves. He sticks a little too close and it's made me wonder if he's always lingering so I don't put him on my list of people who tried to kill me, my father, or both.

"Anything to report?" I ask to remind him that he should be worrying less about me and instead looking for who wants to take out the head of our family.

"Still just Dante," he repeats what we've already gone over.

"There are a lot of others. How about Antonio La Rosa?" I glance around the courtyard we're walking through to make sure no one is around.

"I don't think so. Word is he's trying to get his sister to behave and marry you like she's supposed to." Giovanni shakes his head, so sure to scratch him off the list already.

Thankfully for Giovanni's sake, we walk into the weaponry classroom. For the first time since stepping foot on the Sicuro campus, I feel at peace.

All the knives are locked away under glass partitions and the urge to break the glass and touch each one is overwhelming. I want to hold one like a fucking addict wants one last hit. I've had a knife or gun on me every day since I became a made man. Having to give them up when I stepped on campus left me feeling naked. The fact that I've killed with only my bare hands before is the only thought that puts me at ease.

Mr. Smith walks in, and I'd bet every weapon in this place that's not his real name. The man is pure-blooded Italian. He's got dark-olive skin, deep-brown eyes, and the top two buttons of his shirt are undone with a gold chain peeking out around his neck. His slacks are tailored to his muscular thighs, and his shoes are Berluti leather sneakers. Something about this guy doesn't read college professor to me. I'm not exactly sure why, but something's pinged my radar.

"Quiet down, everyone." He rounds the front of his desk and sits on it, pulling out a piece of paper.

Each guy settles in his seat, and we face forward. It's odd not to see the women in this class with their short plaid skirts and tight white blouses. Giovanni leans in to whisper and I shoot him a curt look to fuck off.

If my reward is to touch the weapons, I'll be the best student this guy's ever had.

Mr. Smith names students and each guy says, "Here."

"Costa," he says.

Giovanni and I both say, "here," causing Mr. Smith to look. "There's two of you now?" His eyes lock with mine for a second before they go back to the paper. "Marcelo." His tone is different than when he read the other names.

"My cousin. Late transfer," Giovanni informs him.

I crack my neck to keep from hitting him for speaking for me.

Mr. Smith lifts his head, but this time, his eyes aren't centered on me. He's doing the trick of looking over my shoulder to make it look as though he's looking at me. But we both know he's not. Then he smiles. "Nice to have you in class."

"Thanks," I say, my alarms blaring as I wonder if I need to worry about this guy.

He continues through the roster, and when he's done, he sets down the paper and clasps his hands between his legs. "This is weaponry class, and you will learn how to protect yourself and kill, but remember Sicuro Academy's rules—no violence is permitted against another student or staff member. We will spar, but if you deliberately pierce your partner, you're out of the class for the semester."

Everyone nods and my hands itch, hoping I'm getting closer to holding a weapon.

He pulls a set of keys out of his pocket, going to the cabinet holding the small knives. "During the semester, we'll work from small to bigger weapons. The more I'm assured I can trust you, the more you'll have to work with. Although I dare one of you to come after me." He looks back at us and winks.

The class laughs, but Giovanni raises his eyebrows at me. Maybe that's what I sensed when he looked at me: fear. Because if he's Italian, he could very well know my reputation around knives.

"Pick a partner, then one of you come up here and sign out a knife. Remember, each one is numbered, so if one goes missing, I'll know who has it."

I roll my eyes at the number of warnings we're getting. I nod to Giovanni and he rises from the desk and goes up, pushing his way through to the front.

"After your partner gets his knife, go to the mats in the back," Mr. Smith announces. Once every partner set has their knife and is on the mat, Mr. Smith comes over and stands with his arms crossed. "Okay, guys, let's see what you've got. Remember, this is sparring, but I want to see where you are now so I can see the progress by the end of the class. Midway through, we'll switch and your partner will have the knife. Ready? Go."

Giovanni starts out with the knife. I've wrestled with him so many times since childhood I can predict every move ten seconds before he makes it. Don't get me wrong, Giovanni is a feared man, especially in a shoot-out. You want him on your side in a gunfight because it's like he's on a suicide mission the way he walks into the fray and fires away. But knife fighting and fistfighting aren't really Giovanni's thing. I think because I excelled at it at a young age, he kind of gave up on it instead of fighting to be better.

"Remember, the opponent without the knife, you want that knife. Feel free to use any trick you have in your arsenal to retrieve it."

"Fuck!" someone shouts from behind me.

"Now, no one is to leave with blood on themselves from fists and kicks though."

I'm not sure what this guy expects of us, but I slide my leg and get Giovanni's feet out from under him and he falls to his back. I snatch the knife from his loose grip.

"Damn it," he mumbles.

"Good work, Mr. Costa. Now switch." Mr. Smith signals to us with his hands.

Giovanni gets lazy, as I knew he would. He's either trying to make me look good, or he's given up. I'm half tempted to believe the latter because he does that sometimes. And like every time, it pisses me off.

Once I get him on his back with the knife right above his heart, he says, "I give."

"Well done, Costa. Anyone want to take on another partner?" Mr. Smith asks the room.

"I will."

I look across the room to the hand that's raised. Dante Accardi. How did I miss that fucker?

"All right, Mr. Accardi and Mr. Costa, get on the center mat. Everyone else, have a seat. Let's start with Mr. Accardi with the knife."

Dante looks me up and down, stepping on the mat. I'll be happy to teach this piece of shit a lesson.

"Ready, boys?" Mr. Smith asks. "Go."

Dante circles me like a pussy while I step forward to knock the knife out of his hand. The blade is no longer than three inches and wouldn't do much harm to either of us. He moves it back and the guys all make noises to suggest he beat me.

No more games then. Every fucker here needs to know who they're up against. I kick Dante's foot out from under him, grab the wrist of the hand holding the knife, and slam it on the mat before securing the knife in my own hand. Then I pretend to use it on him.

"Holy shit," someone says.

"What was that, a second?" another student asks.

"That's my cousin," Giovanni brags.

Mr. Smith claps. "Well done. That was very fast."

Dante pushes up off the mat, cheeks red in either anger or embarrassment. "Get the fuck off me." He flings his arm my way and hits my eye.

I grab him by the front of his shirt and slam him back down on the mat. "You hit me, stronzo."

There's a flash of fear in his eyes, but it only lasts a second because a man like Dante, next in line, can't be afraid of anyone or anything. "Fuck you. It was an accident." His hands go to my wrists, but I refuse to let go.

"That's enough. Let go and walk to your separate corners." Mr. Smith comes to stand by us.

I lean down and whisper in Dante's ear, "Remember this the next time you have the balls to say anything to my fiancée. I'm sure you've figured it out here today, but I don't need weapons to kill." I take my hands off him, but first, I toss him so he falls back to the mat one last time.

The bell rings.

"Well done. Next class, I'll show you all some techniques. What I saw you doing that you can improve on."

We all hand in our weapons before anyone is permitted to leave the classroom. I'm on a fucking high from being able to fight, to strip someone of their weapon. I thought I felt good after Lorenzo the other night, but this weaponry class was fucking awesome.

It's lunch hour, so we head to the dining hall, and I sit with my friends. I'm already at the table when Mirabella walks in with Sofia. That plaid skirt she wears is going to be the death of me. I watch as it swooshes while she disappears through the line for food. Giovanni's bragging about my performance in class to Andrea and Nicolo while I stop myself from seeking her out in line. What the hell is wrong with me?

I wasn't all that happy to take a bride when my father told me the arrangement he'd made with her father. Yeah, Mirabella is fucking beautiful, but me, a husband, at only twenty-one? I knew eventually it would happen, and more than likely, I would be arranged to be with someone, but I figured I had more time. Family rules dictate that as the head of the family, I must have a wife, so I'm not going to argue about it now like I had with my father when he first informed me.

Mirabella walks past me with Sofia, pretending she doesn't feel my gaze on her. But as she sits down, her eyes lift for the briefest of seconds and find me before concentrating on whatever Sofia is telling her.

A few guys I don't know, and some I do, whisper about me as they walk by.

"I swear, you're the talk of the school," Giovanni says.

"He already was when he resurrected from the dead," Nicolo adds.

"All I have to say is thank god we're on your team," Andrea says with a laugh.

"He hardly fought me. He better come out of weaponry class a lot fucking faster than he came in," I mindlessly say. Maybe New York is harder than the other territories, but I was faster than Dante at eight. "I forgot something in the dorm. I'll meet you in class."

I grab my tray, empty it, and put it on the conveyor belt line like the good boy I'm expected to be. On my walk across campus, a few guys sidestep to get out of my way, and a few nod in a way-to-go motion. Having power back feels good. Even in the confines of this place, everyone knows who I am and is afraid to cross me. Well, all but one.

I'm in my room, changing out of my uniform, when there's a knock on the door. I really hope it isn't Giovanni because I need a fucking break. I open the door and try to hide my surprise when Mirabella is standing there.

"Principessa," I say.

"We need to talk. Can I come in?"

Hmm. So polite all of a sudden. She must want something.

I step aside, open the door, and she walks in. I'm not sure what I did to deserve this visit, but looking at her skirt swoosh while she walks past me, I know one thing—I won't let it go to waste.

CHAPTER NINE
MIRABELLA

I push past Marcelo, and his purely masculine scent wafts to my nostrils. I'm not sure if it's cologne or maybe a mixture of body wash and his own natural scent, but I've noticed it a few times and each time it draws me to him even more.

I'm mad I'm even here right now, but my brother's words repeat in my head about how if I play along, then maybe my future husband will bow to some of my whims. I still don't plan to marry Marcelo without a fight, but this conversation will give me a good idea of who I'm working with.

"I figured the first time you'd be in my room, it would be because I dragged you here." He crosses his arms, and his biceps stretch the sleeves of his white uniform shirt. When he clocks me noticing, a small smirk plays at the edge of his mouth.

"I'm here to *talk*, nothing more." Jesus, I'm trying to be nice to further my cause, but this man makes it so damn difficult.

"I can't imagine what you want to talk about." He motions to his bed for me to take a seat.

As if.

When I don't move, he shrugs and sits on the side of his bed, leaning back on his hands and looking completely unaffected that I'm in his space. "Say what you came here to say then."

It takes me a moment to swallow my pride. I'm prideful by nature and the older I get, the more I don't like asking anyone for

anything. Especially because the odd time I have, I've always gotten
a hard no.

"I heard you kicked ass in weaponry class today."

A cocky smile transforms his face. "Did you expect any less?"
There's a glint in his eye that tells me he enjoyed having his hands
on a weapon today.

"Well, while you guys were having knife fights, we girls were
sent back to the 1950s."

A line forms between his eyebrows in question.

"Today we went over the syllabus, and this semester, we're going
to learn how to properly plan and host parties, all about child-rearing,
and how we can best support our future husbands when they return
home from ruling the world." Marcelo laughs and my hands clench
at my sides. "It's bullshit. It's not funny. It was supposed to be different, being allowed here."

"And you kept that temper of yours in check? I'm surprised you
didn't cause a mutiny."

God, I hate how well he appears to know me, even though there
are deep layers he won't ever get to know. "I put my earbuds in and
listened to music while the professor droned on. Otherwise, I probably would have revolted."

He laughs again, and for some reason, it draws me closer to him.
"Going to be pretty hard to pass the class if you have no idea what
the professor's been talking about all semester, isn't it?"

"I don't want to pass the class. What? Are they going to point out
I didn't boil my potatoes long enough, or the dress I wore was too
revealing and turned on my husband's guests? It's all bullshit."

He studies me. "What is it you want then?"

Ack. He reminds me of my father and the leader of every other
family I've ever met—straight to the point.

"I want to make a deal." There, I said it. No turning back now.

"Intriguing." He sits up, his curiosity piqued. "What kind of deal?"

"The kind where you teach me what you're learning in weaponry class, and I give you something in return." His gaze drifts over my body and my treacherous nipples harden under his attention. I have the distinct urge to press my thighs together. "Not in exchange for my body."

He frowns. "What then? What could you possibly give me that I'd want except your body?"

Ugh, these fucking men. When will they ever see us for more than a pair of tits and an ass?

"My compliance."

He nods as if I'm his fucking peon. "Go on."

I decide to pick my battles and that's not one worth fighting right now. "You've made it clear that you want me to stop fighting our impending union. If you teach me everything you're learning in that class, I won't fight you at every turn and I won't shit talk you to everyone."

He's silent for way too long, eyeing me. His gaze is so intense it almost makes me believe that he can see into my brain and know what I'm thinking.

"How do you figure I'm going to get a knife and a gun out of class? They're under lock and key and they monitor with alarms, I presume."

I shrug. "I'm sure you'll figure it out."

He smiles in a way that tells me he'd likely already worked out a way to retrieve them before I offered this deal. "We wouldn't be able to shoot any bullets on campus. Someone would hear."

I step forward, desperate and feeling as though I almost have him. "We could go to the woods where the party was. Or farther. And we don't have to use bullets every time. I want to know how to handle a gun, how to pull it out quickly and pop the safety, how to use it as a weapon without firing it. There is a lot you can show me without firing any bullets."

He rubs his palm against the stubble on his face. "And in turn, you'd come to heel? You wouldn't cause me any further problems or show me any disrespect?" He arches a dark eyebrow.

The word *heel*, like I'm a dog, makes me bristle, but I don't address it. I almost have him, I can taste it. "Correct." Then I think of an easy out for him if he ever wanted to renege on our deal without technically not fulfilling his part. "And you have to agree not to send me home to my father. I get to finish out my schooling here."

"Tell me, why do you want so badly to learn how to handle a weapon when you'll be married to one of the most powerful men in the country?" He's studying me, and I can tell he really wants to know the answer.

"I want to be able to take care of myself."

"You sure it's not just so you can try to take care of me?" He arches an eyebrow.

"You won't be with me twenty-four seven. I'll be a target just by being your wife." What I don't say is that I want to be an asset to the family, the same as any of the male members are.

"You'll be protected at all times. Even the house will be protected."

"Pretty sure you and your dad had protection with you when he was killed. Things don't always go according to plan." I hold his gaze, waiting for an answer.

He nods slowly, assessing. "That's a lot to ask of me for so little in return. I think you need to sweeten the pot." His gaze runs over my body again.

"I'm not going to sleep with you."

"*Yet.*"

We stare into each other's eyes, feeling the other one out. I refuse to be the first one to speak. If I do, I've lost.

Finally, after what feels like an eternity, he nods. "You have a deal on one condition."

Excitement is like a swarm of bees in my belly. "What condition?"

"One kiss. You have to agree to seal the deal with a kiss."

Air whooshes from my lungs. Not because I don't like the idea of kissing Marcelo, but because I worry about controlling myself. But it's a small price to pay to get what I want. I didn't promise I wouldn't still be looking for a way out of this marriage, just that I would be agreeable and not disrespect him in front of others.

"Deal."

The word no sooner leaves my mouth than he stands from the bed, wraps his hand around my wrist, and tugs me forward. We're standing with our chests touching and my head is cocked back to look up at him. My lips tingle in anticipation as he slowly lowers his mouth to mine.

The first touch is gentler than I expect, a brush of his lips against mine. Then his hand is in my hair, and he quickly intensifies the kiss. His tongue forces past the seam of my lips, but rather than feeling like an intrusion, it stokes the heat between my thighs to new levels. Our tongues tangle for dominance. Within seconds, I let him lead, a small whimper sounding from my throat when he squeezes my hair tighter.

But the bite of pain rachets my need even higher until my hands coast over his body—the hard planes of his chest, the wide breadth of his shoulders, the short hair on top of his head.

Marcelo's hands trail down my back, grabbing the globes of my ass, squeezing hard, and he groans. A groan that travels to my clit. One hand moves around my waist to the front, where he slides under my skirt and gently runs his fingers over the damp fabric of my panties.

I should stop him. But I have never in my life wanted someone as badly as I do in this moment. Right now, I can't think of any reasons why this is a bad idea, why this will undoubtedly make things more complicated. All I can focus on is how I want him to do more to me.

He growls when he feels how wet my underwear is because of him, and I sink into his strong hold, widening my stance for him. But he abruptly ends the kiss, backing up to sit on the edge of the bed again. "Come here."

His order leaves no room for argument. To my surprise, unlike when a man normally bosses me around, no part of me wants to disobey him. I do as he says, almost as if I'm in a trance.

When I reach him, he slides his hands up under my skirt and slowly lowers my panties until the thin fabric is draped over my shoes. Without his request, I step out of them. The pleased expression on his face makes me want to bask in the fact that I've done something he likes. If only I could understand my actions.

But I don't have time to think about it because immediately after I've stepped out of my panties, he says, "Let me see my pussy."

He holds up my skirt and stares between my legs. His nostrils flare and he leans in until his nose is pressed between the juncture of my thighs. He inhales deeply and I almost come on the spot.

"Every part of you is beautiful. I knew it would be, angelo." He lets the skirt drop and slides his fingers through my slick heat, resting on my clit.

I hold on to his shoulders as he works me. At first, he allows me to remain how I'm standing, but after a minute, he places my foot on his thigh, opening me up to him. His fingers continue to glide over my swollen bud and rim my entrance, but they never breach the opening, leaving me panting and desperate for more.

I look, but can't see exactly what he's doing because my skirt is in the way. Somehow, that makes it even more erotic.

Marcelo studies me. He's not watching his movements, but instead he watches my reactions. His dark eyes are glazed over as if he's on drugs, but I know the only thing rushing through his bloodstream right now is pure lust for me, and it turns me on more than I would have imagined.

He glides his fingertips over my clit again and around my entrance and I squeeze his shoulders under my hands. "Marcelo, please . . . please."

His eyes show delight over the fact that I've been reduced to begging, but the need to have him inside me, if only his fingers, claws at my insides like a beast waiting to be unleashed.

"Anything for my future wife." There's not even a moment for his words to annoy me because he pushes one, then two, fingers inside me. "Mio Dio, you're so tight. I can't imagine how hard you'll squeeze my cock, dolcezza."

While he works his fingers in and out of me, his thumb toys with my clit and the dual sensations overwhelm my senses. It's not long before my legs feel like jelly and my hands grip his shoulders even harder.

The room fills with the sound of our heavy breathing and the scent of my arousal.

The last thing I see before my eyes drift closed is the satisfied smirk on Marcelo's face. He curves his fingers inside me to hit my G-spot and I detonate.

I come on his fingers, my hips jerking. "Oh fuck, oh fuck, it's so good."

My climax sends me spiraling into bliss and every molecule in my being basks in the glory. It takes me a few moments to come back to myself, and when I do, I find that I'm straddling Marcelo on the edge of the bed. His hard length, still tucked inside his pants, prods my center from below.

It's seconds before how big of a mistake this was hits me. The urge to run is overwhelming, but I force myself to act unaffected. I don't want Marcelo to think he got one up on me. So rather than bolting out, I push up off him and pick up my panties from the floor. Then I slide them on with as much dignity as one can muster after you've let the guy you supposedly hate finger fuck you in the middle of your lunch hour.

He stands from the bed and grips me by the waist, pulling me into him. "Care to return the favor?" He adjusts the hard length in his pants and nods toward the floor.

I smile. "There's something you should know about me," I say in a sweet, sultry voice, trailing my hand down his chest over his tie until I reach his hard cock in his uniform dress pants. I grip it in my palm over the fabric and squeeze.

"What's that, dolcezza?" He swallows hard and his voice is rough.

"I don't get on my knees for any man." I release him and spin on my heel, adding a little extra sashay to my ass as I leave.

CHAPTER TEN
MARCELO

The bang on my door wakes me from a deep sleep and I roll over, but too much, apparently, because I fall to the fucking floor.

"I hate this damn small bed." I stand and throw my pillow back on the bed before stomping over to the door to have someone's head.

I whip the door open to Mirabella standing on the other side. Her gaze roams down my chest, concentrating on my abs and the way my sweats hang low on my hips. She certainly looks like a woman who wants to get down on her knees right about now.

But then I notice that she's wearing a sports bra that shows off her amazing tits and skintight workout pants that show off her perfect figure.

"It's Saturday." Normal people our age sleep in on weekends. Hell, back home, I slept in every damn day. My line of work doesn't exactly require me to be up at dawn.

"Yeah, I know. Sofia's still drooling all over her pillow, but I'm just too excited." She walks into my room as if I invited her.

"Unless you want to help me out with my morning wood, I suggest you leave." I shut the door and deny my urge to flick the lock.

Her gaze falls to the bulge in my sweats. "That's not part of our arrangement."

"Yeah, I was thinking about our little arrangement and I think maybe we should renegotiate." I sit on my desk and prop my feet up on the chair.

"No way, you agreed." She points at me.

In reality, one thing about the Mafia is that a handshake means something.

"That was before your panties were soaked and you were coming on my hand."

I jerked off twice last night, and still, it wasn't enough. The thought of her slick pussy and my fingers gliding through her warm heat . . . how her eyes fluttered shut when she came, and her inner walls tightened around my fingers. Damn, I can only imagine how good it would have felt for her to come on my cock.

"Well, surprisingly, you're a good kisser." She turns to look out the window, her cheeks pink.

Amusement warms my chest. "Is that a compliment?"

"No," she snipes. "I just thought you'd be one of those selfish lovers who gets off and leaves a woman to finish herself." She turns to face me. "Are we going to train or what?"

I lift my hands. "When did you expect me to get the weapons between lunch yesterday and right now?"

Her shoulders sink. She's like no other woman in the Mafia I've ever encountered.

"Why do you want to learn to use weapons?"

She shrugs. "I want to protect myself."

I stand from the desk and walk closer to her. "And how do I know you won't use what I teach you against me?"

She backs up a step, her face paling. *Interesting.* "Guess you'll have to trust me."

I tilt my head. "You know as well as I do that you can't trust many people in our world."

Her lips form a thin line. "Don't you want a wife who can protect herself and you if need be?"

A laugh escapes me. "*You* protect *me?*"

Her eyebrows rise. "What? If you got ambushed, wouldn't you

want someone who has your back rather than some woman who cowers in the corner?"

I drag my hand down my face. That woman who cowers in the corner is my mother. She allowed my father to do whatever he wanted as long as she wasn't bothered. Hell, she was probably more scared of him than she was of any of his enemies. If I wasn't her only and favorite son, she would've been my top suspect as to who tried to kill my father and me.

"Unless you want me to teach you to fight with your fists, you're out of luck until I can steal a weapon."

She thinks for a second then jerks her head up and down. "Fine. That'll do. I do kickboxing on a regular basis, so I think you'll find that I don't need much help there." Another laugh falls out of me, and she puts her hands on her hips. "What?"

"A kickboxing class where you're kicking and punching the air?"

Her eyes narrow. "It's highly effective. You wouldn't know since you probably spend your time in the weight room."

I shake my head, grab a T-shirt from my dresser, and throw it over my head. Then I proceed to put on my socks and shoes before grabbing my school ID. "Let's go then."

"Where are we going?"

"To the gym. So apparently, you can kick my ass." I roll my eyes and open my door.

She stares me down but walks through it and waits for me to lock my door. I wave my hand out in front of us.

"Ladies first. Oh wait, you want to be an equal, right?" I stroll right past her to the elevator.

When we arrive at the gym, other than a few early risers like Mirabella, there's hardly anyone here and no one is paying us much attention. Nevertheless, I reserve us a private room with a foam mat and no windows for gawking spectators.

During my online tour with Nonno, I read that these rooms are private so that no one can study the way someone else fights because, upon graduation, most of the people we've gone to school with will be our sworn enemies.

I open the door of room number three and this time, I am a gentleman and allow her to enter first.

She jumps up and down on the mat. "This is awesome. How come I didn't know about these rooms?"

I raise an eyebrow at her.

"Oh yeah, we were granted admission, but not to every facet of the academy. How very kind of them." The anger is clear in her tone.

Although I don't understand why she wants to learn to fight or be more involved in our way of life than she has to when she could live a relatively quiet, lax life—one of privilege, wealth, and excess—it's abundantly clear she does want her hands in the mix.

"Let's get started. Show me your moves." I raise my chin at her.

She puts up her fists and they're so small they don't even cover her face. We jog in a circle around one another, and when I raise my eyebrows, she throws a punch that I easily dodge.

"Whoops," I say with a grin I know will piss her off.

Her beautiful blue eyes narrow, and this time, she throws a leg at me. I grab it, causing her to jump up and down on one leg in front of me.

"Marcelo!" she yelps.

"I'm your opponent. What will you do now?"

She throws another punch, but as long as I have her leg straight out in front of her in the air, she has no chance. She falls to the mat on her back and I crawl on her. We wrestle until I pin her with both my hands on her wrists.

"That class of yours should teach professionals. Those MMA fighters could learn a lesson or two from you." I laugh at her expense.

When I loosen my grip, she slides out from under me and crosses her arms. "You think you're so funny, but this is important to me."

"Why?" I put my hands at my hips.

"I don't want to be one of those wives who play stupid that their husbands are using them. They go out and have fun drinking and strip clubs or seeing their mistresses. I want my marriage to be different."

I sigh and run a hand through my hair. "You want the impossible."

She sits on the mat and crosses her legs. "Not with a guy who wants something different than we've witnessed our entire lives." Her eyes sear into mine and she's questioning me directly now. I wish I had an answer.

"I just don't think it's possible."

Her eyes study the floor, but she recovers fast. My assumption is that she knows how ridiculous what she wants sounds. It's like a fucking fairy tale.

"So I could use some work on hand-to-hand combat too. But we both know that no one fights fair anymore."

I sit on the mat with my hands behind me, holding my torso up. "You're right about that. But if your gun or knife gets kicked away, you only have your hands. You need to know how to kill a man with your bare hands."

She bites her lip. "Like you?"

"What, you want me to admit to you that I've killed a man with my bare hands?"

"I'm wondering if the rumors are true."

I stand and wipe my ass. "Why would I admit something like that to a woman who apparently hates me?"

She scoffs and stands. I prepare for some smart-ass comment, but she must really be desperate because she merely tries to get us back on track. "Whatever. Will you at least show me one move to protect myself?"

I blow out a breath. "Fine. First off, put your fists up high in front of your face. Your hands are small, but it's a start."

We end up sparring, and she's a surprisingly quick learner, although she never gets me down on my back. Even though I knock her to her back numerous times, I don't try anything. For some reason, I want her to make the first move next time. Maybe it's the fact that she thought I'd leave her hanging yesterday and was surprised when she came so fast from only my fingers.

When we're done, I tell Mirabella that I'm going to the locker room to use the bathroom and she heads to the smoothie bar.

I'm washing my hands when I overhear some guys talking in the shower area. At first, I don't pay too much attention, but then I hear my name.

"Aren't you scared Costa will try to overpower you? Then he'll control half the country."

I quietly creep over and look around the side of the wall. Both men are in their own showers with their backs to me. When one of them turns, I can tell from his profile it's Antonio La Rosa, Mirabella's brother.

"I just need Mirabella to marry him," he says. "After that, it wouldn't be the worst thing in the world if someone tried to off him again."

The other guy—who I can't get a look at—laughs. "You're crazy. He's already cheated death once."

"I'm well aware. Why do you think my dad wants him to marry Mirabella? I'm waiting for my reign, and unless someone tries to kill my father, I won't have my chance for a while. Father is already putting me in charge of a lot."

"Mirabella is going to be a thorn in Marcelo's side," the guy says.

Antonio smiles to himself. "Maybe it'll be enough that he'll kill himself and save us the trouble." He laughs and my hands tighten into fists. "She's not gonna make it easy on him, but she has to marry him. I've told her as much."

"And if she doesn't?"

"Then I guess it's who takes out who first. Northeast versus Southeast."

They rinse the shampoo out of their hair, and it takes everything in me not to go in there and slam each of their heads into the tile until I watch red wash down the drain.

So Antonio thinks he might have a chance to get rid of me someday? Fool.

Has he already tried once?

I don't think so. Having me dead would only be to his benefit after I marry his sister. Unless he tried to weaken the family by taking out my father and me at the same time, then planned to attack when we were susceptible.

I walk out of the locker room and run into Mirabella, who holds out a smoothie to me. "As a thank-you."

"For what? Getting you off last night or having you on your back for the past hour?" I eye it, wondering if she poisoned it.

"Why do you make everything sound dirty?" She sips her green smoothie and walks out of the gym.

"You have no idea what dirty is." But I'll be the one to show her.

Goddamn it if her cheeks don't pinken again. I've never been more desperate to have a woman underneath me—and I've never been a desperate man.

CHAPTER ELEVEN
MIRABELLA

The next morning, I roll over and groan. My body is so sore from my workout with Marcelo yesterday that you'd think I wrestled with a lion.

I thought I'd have him in speed or reflexes, but he's fast. It took him no effort to overpower me. I'm mortified by how confident I was in his bedroom talking about my kickboxing experience. He must've thought of me as such a stupid little girl.

But because of our positions, I don't have the real-world experience he does. All my lessons were taught in a posh, climate-controlled gym in Miami.

A long-suffering sigh leaves my lips.

"You all right over there?"

I turn and face Sofia's bed. "I'm surprised you're up. You didn't get in until late."

Her gaze darts away from mine. "Some of the crew decided to have a little party in the lounge downstairs after the coffeehouse thing."

We were both supposed to head down to the commons last night because the academy was putting on a coffeehouse night, but I opted out at the last minute. Being around a bunch of people, potentially Marcelo, didn't appeal to me. Especially because a part of me was hoping I'd run into him.

I need to reevaluate and figure out how to get out of this engagement because that is still the plan, even if Marcelo's body calls to mine in a way I've never experienced before.

It's Sunday, so I'll get my one phone call. I fully plan to speak with my dad. I'm not sure whether he knows Marcelo is alive or not, but I have no doubt he'll still expect me to marry him once he does.

"Did you have a good time?" I ask Sofia.

"Yeah." Something about her voice tells me she's holding back information.

"But . . ."

She sits up with her legs crossed and faces me, pulling her hair into a messy bun with the elastic that's on her wrist. "But Aurora Salucci was all over your brother all night."

I pretend to gag. Aurora is the same age as us and went to our elementary and high schools. Her dad has been my dad's underboss for many years, so she's always around and she's always a total mean girl. I think she's jealous of me.

At first, I was nice to her and would try to get along, but she made it clear she had no interest. She was on the yearbook committee at school, and in my sophomore year, someone replaced my headshot with a picture of a pig. Back then—pre–nose job—my nose tilted up a bit. In second grade, some of the boys used to make oink noises at me until my dad stepped in. I don't know what he said to the boys' parents or what he threatened, but I have a pretty good idea. Regardless, anyone who'd known me for a long time knew it was my biggest insecurity. She never admitted to it, but Sofia and I are sure it was her.

I didn't ask my dad to step in because I didn't want him drawing more attention to it. And because he'd promised me a nose job for my eighteenth birthday.

"What the hell is she doing around Antonio?" I push up off the mattress and face her, leaning against my headboard.

She frowns, then shrugs. "Not sure, but she made it really obvious that she was into him."

"I hope he didn't fall for her act."

"He wasn't hating the attention." Her voice holds more bitterness than I'm used to hearing from her.

"I'll talk to him."

I want to ask her whether Marcelo was there and, if so, what he was up to, but I refrain. I haven't confessed to Sofia what happened between Marcelo and me in his room the other day. I don't know why. Embarrassment, maybe? Here I am talking all kinds of shit about how I'll never bow down to him, acting like a tough girl, and the second he lays his hands on me, I'm a willing partner. More than that even—I would've done almost anything he asked of me in that moment. Thank God he didn't try to sleep with me. I have a feeling there would be no coming back from that.

"What do you want to do today?" Sofia gets off the bed and makes her way over to our bathroom.

"I have some homework to do, but I need to talk to my father."

She nods. "Want to go grab something to eat from Café Ambrosia?"

"Sure thing. I'll get ready to go when you're done in there." I stand from the bed and stretch.

"Sounds good." She disappears into the bathroom and I reach for my phone off my nightstand.

The only text I've missed is from Lorenzo. A small thread of disappointment weaves through me that Marcelo's name isn't on my screen. But what the hell does he have to text me about anyway?

I open Lorenzo's message.

LORENZO: We need to talk. Why are you avoiding me?

I sigh. He's right—I have been avoiding him since last weekend. I'm not in love with Lorenzo, but I do care about him, and I don't want Marcelo causing any more issues for him. Now that I have a deal with Marcelo, I can't be seen talking to Lorenzo or hanging around him anyway, so I need to let him know that nothing will be happening between us again.

I quickly type out a response.

ME: Sorry, first week of school has me swamped. I didn't want to do this over the phone but maybe it's best. We can't be seen together again. Whatever we had is over.

I hit Send, knowing Lorenzo likely won't end it there. He's persistent, but at least it's done now. Then I pull up Antonio's contact, and I type out a message.

ME: What the hell was Aurora doing all over you last night? She's evil incarnate.

I set down my phone and go to my dresser to pick out something to wear. Once I've settled on a pair of sweats and a crop top, my phone vibrates with Antonio's reply.

ANTONIO: Since when do you have your friends spy on me?

He obviously knows it's Sofia who filled me in.

ME: She's right to be concerned when she sees you with a viper like that.

ANTONIO: She's harmless.

ME: You know how terrible she is to me!

ANTONIO: Yeah, but she's hot AF.

I audibly growl at my screen as I punch out my message.

ME: Stay away from her.

ANTONIO: Relax. I have no intention of trusting her.

With a grunt of frustration, I toss my phone on my bed. Sofia comes out of the bathroom. "Everything okay?"

"Yeah, it's just that every man in my life seems determined to drive me crazy. Give me ten minutes and I'll be ready to go." I slip past her into the bathroom.

* * *

Twenty minutes later, the two of us are just leaving Roma House to head to Café Ambrosia when my phone buzzes in my back pocket. I pull it out to read the message, expecting it to be from Lorenzo.

ROMA HOUSE ADMIN: Your weekly call is due to be placed in ten minutes. Please proceed to the lower level, Room 5, to make your call.

I look at Sofia. "Shit, my call with my dad is in ten minutes. I have to go back in."

She gives me a mock frown. "Want to meet me over there when you're done?"

I nod, shoving my phone into my back pocket. "I'll head over as soon as I'm done."

"Good luck," she singsongs as she walks away.

"Thanks, I'll need it." I rush back into the building and don't bother with the elevator, instead taking the stairs down.

This is my first time on the lower level, and I'm surprised to find a security hub of some kind at the front. I spot a bunch of monitors with views all around the outside and inside of Roma House, but before I can get a better look, a woman who looks like she could be one of my many cousins approaches from behind a large reception desk.

"Hi, I'm Mirabella La Rosa. I just got a text about my call."

She smiles. "You're in room 5 down the hall. Close the door behind you and lock it. The room is soundproof, and the line is secure. You have ten minutes."

Clearly this place is designed so that business can still be conducted from campus. At least once a week anyway.

"Great, thank you."

Down the long hall is a bunch of closed doors, twenty or so in total. When I reach room 5, I open the door and peek inside. I don't know what I pictured, but it wasn't an interrogation room. There's one lone metal table in the middle of the room with a phone sitting on it and one chair in front of it. The concrete walls and floor are barren. Obviously they don't want us to linger.

When I sit in the chair, my stomach flutters and I realize I'm nervous about this conversation with my father. I have so much riding on it, and he's never been receptive before. I pick up the phone with shaking hands and dial the number of his burner phone that he had me memorize before I left. It only rings once before he picks up.

"Stellina, how are you?"

My dad has called me "little star" for as long as I can remember. I used to love it, but lately it makes me think he'll always see me as a little girl.

"Good, Babbo. How are you and Mom?"

"Your mother is well. She misses you, but she was excited to hear that she'll have a wedding to plan again."

So . . . he has heard the news about Marcelo. *Great.*

"About that . . . you know that Marcelo is still alive then?" I stand from the chair and pace, unable to sit any longer.

"I was as surprised as I'm sure you were. But this is a good thing for our family, stellina. The merger of the La Rosas and the Costas will mean more prosperity and power for all of us." It's abundantly clear that he's pleased.

My stomach sinks down to my toes. I can already tell how this conversation will end. "Babbo, I don't want to marry him. There has to be another way. Please."

Though I can't see him, I can feel the energy shift through the phone line. "Mira, I'll have no more arguments about this. Now that he's alive, nothing has changed. I've already spoken to his nonno about the upcoming wedding."

Tears well in my eyes. "Please don't make me do this. Please."

I hate resorting to begging, but I'm desperate. My father is the only one who can stop this sham of an engagement. Him and Marcelo's nonno.

"We all make sacrifices for this family. This is yours."

"But—"

"There are no buts! Now this is the last time I'll have this conversation with you. Do you understand? If you bring it up again, I'll pull you from the academy and you will return home. You can wait for Marcelo to graduate or whatever he decides and then move to New York with him."

The phone creaks as I hold it tighter. Swallowing past the painful lump in my throat, I say, "Yes, Babbo."

"Good. Now, would you like to speak to your mother? I can get her if you like." He is back using his pleasant voice now that he's gotten my compliance.

I suck back my tears. "No, I have to go. Tell her I'll talk to her next week."

"All right. Have a good week."

"Thanks."

I'm about to hang up when his voice stops me. "Mira?"

"Yes?" I wipe the tears that fall.

"Make me proud."

"I will," I mumble, hitting the button to end the call and returning the phone to the table.

Making him proud means not being me. How does a person spend a lifetime pretending to be something they're not?

When I reach the door, I unlock it and yank it open, bursting from the room and right into the chest of the person I least want to see right now—my future husband.

CHAPTER TWELVE
MARCELO

"Whoa." I grab Mirabella's arms with both hands to steady her. Her cheeks are red and her eyes bloodshot. I frown. "What's wrong?"

She looks at me and a foreign feeling digs into my chest. "Just who I want to see—my husband-to-be who's risen from the dead."

I raise both eyebrows. After the orgasm I gave her and the sparring, I thought we were on our way toward an improved relationship—one where she doesn't keep harping on our upcoming nuptials and stops making problems for me.

"Phone call not go as you planned? Daddy not willing to roll over for you?" I don't manage to keep the anger out of my tone. She could be married off to a much worse man than me.

She holds my gaze and it quickly turns into a battle of who will turn away first.

The woman down the hall clears her throat. "Mr. Costa, you only have your allotted time. Miss La Rosa, you need to leave."

I release Mirabella's arms and she slides by me, her body feeling better than I like as it runs along mine. "We'll talk later," I inform her.

"Maybe. I have to study." She flips her hair over her shoulder. Since it's not a school day, she doesn't have to wear the uniform, leaving her in a pair of sweats and a crop top. I'm not sure there's an outfit she can't make look good.

I enter the room and dial up Nonno.

He answers on the third ring. "Marcelo?"

His voice is groggy, and he sounds weak. If anyone else knew how unwell he's been the last year, they'd try to take us out. Actually, maybe someone out there does know and that's why they killed my dad and almost got me.

"This a good time?"

He clears his throat. "Of course. Just finishing my afternoon nap. Live up being young."

"I will, rest when you need." At this point, if Nonno dies, the Costa family legacy is solely in my hands and I . . . will be ready when the time comes. I have no choice but to be.

"Tell me how things are there."

I know he's not asking me how my classes are going, so I start right in since time is limited. "I've got two leads. One is Dante Accardi and the other Antonio La Rosa."

He blows out a breath. "Scratch Antonio off your list. He's going to be your brother-in-law and knows if he tried to kill you, that would take your marriage to his sister off the table. Both families need this marriage."

I glance at the clock on the wall that's counting down the minutes I have to talk.

"But if you think he's a threat, sit him down and make sure he knows who holds the power right now—us."

I nod, already planning to do just that. I'm not letting anyone talk shit about me behind my back. "I already plan to."

"And your fiancée?"

I run my fingers through my hair and down my neck, pulling to release the stress this woman puts on my shoulders. Damn it, I want her under me so fucking bad and I'm not used to not getting what I want when I want it. "She's coming around, but it's clear she doesn't want to marry me."

"Foolish girl. Maybe I should give her what she wants. Have her promised to some forty-year-old widower who won't give one shit about her other than her ability to reproduce."

The anger in my grandfather is one I've experienced myself. I want to shake Mirabella to remind her how much worse she could have it and tell her to stop treating me like some fucking monster. She's never seen the monster in me.

"I'll handle it. No worries."

"Let me know if she continues to be a problem. I'm sure her father would want to know."

I blow out a breath. At some point, I have to be the one to handle these problems, not my nonno. Once I'm not on these grounds, the title is mine, which probably pisses off a lot of our relatives. Including my uncle Joey, but he's never seemed to care much. I'm my father's oldest son, so it goes to me.

"Now, this Dante. He's from the Southwest, right?"

I tell him all about what Andrea said about his yacht being docked by my father's. Nonno says he'll do some digging and find out more on his end, but I should keep my ear to the ground.

"And Giovanni?"

I've been giving Giovanni the silent treatment for the past two days. He's constantly following me around and interrupting my conversations, telling everyone at this school not to mess with me. I've told him to give me some space, but he seems determined to be a one-man bodyguard. Either that or be in the loop on what I know.

"He's remaining close."

Nonno says nothing. He worries, as I do, that Giovanni's staying close to make sure no one gets in my ear, which could mean he's guilty of the hit himself. This is the one part of this business I've always hated. The fact you can't trust anyone.

"Well, you're the safest there. There're no weapons and your reputation will take you far before anyone tries to mess with you.

Talk to the La Rosa son, get your fiancée in line, and I'll handle the Accardis."

The clock flashes that I have thirty seconds left. "And we'll talk next week."

"Of course." He sounds more serious than he has this entire conversation.

The line goes dead before I can say goodbye or ask more questions.

* * *

AFTER THE PHONE call with Nonno, I head to the third floor and ignore all the stares from the La Rosa family boys when I knock on Antonio's door.

"Go away," he shouts from the other side and I pound harder on the door.

I hear a thud and assume someone fell on the floor, some giggling, then a naked Antonio with a towel covering his front answers the door. "Marcelo?" He's surprised to see me, as he should be.

Antonio reminds me of myself, although I'm better looking and a helluva lot stronger. He's going to be the leader of his family soon. No doubt, at some point, we'll both be managing our territories on the other side of each other's borders. Add on the fact I'll be married to his sister, and I have to clear the air before it becomes toxic. Make sure we have an understanding.

"We need to talk," I say.

He glances behind him, but the room is dark. I can't see who's in there. "I'm busy."

If your sister would get over herself and stop pretending she doesn't want me, I'd be busy too, I want to say, but I keep that thought to myself. "Half hour. My room."

Antonio nods. "Done."

He shuts the door and I head to the elevator. When it arrives to take me up to my floor, Giovanni, Andrea, and Nicolo are all in there with drinks from Café Ambrosia.

"We knocked on your door," Andrea says.

"I had my phone call," I answer, stepping in with them.

"What did Nonno say?" Giovanni asks. "When I called, Nonna answered and talked to me about how her sister is trying to steal her gravy recipe." There's a bitterness in his tone and I don't blame him. I would struggle being in his shoes.

"God, I miss her gravy." I place my hand on my stomach.

We all grumble because the food here isn't the same as the feasts we get at home.

"Sunday dinners." Nicolo shakes his head. "What I wouldn't give for a decent meatball right now."

The four of us groan, dreaming of a good Italian dinner the entire way up to our floor. Once the doors slide open and we file out, I tell them to come to my room. They migrate to their usual places, Giovanni leaning along the wall by the door.

"Nonno is going to handle Accardi, and I'm talking to Antonio to-day, but we have to keep digging. Neither of those two is for certain."

They all nod in agreement.

"No one's saying a damn word. The girls all talk about how lucky Mirabella is and the guys all hate you because you have more power than them. It's a no-win," Nicolo says.

"Maybe we need to look beyond the Italians," I offer up. "Maybe the Russians. They've taken over some of the clubs in the city recently."

Andrea's eyes widen and he nods. "That's not a bad idea."

"I have some Russians in a few of my classes," Nicolo says. "I'll keep an ear out and let you know if I overhear anything that's useful."

I point to him. "Perfect."

At times like this, I would never think one of my own could have plotted my death, but at the same time, it's been proven time and time again that people always look out for themselves first.

A knock on the door has Giovanni going over to answer it.

Antonio La Rosa stands in the doorway, looking around the room. "This an ambush?" If it were, he doesn't sound too concerned.

"Done already?" I ask with a smirk.

"You know the drill. Once we're done . . ."

I nod to the guys to leave and they file out. Well, Andrea and Nicolo file out. Giovanni stays. Antonio walks in and sits in the chair Andrea just got up from.

"I'll catch you later," I say to Giovanni, and he looks at us before blowing a breath and leaving.

Once the door is shut, Antonio points toward it. "Isn't he your second-in-command?"

"He's my cousin." I grab the chair from my desk, turn it around, and straddle it, facing Antonio. "I heard you yesterday."

I cut to the chase because I don't beat around the bush. My time is too valuable for that.

"Yesterday?" His eyebrows crinkle.

"I was in the locker room when you were showering." I spear him with my gaze, but he doesn't balk the way a lot of other men would.

He nods and sets his eyes on me. "You can't actually think I was serious."

His tone is unaffected, as though he's not at all concerned about what the outcome of this conversation could be. I don't think he's an idiot, so I doubt that's the case.

"I'm not sure what to think. It's the reason I sought you out." I stare at him, and finally, he shows some sign of being uncomfortable—

fidgeting in his seat. It's a telltale sign that he's not been as conditioned to be under scrutiny as I am.

"I got pissed when he said you'd somehow overthrow me and own half the country. But I'm on the same side as my father here. We agree that the merging of our families is a good thing."

I give him a curt nod. "One day it will be us working side by side."

"And I look forward to that. In the meantime, I've been telling Mirabella that she needs to stop protesting the upcoming marriage to you."

I hold up my hand. "Let me handle her. The more everyone keeps shoving me down her throat, the more she won't want to do it."

"Man, it's our first week and you already have her figured out." He laughs.

"As far as me and you?" I arch an eyebrow.

He holds up both hands. "I swear on my family you have no reason to worry that I'm coming for you. It was strictly locker room talk."

"Okay then." I believe him. As much as I believe anyone.

He stands from the chair. "I'd like us to be cordial while we're here. I'm going to be your brother-in-law and we'll work side by side."

I rise from my chair and shake his hand. "I'd like that too. I just need to find out who tried to kill me so I can be at ease again."

"I'll keep an ear out, and if I hear anything, I'll let you know."

"Appreciate it."

We shake hands again and hopefully we've come to a mutual understanding. I'd hate to have to take out my future brother-in-law. It'd be a buzzkill at the wedding.

I open the door to see Antonio out and we're both surprised to find Mirabella leaning against the wall in the hallway, talking to Giovanni.

She turns to us, her scowl firmly in place. "Weekly meeting to dictate my life?"

Her head tilt and sarcastic lilt are sexy as fuck and all I want to do is throw her over my shoulder and lock us in my room. But knowing her, she probably has a shiv in her pocket and would gladly shove it into me.

CHAPTER THIRTEEN
MIRABELLA

My blood was already hot after my phone call with my dad, but now it's boiling.

I came up here to see if Marcelo had some time to train me, but Giovanni stopped me before I could knock on the door, telling me Antonio was inside. It takes everything in me not to pound down the door.

But I decide to let them have their little talk. I'm not the type of person who makes a scene so that everyone will pop their head out of their dorm rooms to see who's screaming in the hallway. That doesn't mean that I'm any closer to accepting my fate. The same fate he and my brother are probably discussing right now. Another reminder that I have close to zero agency over my life.

At least if Marcelo keeps training me, I'll get closer to my goal—being an active participant in the family business. Maybe down the road things will change and I'll be able to step into the role I was born for.

I still remember my dad's laughter the first time I asked him about taking over a part of the business. He told me there was no way I would be able to do the kinds of things it takes to stay in power. But he has no idea what I'm capable of. No one does. It's not like I'm asking to go out on hits or to shake down people. I just want to matter in a way that has more to do with my mind than my gender and ability to produce an heir.

The door opens and the two of them are laughing with one another.

Antonio must see something in my expression. "Relax, sis. Your fiancé and I are just coming to an understanding."

Jerk. He's using the word *fiancé* to annoy me.

"Why do I feel like this understanding of yours has everything to do with me? It sure would be nice to be included in these conversations once in a while rather than be wheeled and dealed like a trading card behind closed doors."

Antonio pats me on the shoulder. "It's nothing you need to concern yourself with."

I roll my eyes and push past him, making sure to knock my shoulder against him as I walk into Marcelo's room, not making eye contact with him. When the door clicks shut behind me, I turn to find Marcelo sitting in a recliner.

"Back for another round, dolcezza?"

I ignore his taunt. "What were you and my brother talking about?"

He continues to scroll his thumb down his phone screen, not bothering to look at me. "Like he said, nothing for you to worry about."

I step forward. "Don't do that."

He finally puts down his phone and arches an eyebrow, looking unimpressed. "What happened to our agreement? I thought you were going to be an amenable fiancée from now on."

"In public, yes. In private, I'm still me."

He chuckles. "I'd expect no less."

"Well, what were you discussing?"

He leans forward, resting his forearms on his knees. "Nothing to do with you."

My eyes narrow. "So when we're married, this is how it'll be? Everything so secretive? I'm just supposed to remain in the dark?"

He shrugs. "Of course that's how it will be. What happens in business is nothing for you to worry about."

I want to tell him that that's not how I want things to be, but I don't trust him not to react the same way my father did. And somehow, if Marcelo laughed in my face right now about me being an active member of our crime family, it might break me. This first week of school is not at all going how I thought it would.

"Whatever. You two cook up your little plans. I don't care." I cross my arms.

He smirks and watches my every fidget. "I think you do care." He stands from the chair and saunters over to me. "Tell me, what is it you're afraid to tell me?"

Marcelo steps so close that I'm forced to uncross my arms so I don't touch him, leaving our bodies less than an inch apart.

"Not trusting you is different than being afraid of you." I raise my chin and meet his eyes.

He nods slowly. "As your future husband, don't you think I should know?"

I should argue that we won't ever be married, but for some reason, my throat closes around the words. I stare at him long and hard.

"C'mon." He trails a finger slowly down my cheek. "Tell me."

Should I? If I'm honest with him, will he use the information against me to make my worst nightmares come true? I stare at him a while longer, and before I make the conscious decision to clue him in, the words spill from my mouth. "I'm afraid I'll become like my mother and every other woman I know in our life."

His finger trails back and forth where my collarbones meet. The sensation of his skin on mine causes a ripple to run through my body. "And how is that?"

"It means that I'll be trapped in a mansion somewhere while my husband goes and does what he pleases. That he'll have no respect for me or my wishes in what I want in this life. That I'll have no say in making the decisions that affect my future. That I'll likely be in a loveless marriage, being used for your pleasure and not mine. I'm not sure a man in your position can even comprehend all that it means." I hold my breath, waiting for his reaction.

"You must know that there's no room for love in our world." His voice is soft and almost regretful, as if he can't do anything about that one.

"I know I can't ever hope for that, but at the very least, I should have an equal partnership."

His eyes roam my face for a few beats while he trails his thumb up and down my neck.

"Can you promise me we'll be equals, Marcelo?" I hate the pleading note to my voice, but I need to know how he sees this playing out.

"I promise that you'll have everything you'd ever want. I promise you that I'll protect you and our children with my life. And I promise you that you'll be my queen. But I can't promise you equality because that requires trust, and trust is hard to earn in our life. And even then, people flip. The only person I trust wholly is me."

My shoulders sag. It's not like I expected him to answer any differently, but hearing it out loud feels like a blow to the chest. "Sounds like my greatest fear will be my reality then."

Perhaps it's time to accept my fate, but I've been fighting against it for so long I don't want to give up. Maybe if I prove to Marcelo that he can trust me, maybe if he sees that I'll protect him as he will me, his thinking will change.

Before I ended up at the academy, I thought my best course of action was to try to end this marriage before it started. Maybe I actually need to change the confines of the marriage. Maybe if Marcelo sees how valuable an asset I can be to him, I'll earn his trust and, in turn, become an equal in our marriage.

CHAPTER FOURTEEN
MARCELO

It's midweek, and after talking with Nonno, I remind myself that I'm here to collect intel on who killed my dad and attempted to kill me. But my mind is occupied with Mirabella, which is annoying and unnecessary. She's mostly fallen into line, and after the wedding, we'll have plenty of time to do this whole "I hate you, I want you" thing. The sooner I figure out who was behind the car bomb, the sooner we're out of here.

"Hey," someone says from beside me.

I whip around to find Giovanni. "Fuck, man, I almost crushed your windpipe."

The fact that I was so in my head I didn't even notice his approach is unlike me and more than a little concerning.

He doesn't flinch as he keeps in step with me toward our third-period classes. "I came by your room last night. Where were you?"

"In my room. What time?"

He shrugs. "Like ten or something."

"I was sleeping."

"Sleeping?" He looks at me, forehead wrinkled. "What the hell are you doing sleeping at ten at night?"

I run a hand down my face. I wasn't sleeping. I've been sneaking out, figuring out what times the guards change shifts. We're allowed to walk around campus at night, but if I ever have to escape this place without anyone knowing, I have to make sure I don't get caught. Plus, it relaxes me. Reminds me of when I used to walk at night in New York City to clear my head. But Giovanni can't know any of this.

"I was drained."

"Huh . . . okay, well, just wanted to make sure all is well." He pats me on the back. "Gotta get to history of generations. See you later."

"See you," I say, annoyed he's still playing mother hen to me.

I enter my computer science class and sit down behind the computer I've been assigned. So far, I'm not killing it in any class but weaponry, but this class is the worst. What normal businessmen use for business doesn't work for us. It's not like we put together contracts for our agreements or use spreadsheet software for our books—at least not our real books. This class is all about hacking and writing computer code that steals people's information, setting up fake accounts for online businesses to clean money. All shit my father didn't bother to show me. He was always more concerned that I had a strong backbone, an irate temper, and knew a thousand ways to torture and kill a man.

Professor Bowers stands from her desk and asks everyone to sign in to their computer. I'm busy looking for my letters and poking each one when Mirabella rushes through the door. Her long hair is a mess from the wind and she's panting for breath.

What the hell is she doing here? She wasn't in this class last week.

"Ah . . . here she is." Professor Bowers smiles at Mirabella. "Ladies and gentlemen, I've asked Mirabella La Rosa to help me out this semester after what she showed me the first couple of days. She's an absolute whiz on the computer and I could use the extra pair of hands to assist."

Just like every other time Mirabella and I are in the same room, our eyes find each other and electricity crackles between us.

"I'm sorry I'm late, Professor Bowers. I—"

Professor Bowers waves off her concern. "No worries. Why don't you sit over there?" She points at a desk that's clear across the room from me. "You can do the exercise and then go around and help anyone who needs it."

Nervousness pricks at the back of my neck. So far, no one knows my inadequacy with modern technology. The only thing I know about computers is that the feds can get any information they want out of them. But for some reason, I don't want Mirabella to know this about me. I'm going to be her husband, her life will be in my hands once we're married, and I don't want her thinking less of me.

Mirabella does as instructed and sits where I can no longer see her. Damn shame. The class was starting to look up for a second there.

Miss Bower reveals the steps for the assignment on the white-board and everyone gets to work. I can't even find the cursor for my mouse on the screen. I circle it a bunch of times and nothing. I growl from frustration when it suddenly appears. As I'm busy try-ing to follow the directions, a message box pops up on my screen.

You sound frustrated over there . . .

I look around the class, but no one is paying any attention to me. I type a message and hit the reply key.

Who is this?

A message pops back before I can blink.

If I give myself away, what do I get in return?

What the fuck? My fingers hit the buttons as I find them. I glance to my right where the girl next to me can type without even looking at the keyboard. That feels like a superpower right about now.

Hard to find those keys, right?

My jaw clenches at the taunt.

> I'm fine.
> Then why all the noises?
> Who the hell is this?

I have no idea how to get this message off my screen.

> Your fiancée.

I blink double time at the screen. I want to stand to see her face, but I don't have to because she sends a picture of herself with a look of shock on her face. I guess she is pretty good with these things.

> Amazing, right? Someone with a vagina being so much more skilled than all the dicks in the room?

This woman and her need to be seen as an equal.

> I can't deny that I'm impressed.
> Especially since you're a hunt-and-pecker.
> What did you just call me?
> Relax, big guy. Your fingers on the keys . . . you hunt and then peck.

I blow out a breath.

> Not my fault my fingers are too big for these little things.
> I bet you say that to all the girls.

Actually, the girls like my big fingers. You do too,
remember?

The message block screen goes pink, and I think it's to signify
she's blushing.

Don't be embarrassed. They're going to be all yours
one day.
I'm not naive enough to believe that.

My head tilts and I glance at Miss Bower, who's back at the front of
the room giving directions about the next step of the assignment when
I've yet to finish the first part since my attention is on Mirabella.

What does that mean?
You guys try to hide your goomahs, but we know. We
know all about the other women.

I blow out a breath. I shouldn't be surprised she thinks I'd step
out on her like every other made man, but has Mirabella looked in
the damn mirror? No way I'd ever get anyone hotter than her. And I
question whether I could ever have the kind of chemistry we share
with anyone else.

Ahh so you assume I'll do that too?
I can't think of one man I know who is faithful, can you?

I take a moment to think. Surely there's been someone, but even
my nonno had a woman on the side. He wasn't one for the nonstop
strippers and hookers like my dad and his generation, but once I
was old enough to be involved in the business, I saw Nonno with
other women.

I'm not them.

It's a power thing. Men like you like power and women like them like to tell you how hot your power is. They put you on pedestals and you Neanderthals eat it up.

So, you think I'm going to have affairs?

I ignore the part of me that likes the fact that she seems to care. Some wives don't. They're happy to take the money and the prestige that comes with their husband's position in the family and let him get his rocks off elsewhere. But I like the idea of Mirabella being jealous.

I know you're going to have affairs.

The entire screen switches to show newspaper article after newspaper article of famous made men with their goomahs. But she didn't need to show me that. I still remember the day my mom took me and found my dad with some woman in a casino hotel.

My parents weren't an arranged marriage like I am to Mirabella. They were, or so my mom thought, in love. She took me up to the hotel floor, where two guys were standing by the door of a room. She banged and screamed while they tried to get her to go back to the elevator. I watched from down the hallway as the door sprang open and my dad stood there naked with some woman wearing bright-red lipstick that matched her heels.

My mom went in after him, crying and wailing, beating on his chest. He let her in, and twenty minutes later, she came out of that room a different person. She took my hand, led me down the elevator to our vehicle, and we never spoke about it again. I told myself as I got older that I wouldn't do that to my wife.

Think what you will. I can only prove you wrong.

Another bunch of pictures get pasted up on the screen, but these are all from social media and they're all of me and different women.

> ???
> I'm not married . . . yet.
> You'd give all this up for me?

She posts a bunch of pictures that show me with one specific woman I'm photographed with a bunch of times—my mom's best friend's daughter.

> It's not what you think.
> I'm sure.

Professor Bowers walks by my desk and smiles at me. When I look at my screen, the assignment is back on there and the chat box is gone.

Fuck, I had no idea it would be this much of a turn-on to find out she's this good on a computer.

Once Professor Bowers is out of sight, the text box pops up again.

> I'll let you get back to work. Good luck.
> This conversation isn't over.

She's sorely mistaken if she thinks it is.

> There isn't much to say.
> Except that I'm a manwhore? You don't know me at all.
> Reputations are pretty accurate in our life, no?
> Apparently not mine.
> So . . . your hands aren't lethal?

My jaw flexes.

> Come for a midnight walk with me tonight. We'll sneak out of the dorms and I'll tell you about the real me. You clearly have your own secrets.
> Who? Me?

A GIF comes up of her smiling and batting her eyelashes.

Professor Bowers claps from the front of the class. "Okay, everyone, that's all for today."

I find myself desperate for an answer, so I hurriedly type.

> Midnight?

There's a pause and I'm not sure what her answer will be. Professor Bowers is talking about leaving the screens open so she can check to see everyone got to where they were supposed to be. Great, a fucking *F*, but at least I spent my time in a productive way.

> Sure.

The message box closes, and then I spot Mirabella getting up and start walking around to see if anyone needs any assistance. I glance at my neighbor's screen and back at mine to see that our screens match. Mirabella did the assignment for me and now I'm almost fully hard because apparently my future wife is a goddamn genius.

CHAPTER FIFTEEN
MIRABELLA

I creep toward my door, open it, and sneak out into the hall as quietly as I can to not wake Sofia. Marcelo leans against the wall across from my room with one foot propped up.

While wandering the grounds this late isn't forbidden, it would raise some red flags because we're a man and a woman. The patriarchy is hard at work at Sicuro Academy, trying to keep their daughters' virtue intact. At the very least, security would stop and question us if we're caught, and I don't want the hassle or their increased interest.

"I see you dressed the part." Marcelo looks as casual as can be, a smirk tilting up one corner of his lips.

I shrug, glancing at my black leggings, thin, long-sleeve black shirt, and black shoes.

"Let's go." He pushes away from the wall and encases my hand in his large one.

I don't pull away, even if I feel I should. The idea that I'm growing more comfortable with his touch irks me. The fact that I almost crave it is unspeakable.

Rather than the elevator, he leads us to the stairwell, which we take to the ground level. Once we're standing at the door that leads from the stairwell into the lounge area of Roma House, he stops and peers out the small window.

"There are cameras on the stairwell doors. Why didn't we take the elevator?" I ask quietly.

He looks at me over my shoulder. "Just relax. I've been doing this for days now. I'm pretty sure I figured out their sequence."

Huh. It's not a bad idea to test his theory.

"So, what's the plan now?"

He takes my hand again and pulls me forward, then positions me where he wants me by the window with his hands around my waist. I suppress the full-body shiver from having him pressed against my back, his hands on my waist as he towers over me.

"See that door tucked in the corner to our right?"

I nod.

"We're headed there. It's never locked, and from there, we'll sneak out the window. There's a blind zone in the cameras there. Then we should be good."

My heartbeat speeds up. This is way more fun than being sequestered in my ivory tower at home.

"Follow me." He reaches around me and turns the doorknob.

We slip out into the lounge and quickly make our way to the door in question, sticking close to the wall. When we slip into the room, he quietly closes the door. The lights are off, but I'm fairly sure it's the study room.

Like a panther, he stalks over to the window, slides it open, and helps me through it. It's a little higher off the ground than I expected and I almost yelp before I land on the soft grass. He follows, leaving the window open a few inches for our return.

Without a word, he takes my hand again and leads me across the grass. We don't speak again until we're a ways from the school and come upon a large pond with a good-size gazebo. It's built of stone with concrete shingles and has a castle-like appearance. The long rectangular main portion connects to a circular end where the roof reminds me of a turret.

"I didn't even know this was here." I admire how the moonlight glimmers on the still surface of the pond as I step up into the gazebo, which has dim torchlike lights on each pillar inside. Being raised higher gives me the perfect view of the pond.

Marcelo leads me to the end, inside the circular portion. "I discovered it a few nights ago."

I let my hand drift over the coarse stone. "I like it."

Marcelo leans against one of the pillars closest to the pond, arms crossed, staring at the smooth water, so I sit on the bench wrapping around the interior of the structure.

"Tell me where you learned to be so good on the computer." He jumps right into the questions I knew he wanted to be answered.

"You'd be amazed what you can figure out from the internet."

He turns his head to look at me. "Your father allowed it?"

I shrug. "My dad doesn't know enough to restrict my access."

He nods knowingly. "I get the impression you can be devious. Not exactly a quality one wants in a wife."

"Unless she's using it in your favor." I give him a challenging stare.

He chuckles and pushes away from the column, coming to sit by me.

"Why do you want to be involved in the business so badly?" He studies my face as though I'm an enigma to him.

I'm sure I am. Most women I know want no part in the dangerous lying, cheating, and stealing that goes on in our world. "Because I know I won't be content waiting for my husband to come home. I have something of value to add and I'm good at it. I need some kind of purpose in my life."

"You don't consider raising our children purpose enough?"

Every time Marcelo mentions "our" children, a little flutter erupts in my belly.

"I'll love my children and do anything for them. But if you're asking whether picking out their clothes and telling the chef what meal to prepare them and helping them with their homework will fulfill me, the answer is no. I need more. Wouldn't you?"

My statement would sound sacrilegious to some, but it's the honest truth. I didn't grow up dreaming of planning my wedding and brushing my children's hair. I have no doubt that when I have children, I will love them with my whole being, but staying home to mother them full time has never felt like my destiny or something that would fulfill me completely.

Marcelo's lips press together, and he doesn't say anything.

Good. Maybe if anything comes out of this, he'll reconsider this marriage.

"I thought we were here to talk about you?" I'm more than curious to hear what Marcelo has to say. Sure, a lot has been said about the man, but not all of it matches up to the person I'm starting to know.

"What do you want to know?" He scowls. "Seems you had me figured out earlier today."

I roll my eyes. "Tell me what I've got wrong then."

"I already told you that you're wrong about the women in my life."

I stand from the bench. "I'm out of here if you're not going to be honest with me."

He nabs my wrists and yanks me back down, our thighs touching. "You'll leave when I say we're finished."

Something about the glint in his eyes tells me I shouldn't push him this time.

"All right then, convince me how you're such a virgin."

He shakes his head. "I'm not declaring myself a virgin. But the pictures you sent of that one particular woman are nothing. She's my mom's best friend's daughter and we grew up together. She's like a second sister to me and nothing has ever happened between us. The rest of them . . ."

"I can guess," I grumble and cross my arms.

"I was unattached. We weren't engaged yet and I was free to do what I wanted. But believe me, I didn't have a ton of time to chase pussy. My father was busy teaching me the business and making sure I was ready to take it over someday. Even before my grandfather fell ill and handed the power to my dad, Dad was obsessed with the idea of me being ready to lead when the time came. I had my fun, but not as much of it as you seem to think."

"Let's say I believe you. That doesn't mean that once we're married, you're going to be faithful to our vows. Especially if I'm not giving it up to you."

Marcelo full-on laughs and my cheeks heat in anger. "Mark my words, dolcezza. You'll be fucking your husband, and you'll be dripping wet and begging for it every time."

His crass words heat the blood in my veins, pumping desire throughout my body.

"We'll see about that." I shift in my seat, pressing my thighs together.

Marcelo, the jerk, notices because he barely manages to keep the smirk off his face. "What else do you want to know?"

"Is it true what they say? Do you kill men with your bare hands?"

His eyes meet mine as though perhaps he's figuring out whether he can trust me with this or not. "It's true."

I thought so. It doesn't escape me that I *should* be horrified by this truth, but I'm not. Maybe I've been conditioned over the years and seen too much in my own family. Besides, I know the people he's killed weren't exactly innocents themselves. "What's it like?"

He arches an eyebrow, surprised. "The act itself isn't as difficult as you think. Squeezing the life out of someone, cutting off their airway, that's the easy part." His hand settles on the base of my neck, and he squeezes gently. "The difficulty comes in watching the life leave their eyes. That's something you don't forget."

"I know you're trying to scare me." My voice is quiet. "But you don't."

He ignores my statement. "Do you think you have it in you to kill someone, Mirabella?"

I meet his gaze. "If it came down to it, I know I do."

He chuckles and lets his hand drop.

"What was your father like?" I ask.

He sighs. There's more than I can interpret in that sound, but instinct tells me they had a complicated relationship.

"He was stubborn and pigheaded and had zero respect for women. But he'd also do whatever it took to keep the family on top and make sure everyone was protected. Surprisingly, he was a man of his word, but he was gluttonous and always wanted more of everything—more power, more money, more women. Nothing was ever enough for him."

Everything he says echoes all that I've ever heard about his father. "Are you sad that he's gone?"

Marcelo looks at me with what seems close to vulnerability and shakes his head. "No. He was getting into some shit I didn't agree with and was becoming sloppier and more selfish as the years went on. When you're the head of the family, you have to think of the organization as a whole, not just yourself."

I have an idea what he might be referring to and disgust turns my stomach. "He was a product of his environment. No doubt you'll be the same in twenty or thirty years."

His fists tighten at his sides, and through clenched teeth, he says, "I will *never* be my father, Mirabella. In that, you can trust."

He says the words with such conviction I can't help but believe him.

Since he's being so open and honest with me, I ask him the one question I want an answer to, but that seems a little frivolous. "If you weren't born into this fate, what do you think you would want your life to look like? What would you want to be?"

He ponders the question for a minute but eventually shakes his head. "I have no idea."

I frown. "C'mon. There must be something you've dreamed of being able to do."

He barks out a sad-sounding laugh. "You don't get it. Since the moment I was born, I've been raised to be the person I am today. There are no other options for me. There never were."

For the first time, I realize that maybe Marcelo is as much a prisoner in this life as I am, and I hate the way that knowledge softens me to him.

CHAPTER SIXTEEN
MARCELO

Mirabella and I talked for at least an hour last night, and I find myself growing more fascinated with my bride-to-be. She's unlike any girl I've ever met. What she wants—to be a *real* part of the family—is preposterous and, to my knowledge, has never been done. Still, a part of me wonders whether we'd be stronger if she were beside me at the head of the family than if I were alone.

Something to consider? I'm not sure yet.

Regardless, one perk of your fiancée being the computer teacher's pet is that she has a key to the computer room. Since it's far from my best subject, she's agreed to help me. I think it's likely a ploy to try to prove how useful she could be on the outside, but whatever. It's to my benefit.

"You'll get nowhere if you don't learn how to type first." She puts my hands on the keyboard. "I don't understand how you never learned."

"Like I said, my dad was hard core about making sure I would be ready to take over my responsibilities. I never really had time to be trolling the internet. I can text and shit, but I don't have to sit at a computer—ever. It's not like we correspond in emails."

She laughs, and this warm piercing feeling hits my chest. I caused that smile on her lips and her enjoyment. I'm not sure I've ever made anyone laugh—other than the guys, and even that is few and far between.

"Good point. I can't imagine my dad sitting behind a computer to do anything other than probably watch porn."

I hate to break it to her, but her dad owns the most strip clubs out of the four corners, so I'm pretty sure he's seeing the real thing, but I keep that to myself.

"Okay." She has me put my hands over hers on the keyboard, her long hair streaming over her shoulder like a curtain, blocking my line of sight in that direction. But I'm quickly distracted by her face being so close to mine. "These are the eight keys your fingers should stay on and then venture to specific keys nearby." She types out, *I owe Mirabella for this one.* "Now you try."

I do and have to look at the keyboard a bunch of times and take twice as long as she did. When I turn my head toward her, she's smiling again, but I think it's at my expense. "Careful, I can pin you to the ground."

"And I can probably hack the little electronics you had out in the world to find out more dirt about you and have you arrested."

"Touché," I say, and she concentrates back on the keys.

Computer training is much more boring than the physical training we've been doing. Having her pinned under me wearing nothing more than short shorts and a sports bra is more my style.

When I grow frustrated with all my hunting and pecking, as Mirabella calls it, I push my chair back from the computer and slump into it. "I'm not sure why this class is necessary. I mean, this shit seems so 101. We need someone to teach us what you know."

"If everyone knew what I did, then I wouldn't be useful." She raises her eyebrows while checking her perfectly manicured nails.

When I first saw Mirabella after we were told we would be married, all I saw was the usual Mafia daughter—dressed in designer clothes, perfect nails, perfect skin, perfect hair, and the right amount of jewelry for a Mafia princess. But now, I'm seeing a different side to her, one that doesn't fit neatly into our world. She wants a lot, and even if I'm the one in charge, I can't guarantee I can give her that. My men and my enemies would see me as weak if I treated her differently than all the other wives are treated.

"It's a gift, I will admit," she says when I don't respond.

Mostly because she's crossed her legs and all I can think about is sliding my hand between those luscious thighs and making her come like I did days ago.

"Let's say we didn't marry. What would your plans be? Your dad isn't going to allow you to just take a spot on the payroll."

She blows out a breath. "I know."

"So?" I arch an eyebrow.

"I'm not sure. Run?"

My eyebrows shoot up. "You'd be caught."

"I'm not sure my dad cares enough about me to search for me."

"You forget." I stand and press my finger to her nose. "You've been promised to me. My family expects us to get married. If your father can't get his daughter to the altar, that's a problem." I don't need to voice the underlying threat.

Her chair screeches as she gets up. "Do you have any idea what it feels like to be trapped? I run, they find me. I try to better myself, I'm told to sit down and be quiet. Even my father would come for me. Not because he cares about me, but because he doesn't want to lose a pawn he can play."

I walk over to the wall and lean against it. "You'd want for nothing as my wife. You'd live in a palace with maids and cooks at your beck and call. Shop at the best stores. Eat at the best restaurants. Some women would kill for that life."

"Well, they're not me."

No, they certainly are not. "Don't you think your friend Sofia would love to marry a boss?"

"Sofia and I are built differently." She sits on a desk, her feet dangling. "She'd be happy to play the role of obedient wife." She lifts her gaze, and it locks with mine. "I plan on fighting my way into getting what I want."

I blow out a breath and run my hand over the short strands of my hair. "Damn, woman, you're going to challenge me."

She doesn't turn away but holds my gaze. "I am, but I have a feeling you don't hate it."

I push off the wall, stalking toward her. "It drives me crazy when you push against my directives, but at the same time, I can't deny it turns me on. Everyone in my life is a 'yes, sir' person. So explain to me why my dick gets hard every time you disregard my power over you."

She shrugs in a cute schoolgirl way that doesn't fit her. "What can I say? I'm kind of irresistible." Her eyes sparkle with a mix of mischief and lust.

My hands fall to her knees and I push her legs apart to make room for me. "I can't deny that your father was right when he told my dad there's no woman more beautiful than his daughter." My hand slides up to her cheek and back down to her throat, running my thumb down the column of her neck. She swallows hard and her mouth opens in a small O. "You're so fucking beautiful."

She moans and my hand travels up, my thumb brushing along her lips. She slides out her tongue and wets the pad of my thumb. My gaze is fixated on her as she sucks my thumb into her mouth, twirling her tongue around it as if she's giving me a blow job. She said she'd never go down on her knees for me and with how fucking hard I am from just her mouth on my damn thumb, it makes me crave having her mouth wrapped around my cock.

She releases my thumb with a pop, and I coat her bottom lip with wetness before lowering to kiss her. She's a craving I'm never going to quench. I want her in any and every position.

This time there's no reluctance when my lips meet hers. Her tongue thrusts into my mouth and her fist grabs my shirt, pulling me toward her.

My hands venture down to her short T-shirt. The reveal of her midriff has been driving me crazy all night. She jolts slightly when my hands land on her rib cage. Then she calms as I glide them up over her bra, taking her tits in my palms. A desperate plea falls from her lips when my thumbs graze her nipples through the cups.

God, I'm never gonna get enough of her. I tear down the cups and the weight of her tits fall into my hands.

"God, Marcelo." Her head falls back.

My mouth descends on her bare neck, licking my way up to her earlobe. "Tell me what you want." I pinch her nipples, and her hips rise off the desk and fall back down. "Do you like it rough, dolcezza?"

"Don't take your hands off me."

When I remove one hand, she whimpers until she figures out that I'm sliding it past the waistband of her sweatpants and under the hem of her panties. She's slick and wet and ready. I groan. My dick presses against my athletic pants, but I don't want to get my hopes up until she grips it over the fabric, squeezing my cock.

"Oh my god," she says, referring to my size, I think.

"Pull it out," I order, my fingers running up and down her slit, teasing her entrance.

She does what I say and pulls my joggers down to rest under my balls.

"Now look at my cock while you stroke me."

She tightens her grip and pumps up and down on my dick, sliding the precum over the top with her thumb. I want nothing more than to see her mouth stretched around it, but she'll do it on her own accord, without me pushing her because the satisfaction will be worth it.

"There you go. Faster, baby." I push a finger inside her and her free hand grips my shoulder. "You're soaked. Tell me how I make you this wet. That it's only for me."

Her breathing is labored, and her eyes are closed now. "Only you."

I add another finger, arching just like last time. "Only me, what?" I withdraw my fingers and her eyes snap open in shock. "Marcelo!"

"Only me, what?" I repeat, holding her gaze, needing the words.

"Only you make me this wet."

"And needy?" I reinsert the two fingers and her eyes fall back to closing.

"Yes, and needy. Damn it, make me come."

"Not until you pump my dick and I'm squirting my seed all over you."

A strangled cry comes out of her.

I lean in close. "One day, I'm going to be so deep inside your wet pussy, you'll be begging for me to never stop."

She clenches around my fingers then pumps my dick over and over. Her lips fall to my jaw, casting small kisses, whispering dirty things to me, and I grow harder than I thought possible.

"I can't wait to have your big cock inside me, stretching me wide. Wait until you see my lingerie collection."

"I'll buy you the whole damn store." My breath comes out in pants.

"What's your favorite color? What do you want to see me in?" She arches her hips as if requesting me to fill her even more.

Her free hand goes to my balls and she's on the edge of the desk with her legs wide. I'm not sure if it's the talking or the movement, or a combination of both, that's making this so hot for us.

"Black. Always black."

She slides her tongue up my neck and over my jaw. "Done. I have the sexiest see-through number you're gonna love."

I can't take anymore, my vision swirling as I squirt into her hand and all over her shirt. Cum seeps out and down around my shaft, onto my joggers. But I don't bother with the thought of how we're going to clean this up because she climaxes right after me, riding my fingers as though they're my cock.

I watch as her eyes squeeze shut in ecstasy and she cries out. Her cheeks are pink, and her hair is a mess, and she's never looked more beautiful than she does now, giving herself over to me.

Once she's caught her breath, she stares down at my cock and whispers, "That was so hot."

Then there's a knock on the window of the room and she jerks. Luckily, we're on the other side of a low partition, so all the person can see is the upper half of our bodies.

The janitor opens the door. "The building closes in a half hour. Finish up."

"Yeah, will do." I wave him away.

Mirabella laughs the minute the door shuts and her forehead falls to my chest. Then she rests her chin on my chest and stares up at me. "I'll give you one thing, Costa, you give good orgasms."

"Now I can say the same thing about you. I love that dirty mouth of yours."

She smiles, and for the briefest second, I wonder if maybe we could work out. Could I fall in love with Mirabella La Rosa? Could we change the way Mafia marriages are done? Could I afford to give her the power she so desperately wants?

I don't have a fucking clue what any of the answers are.

CHAPTER SEVENTEEN

MIRABELLA

"You're off to meet Marcelo *again*?" Sofia crosses her arms and cocks a hip.

She's questioned my every meeting with him and clearly senses something is up. I haven't confessed about the time we fooled around in his room because I didn't expect there to be another time. But after losing my willpower yesterday in the computer lab, I could use my best friend's input on what she thinks it all means.

"I am. We have a deal."

Her forehead scrunches. "What kind of deal?"

I fall down beside her on the sofa and confess everything—the deal we made for my compliance, our conversation by the pond, and what happened in his room and yesterday in the computer lab.

When I get to the part about us fooling around, her hands fly up to cover her mouth, eyes wide. "Oh my god, how was it?"

My head flops back on the couch. "Better than I knew it could be. I don't have any experience except with Lorenzo, but it was never like that with him." My phone buzzes from the table and I pick it up to see that Lorenzo has sent me another text. I've been dodging him for the past couple of weeks, but the guy can't take a hint. Clearly, I'm going to have to figure out something else to make him go away.

"Is that Marcelo?" Sofia eyes my phone.

I shake my head and drop my phone back on the table. "Nope. Lorenzo. Again."

She rolls her eyes. "He stopped me on my way back here yesterday. Wanted to know why you wouldn't talk to him. He actually asked me to set up a meeting between you two in secret."

"What is his problem? It's over. I'm trying to help him by staying away from him. Marcelo will kick his ass—rules or not—if he gets near me. Probably even more so now that we've . . ." I don't finish the sentence. I've already given her all the details.

"So, what do you think it means that you guys are messing around with each other now?"

I give her a "duh" look. "That's what I'm hoping you can tell me."

"Well . . . have you considered that maybe it means that you're starting to like your fiancé?" She giggles.

I spear her with a scowl. "I like his ability to make me come, Sofia, that's about it."

"Are you sure?" She cocks her head. "You're softening to him. Even the way you talk about him or say his name is different from before."

My mouth drops open. "It is not!"

She chuckles. "Is too. Don't worry, your secret is safe with me." She winks.

I walk over to my dresser to grab a sweatshirt to pull over my sports bra for my walk over to the athletic center where I'm meeting Marcelo for another training session. He swiped a butter knife from the dining hall to act as a prop for us today.

"I'm not softening toward him. I still don't want to marry him, Sofia."

"Have you considered that maybe this is a good thing? Maybe the two of you can have a happy life together."

I pull the sweatshirt over my head and whip around to face her. "I'll never be happy being forced into a role I want no part in."

She frowns, seeming to think. "I just want you to try to make the best of it. I don't want to see you miserable."

"I know. And I appreciate it. But I won't be happy forced into a life I don't want—no matter how good the sex is."

She walks across the room to give me a hug. "I get it. I just want you to be happy."

I squeeze her in return. "And I plan to be. One way or another." We pull apart and I give her a small smile. "I'm going to be late. I'll see you tonight."

She nods, and I leave the room. The hallway is empty as I make my way to the elevator, leaving me to think about my best friend's words. She knows me better than anyone. Is she right? Am I softening toward Marcelo?

Gone is the heated anger every time I think about him. And I no longer snap back at everything that comes out of his mouth. I figured it was because that was part of our deal, but that's only in public. Even in private, I'm nicer to him, and at times I've been too vulnerable with him.

"Shit," I say as I step into the elevator. *I'm starting to like my fiancé.*

If I'm not careful, I'll find myself pregnant and stuck in a mansion, picking out drapes.

I'm in my head as I walk over to the athletic center. I'm happy for the distance so that I can get some perspective about my situation before I'm once again in Marcelo's orbit.

As I approach the building, Dante Accardi stops me. I haven't talked to him since our run-in at Roma House during the first week of school and that works for me. The guy is a complete dick.

After almost running into him, I scowl. "What the hell are you doing?"

"Glad I ran into you."

I cross my arms and give him a look I hope is full of disdain.

"We need to talk."

I caustically laugh. "We have nothing to talk about." I move to step around him, but his hand clamps down on my upper arm. "I suggest you remove your hand now before I remove it for you."

He throws his head back and laughs. "As if. I think you'll want to listen to me though." His hand drops. "I have an offer for you that's mutually beneficial."

I'd be lying if I said that doesn't pique my interest. "All right. Let's hear it. I have somewhere to be though."

He steps closer to me. "Rumor is you're not happy about your upcoming nuptials."

I arch an eyebrow. "What gave it away?" I deadpan.

"What if I had a better offer for you?"

"Come on, Dante, you have nothing better to offer me than Marcelo. You're all the same, except he runs the Northeast."

He scoffs. "Please. I'm a thousand times the man Costa is."

"I didn't realize this was going to be a dick-measuring contest. Get on with it, Dante."

"What if the two of us got married?"

I laugh until I realize he's serious.

"Think about it, we'd own the border between the US and Mexico from coast to coast. Your father should be equally happy with that."

I look him in the eyes. "You mean *you'd* be happy with that because it would make running drugs even easier. You'd finally have both coasts and full run of the border."

He shrugs. "Maybe so. But it's not like you wouldn't get anything out of it."

"My family wouldn't gain nearly as much as yours. Besides, why the hell would I trade one prison for another?"

He smirks. "Because this warden will give you the keys."

Whatever he means by that, he's serious. It's written all over his expression.

I let my hands fall to my sides. "What's that mean?"

"It means I wouldn't expect you to be a wife. We'd be married in name only, but you could do whatever you wanted. Live in a different house than me. See whoever you want. Go to school, get a job, lounge around the house all day . . . I don't give a shit. You do you, just stay out of my way."

"What about what everyone else thinks?" What would be his motive for this?

Dante shrugs. "It's none of their concern. Besides, you don't think I can keep my people in line or take out anyone who might try to revolt against me?"

He's either as good as he thinks he is, or he's an overconfident idiot. I can't decide which.

"So, what do you think?"

It's not ideal, but it's not a terrible offer. Certainly better than anything Marcelo has said to me.

I shake my head. "My father would never allow it. He wants this alliance with the Costas."

"If you say yes, you let me worry about your father."

"What are you going to do, take out Marcelo Costa?" I laugh.

He arches an eyebrow. Is he serious?

Movement behind him catches my attention and I spot Marcelo standing in the gym's doorway, watching us. *Shit. How long has he been there?*

"I have to go."

Dante looks over his shoulder and spots Marcelo. "Just think about it."

I don't respond, pushing past him. Once I reach my fiancé, I softly say, "Hey."

His eyes only watch Dante's retreating form. "What was that about?"

"Just Dante being Dante. Let's go." I brush past Marcelo, not wanting him to know the topic of our conversation. I'd be an idiot not to at least consider whether Dante's offer puts me in a better position than the one I'm currently in.

Marcelo falls in line next to me. "Maybe the two of us need to have another chat. Seems he didn't get my message the first time."

"Give it a rest with the macho bullshit."

We make our way to our usual room. I remove my sweatshirt so I don't get too hot, leaving me in my sports bra and leggings. Marcelo's eyes heat and he brushes his thumb over my nipple that's peeking through the fabric.

"I'm not here for that." I swat away his hand. "Let's get down to business."

He studies me for a beat then puts me through my paces harder than he has before, almost as if he's punishing me. Thanks a lot, Dante.

CHAPTER EIGHTEEN
MARCELO

Since this is my first year at the Sicuro Academy, I had no idea what was up when we received a mass text about the War Games that are slated to happen this weekend. I go to the only person who will give me accurate information—Giovanni. His roommate, Domenico Accardi, is there to add anything he may have heard from his older brother, Dante.

"Each house picks four guys. Girls have been able to put their names in to participate in the past, but no one ever has, so I'm not sure how it will go." Domenico looks at the ceiling as if he can figure it out.

"Let's face it, the girls are just gonna be our cheerleaders. They can't actually compete against us." Nicolo laughs, and Andrea high-fives him.

I don't say anything because I would've agreed with them until recently. Mirabella has shown me that there are other skills besides your fists and how accurately you can shoot a gun.

"I doubt they'll be part of the team selection," Domenico says, returning us to the conversation. "You'll be picked as a leader." He nods at me. "It's always the most powerful guys from each of the four corners. So, you, Antonio, my brother, and Gabriele Vitale from the Northwest. You each pick one teammate."

"Me!" Giovanni points at himself.

I glance at him but say nothing. I'm sure Nicolo and Andrea assume the same, but I need way more information before deciding.

"Then it's like a Spartan Race of sorts," Domenico says.

"What the hell is that?" I ask.

"You go through different obstacles. Usually, the terrain is rough and can be muddy. You run over walls, shoot arrows, climb under barbed wire. But with the War Games, it's more stuff like making a bomb, marksmanship, shit like that. You want your partner to be strong but smart. Someone who accepts that you're their leader."

"Who won last year?" I narrow my eyes at Domenico.

"Antonio."

I nod. Taking out my future brother-in-law will be a pleasure. Choosing Giovanni as my partner makes the most sense. He's usually with me on the streets and I know what he's capable of. But I'll finalize my decision after I sneak into the arena tonight to see exactly what they have in store for us. I have to win this to show anyone who's coming after me that they have their work cut out for them—I'm the best of the best.

* * *

AFTER MY RESEARCH last night as the workers were setting up the race, I know I need my partner to be fast and under a certain size. There are small openings we have to get through. But by the time the entire academy is watching the War Games begin, I still haven't decided which of my friends will make the best partner.

I'm sitting on the grass with everyone else as Chancellor Thompson talks with fellow students on a platform in front of us. My adrenaline is going, my blood is pumping. I cannot wait for this to start. I've only been here for a few weeks, but so far, besides me giving my bride-to-be earth-shattering orgasms, not much has happened. I'm bored.

"I can't believe some of the girls actually chose to make the dinner." Mirabella sits down close to me, talking to Sofia.

"You can't blame them. Not every girl is here for the reasons you are, Mira," her best friend says. "Most are biding time, getting a Mrs. Mafia degree until they're promised to someone."

I lean forward and quirk an eyebrow. "Fuck the patriarchy again, dolcezza?"

She narrows her eyes at me. "They allow us into the academy, but it's clear they don't want us to partake in the War Games. They want all the girls to prepare you big, strong men a meal for afterward." She shakes her head and I bite my lip to stop myself from smiling.

"The women can compete."

"We can put our name in for consideration, but we still need one of you guys to pick us. As if that's going to happen." She rolls her eyes.

"I chose to be captured," Sofia says, smiling.

"Why?" Mirabella asks her with a scowl.

"Because I think it will be fun." Her gaze lingers behind me.

I look over my shoulder to spot Antonio talking to someone. It's pretty evident there's only one man Sofia wants to free her.

"And you?" I ask Mirabella.

Mirabella crosses her arms. "I put my name in to be selected. I deserve a spot on the team even if I don't have a penis."

I chuckle, but am quickly interrupted by the chancellor clearing his throat in the microphone and asking the students to quiet down. Everyone does what he says and soon the entire open grass area is still, tension filling the air.

"I'd like to welcome all our students to this year's War Games. For those who don't know, four people from each house have been voted in by the administration. Each person will pick a partner to help them compete against the other three teams. Now, we've had a lot of questions regarding the women who now attend Sicuro Academy. As it has been in the past five years, we did not include the women in being able to lead a partnership, but we have allowed them to put their names in to be selected as a teammate. The rest of the women have either volunteered to be a captive or are helping to prepare a big dinner for all the tired men at the end."

"Bullshit," Mirabella says louder than she should. A few heads turn in her direction.

"We're starting with Roma House this year, so when I say your name, please come up here." He accepts a piece of paper from one of the faculty members. "Antonio La Rosa."

Everyone claps and Antonio raises his hand, winks to the crowd, and saunters up on stage. The man has an advantage since he's done this and won before.

"Gabriele Vitale."

Gabriele slides his hand through his dark strands and cracks his neck a few times before joining Antonio on stage. They shake hands, but I can tell it means nothing.

"Third, we have Dante Accardi."

The dickhead jumps up, his eyes seeking out Mirabella. Mine narrow at him. He's toeing the line and he knows it. Then he winks at her. If there weren't so many witnesses, I'd drag him by his hair into the woods and beat him to a bloody pulp.

Once he's up there, Chancellor Thompson sighs into the microphone. "Lastly, a new student this year, Marcelo Costa."

Giovanni puts both fingers in his mouth and whistles. Andrea and Nicolo holler as I wink at Mirabella on my way up to the stage.

The four of us stand there like bachelors ready to be auctioned off.

"Now it's time for you each to pick a partner. You may pick any male partner from your house," Chancellor Thompson says. Before he shifts the microphone to Antonio, his assistant hands him a piece of paper. "Oh yes, thank you, Mrs. Gardner. I almost forgot to let you guys know which of the women have offered themselves up as a teammate, should you decide to pick them." He reads the paper. "Seems we've only had one woman step up from Roma House— Miss Mirabella La Rosa. Bravo for putting yourself out there, Miss La Rosa."

There are snickers from the grass. Some people blatantly search out Mirabella to give her a judgmental look and my hands clench at my sides. The entire thing pisses me off.

"I hope I get to choose before you," Dante whispers, his gaze on Mirabella.

"Do you want to die?" The sharpness of my voice could cut through leather.

Does he really think I'll allow Mirabella to be partners with him? I'm seeing so much red that when the chancellor calls me to pick first, I say, "Mirabella La Rosa." I'm not even sure I understand that I said her name until the crowd goes crazy.

"Everyone, calm down," the chancellor says, pounding his finger on the microphone. "Come on up, Mirabella."

She stands from the crowd wearing her snug yoga pants and sports bra. Her hair is pulled back into a ponytail and she's bare-faced. She's gorgeous, and I remind myself that she has a lot to offer our team. If all else fails, I can throw her over my shoulder and carry her to the finish line.

"Sucker," Dante says. "Did you really think I would pick her?" His laugh only stokes my anger further.

I click my tongue off the roof of my mouth. "She's my fiancée. We're a team. No other woman here has her strength, so what are you going to do when we're out of this prison and in the real world? My queen will kick your queen's ass, I guarantee it."

Dante's face turns red. Chancellor goes down the line and asks the remaining three players for their partners. I purposely don't look at Giovanni because I'm sure he's pissed off at me. Mirabella comes to stand by my side, and I slide my arm around her waist, bringing her closer to me.

She purposely slides out. "Let's keep this professional. You won't regret picking me, I promise. Trust me?"

I say nothing. I can't believe I let Dante get into my head.

"So, here are the rules . . ." Chancellor Thompson says. "This year, you must save one of your own. Work your way through the maze of obstacles until you get to the final, where you must put a bomb together. Please note you'll have to wire it, but the actual explosives on it are not real, so no one get any bright ideas about stealing any part of it. Whoever finishes first with a working bomb gets a key from me and must run to unlock their loved one, who is chained to a tree. All three of you pass the finish line and win."

"What if you don't know how to arm a bomb?" someone calls from the crowd.

Good question. I have a rudimentary knowledge, but I'm no expert.

"Instructions are available, but every time you ask for the next step to be given to you, your team will incur a time penalty and you won't be able to leave that station until it's fulfilled."

We line up at the starting line and I glance at Mirabella, who's trying not to smile. I know she's happy I chose her.

I'm baffled by what the hell is happening to me. I don't have soft spots for people. I don't give a shit what makes her happy or not. She has to marry me no matter what her feelings are. Now I've put my reputation on the line and chosen her as my partner and the other three teams have the advantage of having two strong men.

Her hand on my forearm draws my attention back to her. "I won't disappoint you, Marcelo."

The starting gun goes off and we're running for our lives.

CHAPTER NINETEEN
MIRABELLA

I couldn't believe it when my name came out of Marcelo's mouth, picking me as his teammate. From the reaction of the crowd, I don't think anyone has ever chosen a female before. His expression indicated he was just as surprised as me. But what's done is done and I'm determined to show him that he made the right choice.

Everyone from Roma House watches with avid interest. They're likely waiting for me to shit the bed and fuck this up. Well, they'll be waiting a long time because I'm going to kill this race.

We've already done the mud crawl under barbed wire and trenched through the mud pits that felt as if they'd never end. We've climbed over a fifty-foot A-frame draped in rope where Marcelo put his hand on my ass to push me over the top. Thank God I don't have a fear of heights.

Now I'm heaving for breath running to the Arctic Plunge—a giant pit filled with ice water that we have to wade through to the other side, including fully submerging ourselves to swim through a small opening in the middle of the pit.

We're neck and neck with my brother and his best friend, Tommaso, while the other two teams must be behind us.

Neither Marcelo nor I hesitate before jumping into the water.

My lungs seize up and I gasp from the temperature biting into my skin. It takes me a full ten seconds to move, leaving Marcelo a little ahead of me. I focus on moving forward rather than the roar of the crowd following us down the course. My limbs become numb the farther I move through the ice-cold water.

Marcelo dips below the baffle first and comes out on the other side with a scream.

God, this is gonna suck, but I need to prove myself not just to my future husband but to everyone else watching. This opportunity is my chance to give a giant middle finger to the system I was born into.

So, I duck beneath the water and swim forward. My hands and legs move slower than I'm used to, and by the time I come up on the other side, my lungs squeeze for any last bit of oxygen.

I pop out of the water and suck in a big lungful of air, but my lungs don't expand the way they normally do, and anxiety erupts through my body. Marcelo grabs my arm and drags me toward the end of the pit. After thirty seconds, I catch my breath and shake him off with a grateful smile, irritated with myself that I needed help in the first place.

What feels like forever later, we drag ourselves out of the water and onto the grass. We lie there catching our breath and waiting for the blood to return to our limbs. But my brother's voice yelling at Tommaso to get moving spurs us to sit up because they're about to overtake us.

Marcelo and I rush off toward the next obstacle, but I worry one of us will hurt ourselves since I still lack total feeling in my feet. It's a weird sensation, my body not responding normally. Luckily, by the time we reach the next obstacle—a twelve-foot half-pipe we have to get over—I'm starting to get sensation in my limbs again.

I stare at the monstrosity. Marcelo is so tall he'll take a running leap, grab on to the top, and pull himself over. However, I stand no chance.

"C'mon, I'll boost you over." He motions me closer and bends down on one knee, linking his fingers together.

The idea of Marcelo catapulting me into the air is a little nerve-racking, but there's no time for that because Antonio and Tommaso arrive at the obstacle.

I place my foot into his waiting palms, and Marcelo meets my gaze. "Ready?"

I nod.

"One, two, three." He uses all his strength and launches me up.

I yelp and my arms flail for a beat before it dawns on me that I need to catch the edge at the top, otherwise I'll go crashing down. I set my sights on the wall and I'm just able to grab it, but my grip slips just as my chest and legs slam against the wall.

Fuck, that hurt.

Marcelo is underneath me with his hands on my feet, pushing me up. It's enough to give me the leverage I need and I pull myself all the way up until I'm straddling the wall.

Instantly, Marcelo takes a running leap and catches the edge. His biceps bulge as he uses all his strength to pull his body over the ledge. We both land with a thud on the other side.

"Good thing you're so little. Not sure I could've done that with Giovanni."

I laugh and hop to my feet. He takes my hand and practically drags me to the next obstacle.

"Damn it," I say when I see that it's target practice with BB guns. All the guys on the other teams have experience, I don't.

The instructions state that each team member must hit three BBs into the target area before the team can move on. A quick glance over my shoulder tells me that we still have a slight lead. Tommaso is at a height disadvantage for the wall too, so he's having problems getting over, and I can't see either of the other two teams yet.

"Relax," Marcelo says. "You can do this. Let me get mine out of the way first, then I'll help you."

I nod and watch like a hawk as Marcelo fires off three BBs, each one hitting the target area.

"Impressive," I say.

"Yeah?" He arches an eyebrow and grins, then passes me the BB gun. "All right, square your shoulders, look down the barrel, and line it up with the target. Stiffen your muscles and hold your breath before you pull the trigger."

I nod, doing as he says and firing my first shot. I do a little dance in place when it hits the red area of the target.

"Don't get too excited, you've got two more to go."

The first one was beginner's luck because the next three BBs fly off in different directions.

Marcelo's hands land on my shoulders. He stands behind me, speaking into my ear. "Relax. You've got this." He squeezes my shoulders then lets go.

I line up my shot again, hold my breath, and pull the trigger. It hits the target this time, but I don't celebrate. One more.

Antonio and Tommaso arrive at the BB stop, arguing, but I ignore them. I fire off a shot, but it hits way left.

My brother and his friend celebrate from the station beside us. Obviously one of them hit the target with their first shot.

I draw in a large breath, line up my shot, hold my breath, and fire away. When it hits the target, Marcelo shouts and picks me up by the waist, planting a big kiss on my lips, surprising me. He lowers me and our gazes lock for a beat.

"We should probably move on," I say.

He nods and glances over my shoulder. I can hear the other two teams coming through the woods toward this stop.

We rush off to the next obstacle which is the Cage Crawl—a sixty-foot watery trench under a steel chain-link fence that leaves only a few inches above water for us to breathe.

Physically, this one won't be a challenge, but it'll be a mindfuck.

Marcelo and I share a meaningful look and get into the water as my brother and Tommaso arrive. We wade to where the fence starts, get on our backs, and grip the fencing, pulling ourselves under. I work to keep my breathing even, knowing if I freak out halfway under this fence, I'm screwed.

Everything is going well until Antonio and Tommaso get in. Shortly after, Dante and his partner arrive too. They take no care and small waves ripple over the water. I sputter when some of what amounts to mud water runs over my face and into my mouth. I grip the fencing and stop moving, pulling myself as close to it as I can, coughing the disgusting taste out of my mouth.

"You good?" Marcelo asks, a little ahead of me.

"Yup." I even my breathing again and hear some commotion from the other teams down past my feet.

From what I gather, Dante's partner is freaking out now that he's under the fence and it's somehow affecting my brother and Tommaso.

Whatever. I just need to get out of here. I move a little faster now, leaving my body still except for dragging myself under the fencing with my hands. As soon as I'm standing again, a large breath of relief leaves me.

When I look back, I see that my brother and Tommaso are about halfway through the obstacle and the Vitale team is just arriving. Dante is still screaming at his teammate to get back under the fencing.

With not a moment to spare, Marcelo and I hit the next obstacle—Monkey on Your Back. One partner has to carry the other partner on their back for half a mile. Marcelo and I grin at each other, knowing we have the advantage. It'll be much easier for him to carry me than it will be for any of the other teams to carry each other.

"Told you I'd be helpful," I say.

He shakes his head with a smile and bends down so I can hop up. We make quick work of the half mile, and by the time we reach the final challenge, none of the other teams are in sight.

"Fuck, why couldn't this last one be computer hacking?" he says as he looks at all the wires and parts of what's clearly supposed to be a pipe bomb.

I give him an awkward laugh.

We work through the first few steps before Antonio and Tommaso arrive. Now is where things get complicated.

Chancellor Thompson stands off to the side, ready to give a clue to any team who wants it, but with it comes a time penalty that could very easily lead to a loss, even if you're the first team done assembling the bomb.

"Any idea what we do next?" Marcelo asks me.

I shake my head, frustrated.

"Guess we'll have to take a clue then," he mutters and motions for the chancellor to come over. "We need a clue."

He nods, prim and proper as always. "Very well. If you take it, you'll incur a thirty-second penalty."

"Just give it to us." Marcelo holds out his hand and the chancellor passes him a card.

We read it and I let Marcelo figure out what needs to be done next. The next step is pretty obvious, so I take care of it.

When I check out where the other teams are, Dante and Gabriele's teams don't pose much of a threat to us. But Antonio and Tommaso are at the same point we're at now and haven't accepted a clue yet.

Damn it. I worry my bottom lip, unsure what to do.

I look at my brother, who meets my gaze and holds it.

I'm torn—more than I would have thought I'd be. If I help complete this bomb, it feels as if I'm pledging my allegiance to the Costas. But I've always been loyal to my own lineage, the La Rosas.

My father schooled Antonio in bomb-making, and it's only a matter of time before he figures out that they've given us an extra wire that we don't need. The only reason I know is that I begged and pleaded with my brother to show me what my dad taught him and he acquiesced. Antonio wants me to stall.

"Maybe we should ask for another clue," Marcelo says, drawing my gaze to him.

There's panic in his eyes and a little pleading as well, as though he's counting on me to help. No one's ever counted on me for anything.

I glance back at my brother, who's still watching me, and I squeeze my eyes shut.

"Mirabella, should we ask for another clue?"

What do I want to do? This feels like a moment that's bigger than what it appears from the outside. If I help my brother and plead ignorance, I'm staying true to the woman I walked into this academy as. If I finish this bomb for my own team, I'm pledging allegiance to my fiancé, and that's not what I want, right?

"Mirabella!"

My eyes snap open and I reach for the pieces we need. I guess I'm doing this.

I quickly put together the remainder of the pipe bomb and call for the chancellor to come inspect our work. He does, and when he's satisfied that everything is as it should be, he starts the thirty-second timer and hands us our key.

The finish line is in sight, but we're forced to stay where we are. I can barely stay still as I watch my brother working fast to finish putting his bomb together. His jaw is clenched and I have no doubt he's pissed at me, but I can't worry about that now.

Besides, he's the one who ordered me to play nice with Marcelo.

The crowd chants when the countdown reaches the ten-second mark. Marcelo and I get ourselves into position to sprint as soon as the time is up.

"Three, two, one," the crowd chants.

We race toward the finish line just as my brother's team is getting the approval and their key from the chancellor.

My arms and legs pump and I don't dare look behind me to see where Antonio and Tommaso are. I just keep running. We get to our tree, where Giovanni is locked up. Marcelo uses the key and unlocks him, then the three of us cross the finish line first.

Cheers erupt from the crowd. Before I know it, Marcelo is sweeping me into his arms, his lips on mine.

We did it. I know I proved that we made a good team, but does he see it?

CHAPTER TWENTY
MARCELO

After I'm done accepting the congratulations of everyone in the Costa family, the guys and I head back to Roma House to get ready for Vegas Night. From what we've been told, it's a tradition at the academy after the War Games. We all step on the elevator, and I press the button for our floor. The doors begin closing but spring back open, revealing Sofia and a very muddy Mirabella.

Out of the four quadrants of the US, the Northeast has the most competitors vying for power. With two major cities, New York and Chicago, we have the most enemies, especially when you count the Russians and the Irish. The Northeast have always thought of themselves as the alphas of the Wild West. Not to say Mirabella's father having to deal with the cartels coming up through Miami is easy.

I waste no time breaking the distance between Mirabella and me. My finger glides down her mud-stained arm.

"Will we see you ladies there tonight?" Giovanni asks, his gaze on Sofia.

"You will," she says.

"How about we go together?" I suggest.

Mirabella tilts her head back to look up at me. "Um . . ."

God, those eyes. My body reacts so differently than it did weeks ago when we all first got here.

"Sorry, Costa, girls only. You can meet us there." Sofia swings her arm through Mirabella's and pulls my fiancée toward her.

"Don't be expecting to come home with her." I wink.

Sofia scoffs.

"Do I have to remind you that I'm her fiancé?"

Sofia narrows her eyes as if she's any threat to me. "You boys will be too involved in the gambling."

We all laugh. "It's not as if this is the real Vegas. What will we win? Free cookies from the café?" Nicolo belly-laughs at his own joke, but it's true.

We've all been to Vegas. Even before we were twenty-one, thanks to fake IDs. It's a rite of passage—girls and booze and gambling.

"Tonight won't even compare to when we were there. Remember that escort we hooked up with, Nico?" Andrea blows out a breath, obviously reliving some sordid detail in his mind.

"Well, I'm not a hooker," Mirabella says as the doors open on her floor. She saunters out.

"La Rosa!" I shout, and I'm surprised when she stops to look at me. "I'll be seeing you tonight."

"You'll have to find me first." She bites her lip and walks away.

"Oh, I've got your scent."

The elevator doors shut.

"Jesus, she's just winding you around her finger," Giovanni grumbles.

It only takes a second before we're on our floor, and I breeze past the guys to head out of the elevator first. Not that any of them would stop me. "She's my fiancée. Stop acting like a jealous little girl not getting her daddy's attention."

Giovanni stops at my door. "It's as if you're wining and dining her. She's yours regardless."

"I'm not wining and dining her." I open my door.

"You picked her to be on your team." He crosses his arms.

"And we won."

"I can't figure out why you picked her though."

"See you guys over there in a bit." Andrea waves, knowing my cousin and I are about to fight. Rightfully so, he and Nicolo don't want anything to do with it.

I step into my room and Giovanni follows, shutting the door.

"I don't owe you any answers. I gotta shower." I strip off my shirt. Since I know he won't just leave, I head over to my closet to figure out what I'll wear tonight.

"Why did you pick her over me? We're brothers."

I shrug.

"Marcelo!" I turn and glare at him, and he steps back. "Help me understand. You could've lost."

"But I won. She kept up with me the entire time. If I'd had to carry your ass half a mile, the result might not have been the same." I don't mention the fact that she got us through the bomb at the end. Someone's been teaching her things, that's for sure. Or maybe she's one of those people who are good at riddles and when she looked at the instructions, something just clicked.

Giovanni stares at me.

Blowing out a breath, I lean against the wall. "Listen. Dante threatened to put her on his team, and he needed to know she's mine. It's really that simple. But she surprised the hell out of me, didn't she you? Now, stop this toddler tantrum and go get ready."

Giovanni studies outside the window before he gives a reluctant nod. "She did."

It's killing him to admit it, I know. I'm pretty sure Giovanni doesn't want me to get along with my wife exceptionally well. He wants her to give me a good home like every wife we know, but he wants me out at night with him at the strip clubs, going on trips where we each have our mistresses in tow. Basically, he wants me married, but for nothing else to change.

"Just relax. You're too hung up on why I picked her." I go into my bathroom and turn on the water in the sink.

"Someone mentioned they saw you two at the gym . . . sparring?" he calls to me over the water.

I run water over my face to get the mud off my stubble, then I coat my face in shaving cream to clean up my short beard before I get in the shower. "She asked me for help."

"You're training someone who will have the opportunity to kill you during the night."

I rinse my hands under the water and dry them with a towel before leaning my back against the sink. "You're thinking too hard about this. I'll always be able to take her. Plus, we're . . ."

His eyes widen. "What? You're falling in love with your fiancée?" The audacity in his voice makes me want to laugh.

"I'm not falling in love." I'd never admit that to anyone, including Giovanni. Admitting I have deep feelings for someone only opens up a way for people to hurt me. "We've messed around a few times. That's all." I shrug.

His shoulders relax. "So this is just all about pussy? Thank God, man. I was worried for a second there." He claps me on the shoulder. "I better go get ready too. I'll stop by in an hour and grab you on my way out." He laughs. "I was about to call Nonno and tell him to get you the hell out of here."

He can think what he wants. I keep my smile in place until I hear the door shut behind him. As I stare into the mirror, shaving to perfection, I try to dissect my feelings for Mirabella La Rosa.

Surely it's not love, but it's not just lust anymore either. I hate not being able to put a label on something.

* * *

GIOVANNI AND I arrive at the Vegas Night event that's been set up in the gymnasium. We're wearing tailored black suits and white shirts. I search the room for Mirabella, but don't see her anywhere.

"Come on, let's play some blackjack." Giovanni tugs on my suit jacket.

I smooth down the expensive fabric after his assault. "Kind of boring for no money."

"We can still school the cartels." He nods at a table filled with four black-haired guys.

"Perfect. I've wanted a word with them since their head guy ran into me at the dining hall and I almost pummeled him until both our men pushed us aside."

Sliding into the open chairs, we put down our chips. Sure, there are prizes you can win, but I don't give a shit about that. Unless there's a get-out-of-jail-free prize.

While I play, my gaze searches the doorway every other minute to see if she's arriving. I win another hand. These cartels can't play cards to save their lives. Then again, we grew up playing this game.

As the cards are dealt, Giovanni eyes me because everyone at this table knows there's unfinished business. I clear my throat, earning the attention of the guy who cornered me outside the dining hall.

"Have something to say?" he asks.

"The threat you made," I talk while I study my hand and add chips to the pile.

"Threat?" he asks.

The other three fidget and eye Giovanni. The two of us tower over them and I don't doubt we can take them if need be. But it would still be four against two until Andrea and Nicolo find their way over.

"The one about me being my father. You know I'm at Sicuro to find the killer." I flop my cards down and cross my arms.

The guy bets and laughs. "You're kidding me? If it was us who killed your father, we would have wanted you to know. We don't hide things like you guys."

I glance at Giovanni and he tilts his head like he's probably telling the truth.

"Then why the big scene at the dining hall?"

He throws down his cards. He beat the dealer, so he stacks his chips. "Easy. I needed to make sure you were smarter than your father. That you knew to stay out of our business."

"You don't have to worry about that. I have no interest in it."

The dealer hands out new cards and I pick up mine, as does he. "Good."

That ends that. Cartels are off the list of suspects.

A half hour later, Mirabella appears in the doorway. She's wearing a sequin dress that's so short if she bends over, her ass will be hanging out. I love it, but I don't want everyone seeing what's mine. Her hair is flowing down her back, and her makeup only reveals more of her beauty. I truly am a lucky bastard to be promised to someone so gorgeous.

Our eyes lock and I bite my lip to show her how turned on I am. She smiles and even past her blush, her cheeks flush.

"Costa?" Giovanni elbows me.

I straighten to play my cards then decide against it, tossing them on the table. "I fold."

Standing from my chair, I pass Giovanni all my chips. On my way over to Mirabella, Dante slides in front of her. He grabs her wrist and she pulls it back, but he takes her upper arm and leads her out of the gymnasium.

Anger flows like lava through my veins and I follow them, wanting to know what the hell is going on. When I reach the hallway, I spot them going into a science lab, but the door isn't shut all the way. I stand just outside where they can't see me, but I can hear them.

"Did you think about my offer?" Dante asks.

"I did, and my answer is no."

"You're stupider than I thought. Is this because he threw you a bone today? Because if so, I baited him into that decision." Dante's tone is full of rage.

I wonder what the offer was. I want to storm in there like a bull, but I hold my ground, wanting as much information as possible. My dad taught me a long time ago that the serpent has patience before it strikes. A saying he forgot when he gained more power.

"I'm not going to get out of one engagement to go into another. I don't want to be forced into a marriage at all. Why is that so hard for everyone to understand?" Her voice rises.

That bastard Dante asked her to marry him? Who the fuck does he think he is?

"You're making a huge mistake. He's going to treat you like a servant. Make you get on your knees whenever he wants. Use you like a broodmare to extend his line. Make you arm candy when he needs you, and I bet he'll keep you locked up in the house when he doesn't. You could have whatever kind of life you wanted with me."

"Let's remember, he picked me today."

I bust through the door. "What the hell is going on in here?"

Mirabella's eyes widen, and Dante crosses his arms and widens his stance as if I'd ever be intimidated by him.

"We were talking," Dante says.

"You aren't ever allowed to be alone with my fiancée." I approach him with a caustic look.

Dante stares at me, unthreatened—as any good leader should be. "We had a matter to discuss."

"Which was?" I eye Mirabella. Let's see how faithful she is to me.

I cock my eyebrow when she doesn't immediately answer, and she says, "Dante asked me to ditch you and marry him."

I laugh, a hollow, bitter one. "Really?" I harden my stare on Dante. He merely shrugs. "You can't blame me."

This fucker just made it to the very top of the list of people who might have tried to kill me.

I take his lapels in my hands and slide them up and down. "Oh, but I can blame you. To propose to a promised woman isn't accepted in our world. Surely you know this?"

"She turned me down. What's it matter?" He steps back and pushes his arms down on my hands.

The door swings open and the chancellor stands in the doorway. "Do we have a problem in here?"

Mirabella chews the inside of her lip.

Dante rushes over to the chancellor. "No, sir. Just discussing the race."

"You can discuss it in the gym." He holds the door open wider.

We all file out. Dante peels off, saying he has to use the restroom, while Mirabella and I continue on to the gym. As soon as we step inside, I grab her upper arm and pull her into a dark corner.

"What the hell is going on?" I seethe through my teeth. "How dare you embarrass me after what I did for you earlier?" Picking her could have ruined my entire reputation.

"Nothing. He asked, I said no." She crosses her arms. I force myself not to admire the way her tits push up.

"You sure that's all?" I'm giving up way too quickly. She should be punished for not telling me. So should Dante. I step closer to her, my hand rising to her cheek, and I bend down and whisper in her ear, "Don't ever let me find you in a room alone with another man again, do you hear me?"

"I told you it was nothing." I can tell she's pissed.

"You're mine," I remind her before placing a kiss just under her jawline.

"God." She pushes me off her. "You do not own me."

I push us farther back into the corner and use my foot to widen her legs.

"What are you doing?" Her eyes widen.

I glide my hand between her inner thighs and cup her panty-covered pussy. "We may not be married yet, but . . ." With my free hand, I pick up her hand with my ring on her finger. "This signifies that you belong to me, and that includes this pussy." I run my finger down her center and she shivers, her eyes becoming hooded.

"You're such a Neanderthal." But there's no real bite to her voice.

I slide my fingers past the elastic, so she's bared to me, and circle my thumb over her clit. "Still a Neanderthal? I can get you off here, or we go somewhere else. Which do you want?"

She stares at me long and hard. When I thrust a finger inside her growing wetness, her breath hitches while my throbbing hard-on presses against my designer suit pants.

"If you want my mouth, we better go somewhere else." My thumb continues to assault her clit as I fuck her with my fingers.

She studies me for a long time. For a second, I think she might let me fuck her right here, but she pushes my hand out from under the inside of her dress. "Take me back to your room."

"About fucking time. Try to keep your hands off me on the way." I stick my fingers in my mouth and lick them, savoring her taste. "Damn, I can't wait to have my face between those legs."

"No more dirty talk until we're in your room." She stomps off in front of me. Her ass swaying only makes my dick grow harder and I have to adjust myself before I take off after her.

Finally, I'm going to claim her, and she'll be fully mine.

CHAPTER TWENTY-ONE
MIRABELLA

By the time we reach Marcelo's room, I can't decide whether I'm more turned on or angered by his caveman behavior. But I take another look at him in his designer suit as he closes and locks the door, and I know it's inevitable that I'll end up in his bed tonight.

We've been resisting the tension for weeks now, and after he chose me today and believed in me, I lost all my fight.

"Go sit on the chair, mio angelo." Marcelo's voice is rough with lust.

I do what he says, sauntering over to the upholstered chair in the corner, and his gaze on my ass feels like a brand—I can practically feel it singeing my skin.

When I sit, he draws near, his dark eyes taking me in from head to toe. His steel length stretches the confines of his pants and I squeeze my thighs together to try to stem the throbbing in my center.

He drops to his knees in front of me, and I suck in a breath. There's something intensely erotic about seeing a powerful man like Marcelo about to worship me. His hands trail up the outside of my thighs and hook around the elastic of both sides of my panties before he slowly drags the silk fabric down my legs. He doesn't bother to remove my heels, which makes me feel sexier.

Then he brings my panties to his face and closes his eyes as he inhales. "You smell as good as you taste, dolcezza."

My nipples pucker beneath the gold sequins of my dress. He trails his hand back up my leg and under the fabric of my dress, but instead of continuing to my center when he reaches my hip, his hand remains there, squeezing.

I can't help but raise my hips, desperate for more of his touch.

A low chuckle reverberates through his chest. "All in good time."

Marcelo takes my mouth, groaning when our tongues glide together. One of his hands pushes into my hair and he uses it to leverage my head where he wants it. By the time he pulls away, I'm more desperate than ever for him to touch me.

But he seems content to take his time as he unhurriedly eases the straps of my dress over my shoulders until they fall down to my elbows. The fabric of my dress is caught on the swell of my breasts, and one by one, Marcelo reveals them.

I'm practically heaving for breath, my nipples so tight they ache. But when Marcelo dips his head and takes one in his mouth, pulling on my nipple, it eases some of the pleasurable discomfort and I moan. His tongue plays with the turgid tip and my hand flies to his shoulder, squeezing the hard muscle underneath. He moves to my other breast and repeats the same delicious torture until I'm a panting, writhing mess.

"Marcelo, please touch me." I'm not too proud to beg in this moment.

He lifts his head from my breast with a grin. "So impatient." He clucks with his tongue, and I gaze upon him with pleading eyes.

Marcelo takes me by the waist and drags my ass to the edge of the chair before parting my knees and forcing me to hook my legs over the sides of the chair. I'm completely open and bare to him, and though a feeling of vulnerability accompanies this position, mostly what I feel is anticipation. That first swipe of his tongue can't come soon enough.

"Look at you . . . so wet and needy. Do you need my tongue between your thighs, Mirabella?"

I nod frantically, biting my lower lip.

"Keep your legs like that. You move them and I stop. Understood?" He arches a brow.

"Understood." My voice is a near whisper.

Slowly, he peels off his suit jacket, revealing the fitted dress shirt beneath. It hugs his lean muscles in the most perfect way. He tosses the jacket behind him with no regard for how much it must cost and places his hands on the insides of my thighs before he swipes his tongue from my entrance up to my clit. He hums when my taste hits his tongue, then devours me like a starved man, concentrating his efforts on my bundle of nerves at first.

It takes effort not to close my legs around his face, but I don't want this to end, so I manage to keep them spread, my heels dangling off my toes. When he moves down to fuck my entrance with his tongue, my hand whips down to his head, but he doesn't have enough hair for me to grip. Somehow, that adds to my sexual frustration.

Marcelo brings me to the edge several times before changing his cadence and rhythm, leaving me a desperate mess.

"Marcelo, please," I moan.

"What is it? What do you want?" he murmurs against my sensitive flesh before sucking my clit.

"Please let me come. Please." I need to come more now than I ever have in my entire life. I feel as though I'll die if I don't.

The reverberation of Marcelo's chuckle against my clit makes me gasp. When he pushes two fingers into me, curling them to hit my G-spot, I moan and arch my back. He laps at me while he scissors his fingers inside me. His dark eyes study my every reaction, and with one hard pull on my clit, I detonate.

I cry out as my back arches off the chair, my legs off the armrests and struggling to close around Marcelo's head. He stays in place though, prolonging my orgasm as bursts of electricity reverberate through my body, leaving me limp.

I'm panting as Marcelo pulls his fingers from me and straightens up, dipping them into his mouth and sucking on them. A fissure of excitement makes my core pulse. I am in no way done with this man tonight. I need more of him.

Before I can say anything, Marcelo stands and removes his tie, then unbuttons his shirt. I watch as, one by one, he frees the buttons until his shirt is splayed open. He finally brushes it off his shoulders and it falls to the floor.

God, this man's body is all stealth, grace, and power. He's muscular but not bulky, and his bronze skin perfectly showcases each dip and crest of his chest muscles and abs.

Next, he toes off his shoes then undoes his belt, our gazes locked the entire time. When he pushes his pants and his boxer briefs down to his ankles, I lick my lips at the sight of his thick cock that's stretched toward his belly button.

He's going to feel so delicious inside me.

"Still won't get on your knees for me?" He nods down toward his turgid length.

I shake my head and he arches an amused eyebrow. I'll surrender my body to him tonight, but he won't have all of me. He won't have my complete submission.

"Stand up."

I do as he says without argument and my dress falls to the floor. My heels are already discarded on the ground from my flailing during my climax.

He grips me by the neck, drawing me nearer to him until our naked bodies are pressed against each other. Marcelo takes my lips and I moan into our kiss. The feel of his hot, naked skin against mine makes me wetter. When he gently squeezes, the pressure on my neck makes my nipples harden even more, which I wouldn't have thought was possible.

With his lips still on mine, he walks us backward toward his bed. My legs bump against the mattress and he pulls away.

"Lie down."

I turn and crawl onto the bed while he walks over to the night table, opens the top drawer, and pulls out a condom. He rips open the package with his teeth and widens his stance before rolling the condom down his length. The muscles in his abs and forearms flex with his actions and there's something inherently sexy about it.

He crawls over the mattress toward me until he's positioned over me, his elbows on either side of my head. I wrap my arms around his neck, pulling him down onto me, wanting to feel his warmth and his weight. His cock is nestled between my thighs as he dips his head to kiss me again.

Marcelo's being much gentler than I would have expected. It's not a complaint, I'm just surprised.

"I want this to be good for you," he murmurs against my lips.

"It will be."

Our tongues brush against each other's and he deepens the kiss.

When he pulls back, his intense gaze is focused on me. "This may hurt a bit this time, but I promise that from here on out, it'll only be enjoyable for you."

I stare at him with a lust-addled mind before his words sink in.

Meanwhile, he positions himself at my entrance, barely breaching my opening.

My hands fly up to his chest and I push against him. "Wait!"

His eyes widen and he stares at me.

"Marcelo, I'm not a virgin."

CHAPTER TWENTY-TWO
MARCELO

I sit back on my legs and stare at Mirabella.

"You're what?" I never asked if she was, but I damn well assumed I'd be the first to take her, given that she's promised to me.

She sits up so her back rests on my headboard. "It's so typical that you'd expect me to not have been with someone else. You didn't see me assuming you were some wholesome virgin." She rolls her eyes with disgust.

I run my hand over my head, pulling at my neck. This entire engagement hasn't been typical, but I did not expect this. Sure, I suspected she and Lorenzo had fooled around a bit based on her behavior at the forest party, but she should be lying here ready to gift her virginity to me. Then again, it's not our wedding night and I was willing to take her just the same. But that's not the fucking point.

"Lorenzo?" I clarify. It infuriates me that she picked a stronzo like him to take what should've been mine.

She nods.

My fist clenches at my sides. I stand from the bed and rip off the condom. Talk about a complete mood killer.

"Would you rather I lie?"

A hollow laugh falls from my lips. "And how exactly would you do that?"

"There are ways to break a hymen other than a penis, Marcelo. I could've done it with a tampon or on a bike or something. Some women don't bleed that much." She says it with such derision, as though I'm a fucking idiot for not thinking of that.

I stop my pacing and turn to her. "So what? You want forgiveness because you were truthful?"

"I don't need forgiveness—I've done nothing wrong! You know my feelings on this whole arrangement. You know I'm not the typical Mafia princess who's going to fall to my knees for you."

Isn't that the truth. I'm dying for my dick to slide between those lips.

"I want our marriage to be equal. I proved myself in the War Games earlier today. I showed you my computer skills—"

"I hate to break it to you, but I can find a guy with just as good computer skills and it was just a race today." She opens her mouth, but I raise my hand. "I'm not suggesting you did poorly, but it isn't real life. You have no idea what it's like to have someone die by your hands."

She pulls on the blanket and covers herself. "Maybe I don't but—"

I raise my hand because we're getting way off track. That's a conversation for another time. My dick is deflating, and the mood is dying like a fish flapping on the sand. "I can't say I'm not disappointed that you're not a virgin. I expected a fiancée who'd never been with another man. I don't like it and Lorenzo better make sure to stay the fuck away from you now. Were you already promised to me when you slept with Lorenzo?"

"Not the first time we slept together, but yeah, I was with him a few times after my father told me I'd been promised to you."

My fist connects with the wall, plunging through the drywall.

"Jesus, how many people have you been with?" she shouts, and her tone suggests she's proving a point.

She's not. Not in our world. In our world, I'm not supposed to save myself.

I stare at her long and hard. She's fucking beautiful, and a small piece of me loves her independence and fierceness when it comes to her wanting her way. But the part of me who grew up being told that women don't get a say is fearful of how I can rule as a leader with her by my side.

I sit on the bed and she doesn't come closer, curling her naked self up against the headboard with a sheet. "That's a conversation for another time."

"Because you know it's a double standard."

"Hello, Mirabella! Our entire world is a double standard. I understand people outside of our world think differently, but we're expected to have a relationship where I am the leader of our family."

"And the leader of me?"

I give her a sharp nod. "Yes. And you."

Fairness dictates that she's right—I've had my partners and she's only had one. But I can't help the seething jealousy that feels as if it's eating away at my chest like acid.

We sit in silence for I don't know how long. I would've thought she'd get up and leave by now.

She finally speaks. "I can't change it and I wouldn't even if I could."

I chuckle and stare at my flaccid penis. "I know."

She slides down the bed. "But I never said it was good. I just said I wasn't a virgin."

I look over my shoulder at her and she smiles, biting her bottom lip in that sexy way that drives me crazy.

"What are you implying?" I feel myself hardening already.

"I know already from everything else we did that you're going to show me things, and at least this way, you don't have to be careful with me."

My dick perks to attention. "Was it only him?"

"Only him." She lets the fabric go and it falls to her lap, revealing her mouthwatering tits. "I'll never ask for forgiveness though."

As if I didn't know that. This fucking fiancée of mine is infuriating.

I'm going to fuck the memory of him right out of her head. I'm going to show her who she really belongs to. When I'm done with her, she'll have come so many times there will be no mistaking who her body needs.

I press my lips to hers, immediately getting her on her back. Lorenzo may have had her first, but I'm going to make her wish it was me.

Her fingernails grip my shoulders as if she wants me as badly as I want her. I squeeze her tit, my thumb running over her already pebbled nipple. She moans, and it only elicits a need deep inside me to embed myself in her mind.

She bends her head back, offering me her neck. I sprinkle small kisses on her collarbone until I remind myself she's not a virgin and I don't need to be gentle with her. My teeth nibble down her body, and the way her fingernails scrape my back is a clear sign she's liking this.

"I'm going to fuck you so hard, you'll be so sore you'll think you were a virgin," I whisper along her smooth skin, pinching her nipple.

She yelps but sinks into my touch, her hand diving between my legs and wrapping around my shaft. She tsks then squeezes and pumps my dick back to life. "All your silly expectations."

I wrap my hand around hers. "I haven't forgiven you yet." But based on her sweet smile, I'd say we both know my lips and hands wouldn't be on her body if I didn't. I place my hand over her dripping-wet center and tease my finger around her entrance. "From this day forward, this pussy is mine and mine alone. Understand?"

She moans.

"Say it." I push one finger inside, arch it, and she practically mewls for me.

I growl when she doesn't say the words. I want to taste her again. I just ate her out, but consider me a man obsessed because I'm dying for more of her. I maneuver myself between her legs again, swinging them over my shoulder blades.

"Say it," I demand, my tongue millimeters from her core.

Her head thrashes side to side, denying me my due, and I lick her in one swoop before sucking her clit. I twirl the hard nub with my tongue and her back bolts off my bed. She'd be a reason to grow my hair out, just to feel the tug of how much she's enjoying my mouth on her.

Instead, her hands go to her sides and she grabs the blanket, tugging it tight. "Oh god, Marcelo . . ."

I smile as my tongue continues to assault her, feasting on her pussy like a starved man. I tease her opening, then run circles just inside her walls with my finger.

She pants, her breath hitching every second, and she grinds her pussy on my face. "I'm going to come. I'm gonna come," she chants over and over, as though I can't tell.

I'm the maestro and her body is my song. I'm orchestrating every reaction, every hitch of her breath, every pulse of her core. It's all my doing.

"Let go," I murmur, thrusting two fingers inside her and curling them, which sets her off.

She writhes under me, her body arching off the bed as her hands tighten on the sheets. I watch with rapt attention as her cheeks redden and her skin flushes before her body tightens then slowly relaxes one breath at a time. I slow my movements, wanting her to enjoy every last second of her orgasm.

When I lift my head, I contemplate not getting a condom and sending her off without the satisfaction of having me fuck her, but the urge to be inside her is way too great.

"That's two." I place two fingers up in the air and roll over to the edge of the mattress, whipping open the top drawer of the nightstand and grabbing another condom. As fast as I can, I roll on the rubber and get myself back over her.

I spread her legs wide, hooking them over my elbows, then I slowly slide into her. It takes me a few thrusts until I'm fully seated inside her. I watch where we're joined as I make progress. Once I've filled her, she gasps, eyes wide.

"More than you're used to?" I arch an eyebrow and she narrows her eyes.

She looks as though she might have some biting comment for me, but she never gets it out because I pull out and slam back into her. Her arousal glistens on the condom and the sound of our skin slapping makes me even harder.

I continue that for another couple minutes—sliding out slowly and slamming back in—while Mirabella gazes up at me with half-lidded eyes. When I arch my hips when I'm inside her to hit her G-spot, her eyes fall closed and she moans.

Oh yeah, that's the spot.

"Did he fuck you like this?"

I pick up my pace, and I can tell from the small tremors against my cock and the arching of her back that she's close. When I think she might be right on the brink, I force myself to pull all the way out.

"Ah!" Her eyes whip open. "What are you doing?"

"You didn't answer me."

"Wh—what?"

I bring my hand down between her thighs and rim her entrance with my fingertips. She moves her hips, trying to get me exactly where she wants me, but I pull away until she settles again before placing my fingers back where they were.

"Were you ever this wet for him?" I hold her gaze so she knows I won't give her what she wants until she answers. When I trail my fingers up to her clit and press there enough for her to feel it but not enough for her to get off, she whines. "Answer me, dolcezza, and you can have what you want. Who would you rather fuck you . . . me or him?" I increase the pressure on her clit, and she arches her back.

Her body quits responding and she locks eyes with me. "Were you ever this hard for them? Tell me, Marcelo, did you crave their taste the same as you do mine?"

Unable to help myself, I wrap my lips around her right nipple, sucking it and biting down. Her hand flies to my head, her fingernails digging in. I release her breast with a pop.

"Who, Mirabella?"

"Answer me first, Marcelo."

I play with her clit some more until she's a writhing mess, but she still won't answer me.

"You're so fucking stubborn. Just admit it. Admit you want me more than you ever wanted him."

Her teeth press into her bottom lip and her head whips back and forth. "Tell me first."

"Damn you," I roar.

Her eyes snap open. "No!"

My chest heaves as I stare at her. "Have it your way."

CHAPTER TWENTY-THREE

MIRABELLA

Marcelo flips me so I'm face down on the mattress, then he yanks me to my knees so I'm ass up before he plunges into me. I cry out as he grips my hair, wrapping my strands around his hand and using them for leverage.

He fucks me like a man possessed and it's everything I wanted it to be. At least now I know that I drive him as mad as he drives me. The idea of him with other women makes my chest split in two, and I had to force myself not to think about it for too long while we were talking earlier.

Each drag and pull of his cock in and out of my tight sheath sends fissures of bliss throughout my body. But it's his words as he fucks me that really push me to the edge.

"This pussy is mine. You're mine."

"Never gonna want another man's cock again."

"It's me you'll crave from here on out."

The possession in his voice rattles me to my core, but I'd be a liar if I said it didn't light me up inside and make me feel special.

Marcelo uses my hair to yank me up so that my back is pressed to his chest as he drives into me. Our bodies are sweaty and stick to each other.

His hand leaves my hair and grips my neck, exerting just enough pressure for me to know he could cut off my air supply if he so chose. His other hand pinches my nipple as he brings his lips to my ear. "I'm going to make it so you never want any man but me. I'm the one you'll come to when you want to get off. I'm the one you'll want to praise you and tell you you're a good girl when you please me. And I'm the one who's going to blow your fucking mind with the best orgasm you've ever had in your life."

"God, yes," I pant.

The hand on my breast goes down to my swollen and needy clit, exerting the exact amount of pressure I need. Marcelo's thick cock drags in and out of me at the same time as he circles my clit with his fingertips. I'm so close to finishing, seconds away, when he slows his rhythm, leaving me more desperate than ever.

"Marcelo, please. Please." I'm practically begging now, near tears I'm so desperate for release.

"Tell me the words I want to hear," he grates out near my ear, never slowing the rhythm of his hips.

"Why does it matter?"

"It matters. Say it and I'll make you feel so good."

My body is strung tighter than a piano wire and I know there's no point in keeping the truth from him any longer. I am every bit his in this moment.

"I never wanted Lorenzo as much as I want you!" I almost scream the admission.

He chuckles and kisses my temple. "Good girl."

Then he fucks me in earnest and I realize that he's been holding back. He drives his rigid cock into me like a piston and his fingers go back to my clit. Within seconds, my entire body shakes, the force that is my orgasm overwhelming me.

When my climax hits me full force, vibration radiates out from my core and I cry out. I feel like a supernova exploding until I slowly come back to myself.

I don't know how long I was out of my body, but when I come to again, Marcelo is still inside me, pouring into the condom with a guttural groan. Everything about this man is sexy, even the sound he makes when he comes.

I flop down onto the mattress, my limbs having no strength left. Marcelo gets off the bed to dispose of the condom, but my eyelids struggle to stay open. I fall asleep before he returns.

* * *

I WALK INTO Roma House after dinner the next night as Sofia peppers me with questions about Marcelo and me sleeping with each other.

I slipped out of his bed before he was up this morning and managed to avoid him all day because I went to the library to study. When I spotted him in the dining hall, he was in a deep conversation with Giovanni, Andrea, and Nicolo.

It's not that I don't want to talk to him. It's just that last night was intense and I still haven't decided how I feel about it. Nor have I decided how I want *him* to feel about it. He rocked my world, but will he think the same of me? I feel stupid and girly for even caring.

"Are you going to do it again?" Sofia asks as we step into the elevator.

"We're engaged and will be married someday, so . . ." I punch the button for our floor.

"Wow."

I snap my head in her direction. "What?"

She smiles. "That's the first time I've heard you refer to your upcoming nuptials and actually sound like you're somewhat resigned to the fact that he'll be your husband."

I press my lips together and say nothing because she's right. Ugh. Am I getting soft where Marcelo's concerned?

The elevator dings and the doors swing open on our floor.

"I knew he'd be good in bed. You can just tell," Sofia says and steps off the elevator.

I shake my head and follow her. "And how exactly can you tell?"

She shrugs. "You just can. Something about the way they carry themselves."

"If you say so." I chuckle and open the door of our room. When I take a step in, something crunches under my foot, and I draw back. There's a piece of paper on the floor.

"What's that?" Sofia asks.

I bend to pick it up and see that it's a note addressed to me.

Mirabella,

Meet me at our spot at 10.

xo,
M

Typical Marcelo, ordering me around. But a warm feeling invades my chest at the use of the term "our spot" and the way he signed it with "xo."

Yep. Definitely getting soft.

It's weird that he left me a note rather than texting me. Maybe he didn't want a digital footprint of our rendezvous. Perhaps he thinks the school keeps track of them?

Sofia reads the note over my shoulder. "Oh my god, that's the sweetest. He's under your spell, girl."

I continue into the room and Sofia closes the door.

"What are you talking about?" I ask.

"He was practically devouring you in the dining hall and now this note . . . it's like you've compelled him like vampires do."

I shake my head. "I think you've watched too many *Vampire Diaries* reruns."

"I'm serious, Mira. He's into you. Isn't that a good thing? Like you said, you're going to marry him."

Why don't I hate the sound of that as much as I used to?

I blow out a breath. "I guess it's kind of sweet." My cheeks heat.

"It's totally sweet. A midnight rendezvous between lovers." If we were in a cartoon, Sofia would have hearts in her eyes. "Or a ten o'clock rendezvous, I guess."

"All right, all right. Let's not make that big a deal of it, okay?"

I know I have to meet him. He'll come looking for me if I don't. And damn it if there isn't a small part of me looking forward to it. I guess I have to figure out sooner than later exactly how I feel about what happened last night.

* * *

I'm THE FIRST to arrive at the stone gazebo and disappointment floods me, but that's okay. I am a few minutes early.

I hate that I made sure to freshen up and wear my good lingerie. What happened to the fierce, independent woman I came to Sicuro Academy as? One shot of good dick and suddenly I'm burning my feminist card.

I wait, staring at the water, until I hear footsteps behind me. I turn with a smile, ready to greet Marcelo, but my smile quickly falters.

"Lorenzo?" My forehead wrinkles.

He beams. "You came."

He rushes to me and pulls me into a hug. I'm still too shocked by his appearance to do anything, so I stand pressed against his body for a beat with my arms at my sides before I push him away.

"What the hell are you doing here?"

His eyes are wide and desperate looking. "I had to see you and you keep avoiding me."

I glance around in the dark. "How did you know I've been here with Marcelo?"

"You haven't returned my texts," he says, not answering my question, but the truth is obvious—he followed us.

My forehead creases. "I told you the last time I texted you that it's over. We can't see each other anymore. We can't even be friends. In fact, Marcelo would kill you if he found us together."

I think back to how pissed Marcelo was when he found Dante and me alone, then again when he found out I'd slept with the man standing across from me.

"I'm not afraid of him." He seems buoyed by a confidence he shouldn't have.

"You should be." I move to walk past him, but he snags my arm. Some of the training Marcelo taught me kicks in and I dislodge Lorenzo in seconds.

"Mira, why are you acting so weird? It's me." He sounds confused, which I don't understand.

"Why did you trick me to get me to meet you here after I've made it clear that nothing is going to happen between us again?"

His eyes narrow and there's a weird gleam in them from the dim lighting of the moon. "How can you say that? You and I are meant to be together. We can't let him ruin that."

I shake my head. "Lorenzo, we were never going to be together. You know I was promised to Marcelo."

"You don't even want to marry the guy. You've been adamant about that fact—even to him." He must see something on my face, or maybe it's my hesitation, because his mouth drops open and his eyes widen even further. "You've gotta be fucking kidding me. You like him now? What the fuck, Mira?"

I cross my arms. "I didn't say that."

"You didn't have to. Have you slept with him?"

"That's none of your business."

"Holy shit." He pushes both hands through his hair. "You fucked him."

He looks devastated. Again, I don't quite understand. Lorenzo and I were only ever messing around. Even I knew the chance of me getting out of the engagement to Marcelo was as likely as me being named the head of my family over my brother.

"Lorenzo—"

"No!" His arm swats me away when I reach out to squeeze his shoulder. "This is unbelievable. You sleep with that piece of shit and now you're suddenly all about him? Don't you realize you're just another piece of ass to him? You think he gives a shit about you? A guy like that only cares about one thing—power. You're convenient because you're engaged to him and you're here, but you're just like the rest of the whores he's fucked."

I slap him across the face. The sound of my palm against his skin echoes across the water and the deafening silence in the aftermath feels foreboding.

Lorenzo slowly turns his head back in my direction, and every instinct inside me says to get the hell out of here. I step back. But I need to see this through and make him understand, once and for all.

"Does he know I had you first?" He steps toward me, but I hold my ground. "Does he know he'll never have his wife's virginity? That some other man stole it from him? If he knew, he'd never marry you."

My teeth grind together and my chest heaves in anger. "He does, in fact. And that's just another reason you need to stay away from me."

A sadistic laugh leaves his lips and it's unnerving. I've never seen him like this. "I don't think I have anything to worry about anymore now that he knows you've been defiled."

Now I'm the one laughing, but it's an arrogant laugh. "We're still very much engaged, Lorenzo. And after what he made me feel last night, I can't wait to sign up for a lifetime of *that*."

His hand whips out and latches on to my wrist. "What do you think he'd say if he knew how good you are with computer programs?"

My forehead wrinkles and I stare at him with confusion. I don't know what the hell he's talking about.

"You're mine, Mirabella."

His hand squeezes my wrist. Once again, Marcelo's teachings come in handy, and I easily dislodge him then bring my knee into his groin. It's a cheap shot, but he deserves it after everything he's said tonight.

He bends over and groans.

"Stay away from me, Lorenzo. I am not yours. I'm not anybody's. This is your last warning." I turn and walk away, adrenaline rushing through my veins like river rapids.

"This isn't over between us, Mira! We're going to be together, you'll see!" he shouts.

I don't bother responding. Instead, I leave him there, still moaning in pain, proud of myself for handling the situation on my own as I knew I could.

CHAPTER TWENTY-FOUR
MARCELO

Spending my entire dinner talking to Giovanni, Andrea, and Nicolo about Dante and finding more evidence that he was the one behind the car bomb meant that I couldn't eat with Mirabella. I feel as if she's been keeping her distance from me all day. I didn't like waking up and finding her gone.

I knock on the door of her dorm room, and when I hear footsteps on the other side, I calm the animalistic urge to grab her and kiss her. But the door opens and Sofia stands across from me. Disappointment hits me like a punch to the gut.

"Well, if it isn't Romeo," she says, crossing her arms and jutting out her hip.

"Where's your roommate?" I ask, eager to see the woman I came here for.

Her forehead wrinkles. "She's supposed to be with you."

"What?" I tilt my head.

"The note? You told her to meet you at your spot at ten."

I step in past her as all my muscles constrict. "Sofia?"

She shuts the door and turns to face me. "What?"

"I never left her a note."

Her eyes scrunch up. "Marcelo, you don't have to act all macho in front of me. I think it's romantic and I told Mira the same." She goes and sits down on the chair at her desk.

"I'm not joking. And I really don't give a flying fuck what you think."

She sits up straight. "You should, I'm her best friend. She listens to my opinion."

"You and I both know Mira doesn't listen to anyone."

Sofia laughs. "True enough. Now go . . . your Juliet awaits. You're going to be late if you don't leave right now."

"I told you I didn't write a note." My tone is harsh. For the first time, Sofia looks at me with concern. "How did you know it was from me?"

"It said, 'meet me at our special place at ten.' Signed xo and *M.* I'm assuming you're the only *M* Mira is fucking."

My fists clench. "I better be, but I didn't write the note."

I turn for the door and twist the doorknob. Is she seeing someone else? Or is someone pretending to be me? The same person who tried to kill me? *Fuck.*

"*Dante!*" I bellow and run out of the room.

"Wait for me," Sofia says, catching me at the elevator with her coat half on.

We get into the elevator, and I pull out my phone, alerting the guys I trust most on campus.

> **ME:** Someone pretended to be me and lured Mirabella out of the dorm. Get out and search every surface of this place.

My phone pings immediately.

> **GIOVANNI:** My money is on Dante. He's always checking her out.

"We should probably grab Antonio, right?" Sofia asks as the elevator descends.

"Do what you want. I'm heading to the only place I think she might be. Whoever knows about it has to have been spying on us. You know who spies, Sofia?" I crack my knuckles, prepared to kill whoever has her.

"Who?" she asks in a small voice.

"Dead men, that's who."

"Maybe I'll just run up and grab Antonio." She hesitates in the elevator when I rush out.

But I run right into Antonio. "What the fuck, Costa?"

"Antonio!" Sofia runs to him. "Mira is in danger. Someone pretended to be Marcelo and got her to meet them somewhere outside."

His eyes flash to mine. "What?"

I hold up my hands. "I'm going to check out a place we've visited before."

"The letter mentioned 'their place.'" She pushes her arm through Antonio's. "We should break apart into teams. We can cover more ground that way. I'll go with Antonio."

I quirk an eyebrow at her. Is she more concerned about Mirabella or Antonio?

The elevator dings and out come my guys. Antonio's head is buried in his phone, hammering away a text to his guys, I assume.

"I'm out. Text me if you find her or anything out. One of you better go to Dante's room," I say.

"Why would Dante have her?" Antonio asks.

"Because he asked her to marry him and she turned him down." I raise my eyebrows.

Antonio inhales deeply. "He knows she's promised. He already pleaded his case to my father months before she was promised to you."

I hold up my hands so he knows I don't blame his family in the least. "It's fine. I gotta go. Hopefully she's where I think she is. I'll be in touch."

Giovanni grabs the arm of my sweatshirt. "You can't go alone. What if it's a trap?"

I stop. He's got a point. I could be running into an ambush without a weapon. "Let's go."

All of my guys come to my side. I look back at Antonio.

"I'll check on Dante. I'll text you right after and you can give us your location," he says.

"Where should I go?" Sofia asks.

"Back to your room," Antonio and I say at the same time.

"She's my best friend. I want to come."

I see the agreement in Giovanni's face before he waves her over to us. "You can come with us. But if it gets messy, you're to run back here."

"Okay," she says and rushes to our group.

I hate the fact that I'm gonna show them our gazebo. A spot I found and have only shared with Mirabella once. And now some asshole is gonna ruin that place for me.

I run ahead, the moon lighting my way as we get farther from the main campus and dorms. The white stone structure comes into view and I slow my footsteps, ushering everyone to a spot behind a bush that should keep us hidden. I peek out and don't see anyone in the gazebo, but I can't see everything, so I can't be sure.

I get everyone's attention by hitting their shoulders, then I point at myself. "Going first," I whisper.

They all nod. I slowly rise and tiptoe to the gazebo, hoping I don't find her dead. I'm not sure I could live with the fact that I caused her to die. I'm supposed to be her protector. How did I not think people would see us, know us, and if they want to hurt me, they're going to harm her to do it? It's Mafia 101.

I lift myself up on the back end of the gazebo to peer over the edge of the stone. No one's there. I fall back down and shake my head to the others behind the bush.

I push away the fear that Mirabella thought *M* was anybody but me. She told Sofia the note was from me. I swear, if she's lying to her best friend and fucking someone else whose name starts with an *M*, I'm going to earn my reputation all over again.

Walking around, I see no sign of anyone, and I walk down to the pond and come up empty again. There are no footprints or discarded clothes or any sign of a struggle. I turn in a circle, examining everything again to make sure I'm not missing anything.

"This is your secret spot?" Sofia asks.

Giovanni glances at me in disbelief.

"I brought her here once. It wasn't a big deal. But someone must've followed us. Someone who wanted Mirabella here tonight. It's the only place they could have meant. It could be the same someone who killed my father and tried to kill me." I walk along the water's edge. Nothing.

"Don't jump to that conclusion, man," Nicolo says, but I see the concern in his eyes.

"It's so romantic. That's why she's had stars in her eyes all day. Under that big bravado is a softy." Sofia continues to poke fun and Giovanni keeps glaring at me.

"We fucked last night, okay? Now we're all on the same page." I stare at Giovanni.

"Consummating the marriage before you actually get married?" Andrea chokes back a laugh.

Sofia pokes me in the chest. "Go ahead and act all macho in front of the guys, but you're out here looking for her. I saw it in your eyes when you realized someone else might have her. You care about her."

Jesus, would she shut up? "Because she's my fiancée. She's my responsibility."

"You'd probably like it if we were married and I cut the tongue out of some guy because he kissed you?" Giovanni raises his eyebrows.

Sofia just smiles.

Yep, she'll make a good Mafia wife as long as she doesn't purposely try to make a short-tempered Italian mad with jealousy. Oh, the innocent guys who will die.

A scream rings out in the night air.

"*Mira!*" Sofia shouts and Giovanni pulls her to his chest, covering her mouth.

"What, are you crazy?" he whispers. "We do not give up our location."

I run in the direction of her voice, Andrea coming to one side and Nicolo the other. We're at the edge of the academy, from what I can tell, and there are some trees that anyone could be hiding among.

Soon Sofia and Giovanni join us, walking behind as we investigate anywhere Mirabella might be hiding. If someone has her, he's quieted her now for sure.

We tiptoe through the trees until we hit a clearing.

I blink once, then twice, because Mira is walking straight toward us with a concerned expression.

"Mirabella," I say and rush forward then pull her toward me. I didn't realize how worried I was until she was safe in my arms. "Was that you who screamed?"

She pulls back and nods. "Yeah, I tripped over a branch and fell." She holds up her palm and I see a decent scratch across it. "Scared the shit out of myself."

"OMG, Mira!" Sofia says way too loudly, coming barreling around me and hugging my fiancée.

When Sofia pulls away, I meet Mirabella's gaze again and ask, "What happened?"

What she says makes me want to beat my chest with rage.

"Lorenzo."

CHAPTER TWENTY-FIVE

MIRABELLA

I stare into Marcelo's eyes, and for the first time since I left Lorenzo, the adrenaline leaches from my body and my heart rate slows.

I've never seen Lorenzo act that way. He's always so even-keeled—not much rattles him. But something about the look in his eyes when he realized I'd slept with Marcelo made it clear something had shifted inside him.

I glance behind Marcelo and see everyone staring at me.

Marcelo doesn't remove his gaze from mine when he barks, "Everyone, out of here."

"Marcelo, we should—" Giovanni starts, but Marcelo is quick to interrupt him.

"Get. Out. Of. Here." His tone is lethal.

There are a few murmurs, but everyone departs, and I watch until they're in the distance before I look at Marcelo. His hands are on my shoulders and he's still staring at me with what I think is barely restrained fury.

"What happened?" he asks for the second time.

"I thought you'd left me a note to meet you at the gazebo, but when I got there, Lorenzo showed up. He wanted to talk because I've been avoiding him and not returning his texts." A shiver of revulsion worms through me and I feel oddly vulnerable. "Was I naive this whole time?"

His fingers flex on my shoulders. "What did he want to talk to you about?"

"Me and him. You and me. I don't really know. There was something off about him, but I can't explain it."

Lorenzo's comment about my ability to write code stuck with me the entire walk back. He was definitely off, but the way he said it . . . it was like it should mean something to me.

"Did anything happen with you two?" His hands drop from my shoulder.

My head rocks back in surprise, all thoughts of computer programs long gone. "Are you serious?" My vulnerability turns to anger faster than a lightning bolt in a thunderstorm.

"You're meeting your ex-lover in the middle of the night. What am I supposed to think?" He steps back, shoving his hands into the pockets of his jeans.

I scowl. "You're supposed to trust me, that's what. I just told you I thought I was meeting you." I cross my arms and jut out my hip, completely pissed he would second-guess my motives.

"And how am I supposed to trust you? You flaunted that relationship that night of the party in the woods. And you know as well as I do that you can't fully trust anyone in this life."

"If you want me to marry you, you'll have to find a way." I turn on my heel and march off toward the dorm.

Marcelo's hand clamps around my upper arm and brings me to a halt, whipping me around to face him. "Where the hell do you think you're going?"

"Somewhere the toxic masculinity isn't quite so potent!" I yank my arm from his hold.

Just leave, Mirabella, this isn't worth it.

"Well, what the hell do you expect me to think?" For the first time since he found me, I recognize the glint of fear in his eyes.

"I expect you to believe me. I slapped Lorenzo and kneed him in the balls because he said some fucked-up shit. He figured out that we'd slept together and just kind of lost it. Honestly, he was kind of scary. I'm not sure what he would have done if I'd stuck around. Nothing happened between him and me. For Christ's sake, I gave myself to *you* last night."

He blows out a breath and rubs his hand over his shaved head. "And you were gone this morning." He cocks his eyebrow.

I blow out a breath. "You're insecure?" All I can do is bite down the smile that's threatening to come out. No doubt he finds it less endearing than I do that he missed me when he woke up this morning.

"You leave when I tell you to leave."

I laugh.

I'm not sure if it's my laughter or the fact he realizes I'm right and he might be worried about the same thing I am. Is this thing between us really real? But his anger seems to melt.

"Damn it, Mira! I felt so out of control. I didn't know where you were or who you were with. I pictured you tortured, tied up, pleading for your life from some bastard who just wanted to get to me." Marcelo cups my right cheek with his hand. "I didn't know if you were alive or dead."

The rare display of vulnerability from this powerful man almost leaves me speechless and my chest swells. He does feel the same way I do. "I'm okay now that you're here. As soon as I was in your arms, I knew I was safe again."

His shoulders relax, and he leans in and takes my lips. His tongue parts my mouth and our kiss is slow and sensual. It's not a precursor for him laying me out on the grass and having his way with me. It's just a shared moment between two people who . . . *care* about each other?

He pulls back and rests his forehead on mine. "I'm glad you got away from him." When I cringe, he pulls back and studies me for a beat. "What?"

"I think my ego has taken a blow. I kneed him in the balls and left when he was still incapacitated. Maybe I should have stayed and fought."

Marcelo shakes his head. "Sometimes losing the battle means winning the war. You have to know when to stay and fight and when it's smarter to retreat and live to fight another day. You did the right thing. You had no backup, no weapon."

"I guess." I frown, knowing kneeing and running doesn't feel as good as kicking Lorenzo's ass would have. Speaking of Lorenzo's ass, he's in deep shit. "What are you going to do?"

"I'll take care of Lorenzo. Don't worry, he won't be bothering you again." His features take on a menacing look, the face of a man who can kill someone without blinking.

My eyes widen. "Marcelo, you can't do anything that will get you kicked out of here." If he goes, I know he'll demand I go with him.

"Don't worry. I won't."

But his words don't hold the promise I long to hear.

"Did he . . . touch you or anything?"

I realize what he's asking, and I shake my head. "No." Better not to even tell Marcelo that he hugged me.

"My brain played havoc on me. While we were looking for you, I'd picture you with someone else. Like maybe the note was a decoy so you could fool Sofia into thinking that you were with me, but really you ran off with someone else."

I'm shocked he would admit that to me. Shocked but pleased.

I lay my hands on his chest. Inhaling deeply, I decide to be honest with him right back. Something I wanted to say last night but didn't have the courage. "I think I should explain something to you."

A crease forms between his eyebrows. "What?"

"I didn't give my virginity to Lorenzo because I loved him or had strong feelings for him."

He scoffs.

"It's true."

"Why would you then?" He scowls at me.

"Because I knew I'd be promised to someone and I wanted at least one big decision in my life to be my own choice. I wouldn't get to choose who I'd spend my life with, who I'd have children with, but at least I could choose that one thing. It was something I didn't have to let this life we're in choose for me."

He studies me for a beat, then gives me a curt nod like he doesn't want to discuss it. I'm not stupid. In our life, for him to accept me as not a virgin is a huge thing.

"If I could go back, I'd have waited and given it to you," I whisper into the cool air. "I'd have made the choice for it to be you."

His body relaxes and his hands delve into my hair before his lips seal with mine. It couldn't be more romantic, being bathed in moonlight as we take our time kissing.

When we pull apart, I feel as though this is a new beginning for us. With any luck, the past will stay just that and we can move forward from here.

CHAPTER TWENTY-SIX

MARCELO

I think having been born into Mafia life makes it so that even though I want to trust Mirabella when she says her relationship with Lorenzo was nothing compared to what we're starting, I need solid proof before I can believe it. And today is the perfect day to ask for it because Nonno is coming for parents' weekend. I can ask him to get me Lorenzo's phone records to see exactly what kind of relationship he and Mirabella had, how long it continued, and whether she's telling the truth when she says she cut him off. It might also show me whether he had anything to do with the hit on my father and me.

I sit with Mirabella and Sofia in the courtyard as the limos and blacked-out SUVs pull in one after the other, hiding our parents behind tinted glass.

"Are you excited to see your parents?" I ask my fiancée.

She shrugs. "My father will probably be more excited to see my brother and you than he will me."

"But remember, your mom is bringing all your new winter clothes for you." Sofia nudges her.

I guess Sofia's parents can't make it today, so she's hanging around the La Rosas the entire day.

"And like any good bestie, you'll share." She nudges Mirabella again.

Mirabella looks at me and kind of rolls her eyes. Ever since I went searching for Mirabella last Sunday, I've noticed more and more how much Sofia is like any other woman born into our world. She's kind of whiny and clingy and I'm not sure I like it as much as I expected. I often wonder how she and Mirabella are best friends, with such different views of what they want out of this life.

Just thinking of that night sets my teeth on edge. I haven't bumped into Lorenzo yet and I can pretty much confirm he's avoiding me. The only reason I haven't searched him out is that I have to be smart about how I take my revenge so it doesn't come back to me and get me kicked out of here. Also, Mirabella's got me on lockdown in my bed practically every second we have downtime. I'm not sure if it's strategy or lust on her part. No matter which, I'm not complaining.

The doors open on a new row of vehicles after they've passed all the security checkpoints and Mirabella's dad steps out, holding his hand out for his wife.

"There they are." Sofia points as if they're her parents.

I jump off the table and take Mirabella's hand. I'm thankful they arrived before my family because I need to show Frank La Rosa that he's picked the right person to give his daughter to.

"This is unnecessary," Mirabella whispers. "This isn't 'meet the parents' and you have to make a good impression."

I tighten my grip on her hand. "No matter what, I have to treat your father with respect."

"You're essentially in command now," she says.

"Not yet. Nonno is head of the family until I leave here."

We're talking in hushed tones, but she stops at my last word. I hear her mother in the distance, gushing over Antonio and how big he seems since the last time she saw him.

"Come on." I tug on Mirabella's hand.

"Are you going to leave? Before graduation?" Her face has lost all color and she looks how most of our soldiers do when they see a dead body for the first time.

"That was my plan. As soon as I find who wants me dead and exact my retribution, I'm outa here."

Her mouth hangs open. Why the hell does that upset her so much?

"And if I want to graduate?" she asks.

My shoulders sink. Just when I thought we were getting to be on the same page . . . "If I leave, you're coming with me."

"Mirabella!" her mom interrupts, walking over to us. "You look sick." She puts her hand on her forehead. "Are you okay?"

"Marcelo." Frank La Rosa sticks his hand out to me.

I shake it. "Nice to see you, Frank. I hope your trip in was smooth."

"It was, thank you." He nods to his left. "May I have a word?"

I glance at Mirabella, who rolls her eyes while her mother takes garments out of a bag and holds them up. Sofia oohs and aahs over each item, but Mirabella couldn't look less interested.

Once we're off by ourselves, Frank puts his hand on my shoulder. He's graying around the temples and it's clear he's spent way too much time in the sun, but he has a lean body still, no extra weight at the front, so I'd bet he still works out. Height-wise, I have the advantage.

"First, I want to offer my condolences on your father. He was a great man and a better leader."

I nod. "Thank you."

"Second, I heard there were some problems initially with Mira and I want to apologize for my daughter. I blame her mother. She's spoiled Mira her entire life." He glances at them then back at me. "She asks for too much, doesn't accept her place in this family."

"Yes, she's stubborn . . ." I take a moment to consider how honest I want to be with this man. It's not unheard of for a father to take his hand to his child for embarrassing him or misbehaving. If I told him everything I know about Mirabella, I have no idea what he'd do. And if he lays hands on what I now consider mine, we're going to have problems. "She's come around. Arranged marriages can take time."

He laughs. "Yes, me and her mother, let's just say the apple didn't fall far from that tree. It took me a long time to bend her will, make her realize her dreams of the life she wanted were just that—dreams."

I smile down at him, spotting my mother stepping out of a limo with my uncle. Talk about a woman who learned to bend to her husband's demands. My poor mother. Is that why I've become almost soft with Mirabella? She has unrealistic expectations for our marriage and life, but I find myself attracted to her stubbornness in wanting more for herself.

"Again, she's turned around. Things are going well."

He clasps me on the shoulder. "Good to hear. Good to hear. Her mother can't wait to plan the wedding. We're thrilled to be uniting with the Costas."

I nod. "Us as well. If you'll excuse me, my mom and uncle just got here."

Frank glances over his shoulder. "Your uncle Joey?" he asks, with the tone of someone who's come into contact with him in the past—disdain.

Not that I blame Frank. My uncle Joey is the third and youngest son of my nonno and has no wife or children. Being the third, he's never held any real power, but now that my dad and Giovanni's dad are dead, I assume that if I die . . . I blow out a breath. The list of people who could want me dead gets longer every day.

"Mind if I join you? I'd like to give your mother my condolences as well."

I nod. "Of course."

We walk down the cobblestone path toward them. My mother is dressed in black, but her makeup is perfectly done. Meanwhile, my uncle escorts her with his hand on the small of her back. *Bastard.* He better not be trying to slide in there. I'll kill him myself.

"Marcelo." My mom wraps me in a hug along my middle and squeezes me into her.

"Hi, Mom," I say before kissing the top of her head.

"My boy, I miss you so much."

"I'm sorry about your brother." Frank approaches Uncle Joey first.

"Thank you."

My mom steps back from me and Frank shifts his attention to her. "Vittoria, Livia and I are so sorry for your loss."

Tears well up in my mom's eyes and I wonder if they're real or fake. She has to play the grieving widow, but if I was her, I would've thrown a party on the bastard's yacht then lit it on fire. "Thank you, Frank."

He hands her an envelope, and she puts it in her purse. I catch my uncle watching the entire exchange and I mentally make a note to talk privately with my mom today.

"Is Mirabella around?" my mother asks. "I so look forward to celebrating your union. It's what Sam was most looking forward to this year, our two families joining together."

Frank pats her hand. "Yes, let me get her."

I turn to take care of it, but Mirabella is already walking over with her mother.

When she stands next to me, I wrap my arm around her waist. "Mom, you remember Mirabella?"

My mom's eyes light up. "I do, but not this grown woman. Mio Dio, you're gorgeous. You were just a girl when I saw you last."

"Vittoria, I'm so sorry." Livia approaches my mom and hugs her.

Mom's eyes close and she wipes a tear from her right eye. I swear, if she's not actually upset, she should go to LA and try her hand at acting.

"Thank you, but enough about Sam. Look at what a gorgeous couple they make." She puts her hands out in front of us then kisses Mirabella's cheeks. "And I promise I'm not a wicked mother-in-law."

Mirabella smiles. "I'd never assume that. I love your dress."

The women exchange compliments, Livia gives me a hug at one point, and it's not until Antonio, Giovanni, and Sofia meet up with us that we decide to part ways for the day.

I kiss Mirabella on the lips, lingering longer than necessary but keeping it polite for her dad. To him, she's still a virgin, I'm sure.

"See you in a bit," I say before kissing her cheek.

"Yeah." Her hands grip mine a little tighter.

I swear the look in her eyes says she'd rather be in bed with me than have to visit with our families right now.

* * *

A HALF HOUR later, we're getting a snack from the Café Ambrosia. My mom chose some vegetables and dip because she's forever watching her figure. My uncle, on the other hand, grabbed a stack of cookies.

"Where is Nonno?" I ask when we sit at one of the tables outside, away from anyone else.

"He couldn't make it. The doctors didn't clear him, so he sent me to chaperone your mother," Uncle Joey says.

"Which I didn't need." She smiles at him. My uncle glares and she masterfully recovers like she learned a long time ago. "But I do appreciate it, Joey."

"Just doing what my brother would have wanted," he grates out.

Giovanni gives me a look. He's waiting for me to bring up business.

I slide closer to the table and look around to make sure no one will overhear us. It's mostly the Irish Mafia around, and I'm pretty sure they had nothing to do with my near-death experience. "We need to talk business."

"I'm going to go for a walk. Catch up when you're done." My mom places her hand on mine.

Guilt racks me that I'm spending this time doing business, but this is the way it will be when I take my spot as the head of the family. "Thanks, Mom."

She smiles and tosses her plate in the trash before walking toward the courtyard.

"Uncle, I need a favor. I was going to ask Nonno, but since he's not here . . ."

"What is it?" he asks.

"I need the phone records and text conversations of someone who attends Sicuro. I think he may be linked to the hit on my father and me."

Uncle nods toward the edge of the patio and I rise from my chair.

My uncle, Giovanni, and I head the opposite way to the edge of the patio. No one is on this end thankfully.

My uncle lights a cigarette. "Tell me more."

Giovanni and I both take a cigarette from his offered pack and Giovanni sits on the stone ledge.

"Lorenzo Bruni."

Uncle Joey sucks in a deep inhale of his cigarette and blows it out, turning to face the view of the forest. At first, I think he didn't hear me.

"You should talk to your soon-to-be father-in-law if Lorenzo's causing you trouble. His father works for him." He inhales then blows out more smoke.

"I'm not involving him until I have to." I take a drag off the smoke.

"Why do you think it's him?" He tilts his head.

This is where I should tell him not to question me. That I'm higher than him and he does as I say, but he's my uncle and I've never told him what to do. But he better be prepared not to question me once I'm head of this family, or I'll have no choice but to discipline him.

Giovanni clears his throat, but I quickly speak because I don't want anything involving Mirabella in this conversation. "I don't trust him. We've had a few run-ins, but I have no actual proof. He . . ."

I can see the doubt in my uncle. He knows there's more.

"He's trying to steal Mirabella out from under Marcelo," Giovanni says, and I give him a scathing look.

What the fuck? He's lucky we're in public because my hand itches to backhand him across the face.

Uncle's head falls back. "Ah, I see. Jealousy over the girl. Your father was like that too. No one could go near Vittoria without him wanting to slice their throat. Okay, I'll see what I can do. We have someone on the payroll at most of the big telecom companies. Don't get your hopes up, they could use burner phones. But if we find what you think we might, we go to Frank La Rosa and demand Bruni's head."

"I'll deliver Lorenzo's father his dead son's head to his front porch if it was him."

Uncle clasps me on the shoulder and nods as if he's proud of me. "Did I tell you we found our weapons on the Russians' docks?"

"No." This is something I should have been told way before now.

"Don't worry, I'll handle it for you, what with you locked up in here." He winks.

"Thanks, Uncle Joey."

I wish he would have told me earlier. I'm supposed to be privy to this news, but hopefully Nonno is fully aware.

"Now show me where the alcohol is in this place."

We laugh and Giovanni jumps down from the ledge. "They have a tent set up just off the dorms. I'll take you."

"I'm going to catch up with Mom. We'll see you soon." I toss my cigarette in the outside ashtray and walk over to the courtyard in search of my mom.

Now I just have to keep myself in check until those phone records come through.

CHAPTER TWENTY-SEVEN

MIRABELLA

"I love the YSL sweater you bought, Mrs. La Rosa. I'll definitely be borrowing that one from Mira." Sofia smiles across the dining table at my mom, who preens under the compliment.

"Thank you, Sofia. I wish my daughter was as excited as you are. I put a lot of thought into all the outfits I brought, you know." My mom gives me a stern look of disapproval. She probably wishes Sofia were her daughter. Actually, my entire family probably wishes that.

A wan smile forms on my lips. "I appreciate all of it, Mom. Truly."

We're eating dinner in the dining hall with some other families. So far, most of the conversation has been between my father and Antonio regarding business. Mostly in code words, so we women don't know who or what they're talking about. Even if we did, we're expected to sit here and pretend we can't hear anything. There's a real "don't speak unless spoken to" vibe to this dinner.

"Mira."

I glance warily at my dad.

"I was happy to hear from Marcelo that you've come around and accepted the engagement. It really is what's best for all."

Sofia titters like a schoolgirl and I squeeze her leg under the table. I know my dad is happy I'm no longer throwing up every opposition I can to my upcoming marriage, but I have no idea how he'd react if he knew I've already slept with Marcelo. Best not to find out. If only I had a gag for Sofia.

"As always, I'm happy you're happy."

If he hears any of the sarcasm in my voice, he doesn't show it.

Just because I've accepted that marriage to Marcelo is inevitable doesn't mean that my endgame has changed. I still want some agency over my life, but more than that, I want to be a partner to Marcelo. For the first time since I was told I was getting married, I can see our marriage possibly giving me what I want. I can picture Marcelo and me leading the Costas into prosperity, side by side, as equals. But he has to see it too.

"Well, it's good to know that's taken care of. Now we can set our sights on other things, right, Livia?" He takes my mom's hand and sets them on the table between them.

Unease bubbles in my stomach, and I look between my parents. "What do you mean?"

My mom smiles and looks overjoyed while my dad's chest puffs out and his chin rises with pride.

"We have an announcement to make." My dad looks at my mom, then glances at Antonio beside me. "After much consideration on my part, I've made the decision that Antonio will be wed to Aurora Salucci when he finishes here at the Sicuro Academy."

Sofia gasps while my mouth falls open in disbelief. One glance at my brother's tight grip on his silverware tells me he's not thrilled about this arrangement, but he doesn't say anything and keeps from looking at Sofia or me. Huh, I can't wait to see how this plays out after he told me to bend for Marcelo.

"You can't be serious?" I shout.

My dad's eyes narrow. "Lower your voice."

I lean forward and quiet my voice. "Aurora is the worst! She tried to make my life hell in high school. How could you want Antonio to marry her? He'll be miserable." I look at my brother with an expression of "say something," but he still won't meet my eyes.

My dad leans in. "Aurora's father is my underboss. With you

cementing us in with the Costas through your marriage, Mira, we can use Antonio's marriage to solidify our hold within our own borders. Oronato Salucci is highly respected, and this is the match that will make the most people happy."

I obviously won't get anywhere with my dad, so I turn my attention to my mom. "You're going to let this happen? You know what she's like."

I spent many a night in high school with my mom rubbing my back as I cried because of some mean girl stunt Aurora had played on me that day.

"Your father says this is what's best," she says in a measured voice.

My neck throbs as my blood pressure spikes. I cross my arms and glare at my father. "Do you ever get tired of using your kids as pawns?"

"You will speak to me with respect or not at all, Mirabella. You may be an engaged woman, but until you are married, I'm in charge of you. I can yank you out of here any moment I see fit."

I press my lips together, physically forcing myself not to say anything more.

Aurora Salucci is going to be my sister-in-law. This is unreal.

"Congratulations, Antonio," Sofia says in a small voice and stands. "If you'll excuse me, I don't think dinner is sitting right in my stomach. I'm going to head back to the dorm. Thanks for letting me hang around you guys today, Mr. and Mrs. La Rosa."

"It's always a pleasure to see you," my mom says with a genuine smile.

My dad says goodbye to Sofia, then she's off. I watch her walk away and don't miss the way her shoulders sag and her chin hangs down. My father's news has affected her.

Not surprising, I guess. This is Aurora Salucci we're talking about. My brother marrying her means the two of us will inevitably have to deal with her for the rest of our lives.

"When are you making the announcement?" I ask.

"We'll hold off until you're all home for Christmas break, then we'll work on planning an engagement party."

"I'm already figuring out the color scheme for the engagement party, Antonio, don't worry." Mom forks her salad and smiles at my brother.

"Thanks, Mom," he says blankly.

I'm pretty sure my brother doesn't give two shits about the party's color scheme. Not when he's being saddled for life with the Queen Bitch.

The four of us are quiet as we finish our meals. There's a lot I could say, but my father has made it clear he doesn't want to hear any of it and I know he's serious when he says he'll pull me out of here.

By the time my brother and I wave goodbye as they get into their vehicle to head to the nearby private airport to fly home, I'm bursting at the seams to talk with my brother about this new development.

The moment the driver closes the door on my parents, I turn to my brother. "What the hell? Did you already know?"

He doesn't bother to look at me, just watches the limo drive off. "Dad informed me when he arrived." He shrugs. "It is what it is."

"It's bullshit, is what it is. You can't possibly be thinking of letting this happen."

"It's already been decided, Mira." He stalks off toward the dorm.

My legs have to work double time to keep up with him. "There's no way you want to marry that witch."

He stops abruptly and spins to face me. "You're right, Mira. I don't want to. But the difference between us is that I know what my responsibility to this family is and I'll see it through without complaining. I'm not as selfish as you."

His last comment is like a slap across the face. My eyes narrow on him. "You think it's selfish to want to make a decision as large as who you'll marry for yourself?"

"This is how things are done in our world. You know this. You've been witness to it your entire life."

"It doesn't make it right."

I shouldn't take any pleasure in how miserable he looks, but a small part of me does. Now he knows what it feels like to be in my position. But he's right about one thing. He's obviously willing to accept my dad's proclamation much easier than I am.

"Just drop it. It's not even your life we're talking about."

"The hell it's not. I'm going to have to watch you be miserable every day."

"You just don't like her," he snaps.

"Fair enough, but you should have some say in this. I don't want you to be unhappy."

"You'll be in New York, Mira. I'll be in Miami. Just leave it alone." He walks away, feet pounding the pavement as he goes, hands clenched at his sides.

"If you say so," I mutter.

Then I rewind to what he said. *You'll be in New York*. Damn, I'll be away from everyone I know and love. How had that not occurred to me?

I watch until he disappears from sight, then I begin my trek back toward Roma House. The realization comes in a flash the way things do sometimes when you stop trying to work them out in your head—suddenly, the answer is just there.

Lorenzo's comment about the computer program . . .

Marcelo's comment early on about how they knew the explosion had been detonated using a program of some kind . . .

I stop walking and clutch my stomach, remembering the day Lorenzo asked me to teach him how to write a program to set off a bomb. He told me he wanted to improve his skills so he'd have more to offer the family, work his way up through the ranks by proving himself. I even gave him the code I wrote on a portable drive because he said he wanted to study it and see if he could re-create it himself.

Did I unknowingly give him the key to killing Marcelo's father?

I think of how jealous Lorenzo has been of Marcelo and how out of character he's been acting. Was the goal really to take out Marcelo so that he could be with me?

If I did have something to do with the bomb, what will Marcelo do to me if he finds out? Will it even matter that I wasn't a knowing participant?

I walk again, my mind a jumble of thoughts and emotions. About halfway back to Roma House, my phone buzzes in my back pocket. I pull it out, expecting it to be Sofia or Marcelo.

Rage colors my vision when I see Lorenzo's name after my realization. He hasn't tried to contact me since our altercation last Sunday night. I've managed to convince Marcelo to chill for a bit before he confronts Lorenzo for fear that he'll do something stupid and get kicked out of Sicuro Academy—revenge is best served cold and all that. Most of my negotiation has been through sex, which isn't really a hardship.

I click on the screen to pull up the message, and at the same time, a set of hands wraps around my middle and squeezes. I yelp and flail, my phone catapulting out of my hand and landing on the nearby grass.

"Oh shit, sorry."

My body tenses at the sound of Marcelo's voice. Will he be able to see the guilt on my face?

I turn and smack his arm, trying to act normal. "You scared the shit out of me."

He laughs playfully, and if my heart wasn't beating five hundred beats a minute right now, I'd probably be awestruck by the sight. "I didn't mean to. Well, yeah, I did. I just didn't think you'd spook so easy."

He bends down to grab my phone and passes it to me, but he must notice what text exchange is open on the screen because he tenses.

"I just got it. Haven't even read it yet."

His entire posture stiffens and his jaw clenches when he reads what's on the screen. When he slowly glances back up at me, any of his earlier affability is replaced with the stone-cold face of a killer.

"This guy is a dead man."

CHAPTER TWENTY-EIGHT

MARCELO

Before seeing the text from Lorenzo, I had high hopes of spending the night naked with my fiancée in my dorm room. We've been all over each other this past week, exploring one another and figuring out what drives the other crazy. She's yet to go down on me, but one day she'll bend her will to me.

But all that is out the window as I stare at her phone, rage burning in my chest.

LORENZO: Costa has completely brainwashed you.
You hate him, remember? WE love one another.
I'm not going to hurt you. Can we just talk? I can
make you see if you'll just talk to me.

I hand over her phone before I break it in two. "This fucking guy. What doesn't he get?"

She shakes her head. "He's just seeing something not there. I'm sure he'll stop messaging eventually. I'll keep reminding him."

My hands clench at my sides as I work to control my temper. I don't want to take it out on Mira, but then again, if she hadn't played games, if she had just accepted our engagement from the start, we wouldn't be here.

"This is the final nail in his coffin."

She pockets her phone and nods. "Marcelo," she says in a re-signed voice.

"Are you going to try to stop me?" I stare at her.

She's fidgeting with her phone. "I'm merely suggesting we give this more time."

I take her hips in my hands and lock eyes with her. "Are you mine, Mira?"

"You know there's no one else."

"Answer me with a yes or a no."

She doesn't even blink. "Yes."

"Then that's it. His funeral is coming."

I take her hand to escort her to Roma House. Lorenzo will be a problem for tomorrow. I have to be smart about this. I can't just pop off the way I want to right now. I have to get the guys in on it, do some surveillance, and figure out the best move forward.

"You can't get kicked out of here," she whispers even though no one is around us.

"Trust me, I won't. This isn't the first . . ." I let my sentence die on my lips. I'm not sure how much Mira knows about my reputation and whether it scares her at all. She's said she wants to be a part of the business. She's asked me to train her with weapons. I probably need to find out exactly how involved she wants to be.

"I don't want to go back to the dorm," she says, and I take that as the opportunity to take a detour.

"We need to find another special spot, thanks to that jackass," I grumble.

Her hand tightens in mine. "No, we don't. I'm fine to go back there."

"Are you sure?" I glance at her and she nods.

"Okay."

When we arrive at the stone gazebo, I sit down first and tug her onto my lap. She repositions herself so she's straddling me, her fingers running up and down the back of my head.

"How was your visit with your family? God, your mom is so gorgeous. I see where you get it from," she says.

My hands slide up under her skirt and mold to her ass. I playfully smack it and she yelps, sliding closer to me. "It was fine, except I wish my nonno had come and not my uncle. But I'm glad my mom came."

"She's still broken up about your dad?" She doesn't look at me when she asks, and her body stiffens.

Death is somewhat of a constant in our world. Could it be that Mirabella's now realizing she cares about me and the prospect that someone could take me out is always there? That she could end up like my mom?

"I don't know. They lived a pretty typical Mafia marriage after the first time my mom caught him with someone else. After that night, I don't know what he said to her, but she just smiled through it all, biting her lip when he came home drunk and smelling of perfume or, worse, didn't come home at all. I doubt she's mourning him, but it's only been months. She has to keep up the facade."

Her body loses some of its tension, and she kisses my forehead. "I'm sorry," she says with so much emotion I draw back.

"He was a giant asshole, but thank you."

She unbuttons my shirt one button at a time, squirming in my lap. "Tell me, Mr. Costa, are you a rule breaker?"

My fingers glide under the elastic of her silk panties and squeeze her ass cheeks. "I think you know the answer to that."

Once my shirt is spread open and her fingernails slide down my chest and abs, she starts in on her blouse. Teasing me, she undoes it slowly, giving me a glimpse of her cleavage.

"You're so damn beautiful," I whisper.

I squeeze her ass cheeks again before tearing off her blouse, revealing her tits snug in a satin light-pink bra. I stare at her in the moonlight, my fingers grazing her rib cage under the cups of her bra. Her chest rises and falls, watching me.

"Please, Marcelo."

"My two favorite words."

I yank down the cups and her tits pop out. I waste no time grabbing them and moving from one to the other with my mouth, teasing her nipples with my tongue before biting them. Her head rocks back and her hands strip off me, but only to unhook her bra and let it fall between us.

I'm busy worshiping her upper body while she undoes my pants and pulls out my dick.

"You want this here?" I ask, tapping her ass to lift and using my fingers to slide her panties over. "I have no condom with me."

She stops moving for a beat, but when she lowers a bit, the tip of my dick runs along the length of her center. "I'm on birth control to regulate my periods. But . . . are you clean?"

"Mira, I've been here so far this semester. Even before then, I've always used a condom."

She opens her mouth as if she wants to say something, but doesn't. Before I even realize her intention, she grabs my cock and sinks down on it.

"Fuck," I groan. Having her bareback feels too fucking good. "You're gonna be the death of me."

She stills and meets my gaze for a beat before she moves again. "Good thing I'm going to be your wife. I'll get everything once you're gone."

My eyes flash open and I stare at her cheeky smile. It's the first time she didn't refer to our marriage in a derisive way. It's the first time she's seemed to like the idea.

I thrust up into her hard. "I'm going to fuck you senseless."

She bounces on my lap, her tits right in front of my face. A man could get used to this life.

Then a flashlight shines in Mirabella's eyes, and she blinks from the glare. "Oh shit."

She falls down to the ground, quickly fastening her blouse while I put away my cock and button up my shirt.

"Well, well, Mr. Costa. You'd think I'd be surprised, but . . ." Chancellor Thompson walks the length of the gazebo. "And who do we have with you?"

Mira peeks her head up and raises her hand.

"Mirabella La Rosa." He sounds surprised. I guess he expected to find me here with someone who isn't my fiancée.

"We're engaged," I remind him.

"That doesn't mean I can condone you two messing around. How do you think your father would feel if he knew the school was turning a blind eye to the defilement of his daughter?" He crosses his arms. "But I'm not an idiot. Keep it to your dorm rooms like everyone else, where we can't be expected to monitor your behavior."

This guy hates me.

Mirabella quickly sits next to me once she's presentable again, although she doesn't have a bra on—it's clutched in my hands. "We're very sorry, sir. It won't happen again."

He raises his hand at me. "That's two, Costa. One more and you're out."

My head falls back on a groan. *Asshole.*

"It's not just him here. I should get a warning too."

I stare at Mira as though she has two heads.

"Fine. Miss La Rosa, this is your first warning. Now I'll lead you both back to your dorms."

Once we're at the entrance to Roma House, the chancellor lets us go. Mira is quiet on the way in. I know she's thinking overtime about something in that brain of hers.

"What?" I ask once we're in the elevator.

"I know you're not going to listen to me, but if you get caught beating up Lorenzo, that will be your third strike."

I pull her into my arms. "Dolcezza, I've killed people no one found out about. This isn't the first time I have to do something without getting caught. Plus, if you weren't such a temptation, I wouldn't have two strikes already." I grab her ass over her skirt, and she wiggles to be let free.

"I'm serious, Marcelo."

The elevator doors ding and slide open on her floor. I step out to follow.

She puts her hand on my chest. "I got it from here. Just think about it, okay?"

"Okay." But I have no intention of changing my mind.

She gives me a quick kiss then walks down the hallway. How in the hell did I end up with blue balls tonight?

* * *

BETWEEN GIOVANNI, NICOLO, Andrea and me, we watch Lorenzo's every move for a week. We know when he goes to class, when he goes to work out, which piece of equipment he uses. We practically know every time he takes a shit. Only then do we make a plan for him.

"I say we take him down at night, wear masks, two of us hold him back, and Marcelo kicks the shit outa him. But don't hit his face," Giovanni says.

"None of you are going. This is between me and him," I clarify.

Giovanni shakes his head. "What? That's way too dangerous."

"Yeah, Giovanni's right. We need to do this together. What if he's expecting it and he's got guys with him?"

"In the entire week we've watched him, have you seen him with anyone you think is gonna back him up against us?"

They all shake their heads.

"It's just me and him. I'm going to approach him on the south end of Roma House when he gets back from fencing tonight."

"If you say so, boss." Andrea leans back in my chair and holds up his hands.

It's the first time he's ever called me that and I like it.

"If you guys want, you can be my lookouts. Stand by the front doors and make sure you don't see the chancellor skulking around. That stronzo would like nothing more than to give me my third strike."

"That I can do." Nicolo runs his hands together.

"Okay, we have about an hour before he returns."

In that hour, I throw a rock at the light outside the south end of the dorm. I sneaked into the camera room two nights ago and figured out that as long as that light doesn't go on from its motion sensor, then the camera won't go on either. Then I change into a black shirt and pants and grab some leather gloves, so my knuckles won't show any obvious signs of a fight.

I hear Lorenzo coming, such a creature of habit. He hasn't figured out that works against a person in a business like ours.

As soon as he hits the dark spot, glancing up at the light—probably wondering why it didn't turn on—I reveal myself. I thought about wearing a mask, but I want him looking right at me every time I land a hit. I'll make sure he doesn't talk.

"What the fuck?"

Before he can say anything else, I punch him in the stomach. He crumples and his book bag drops to the ground. He comes back at me with a swing of his own, but I dodge it and land a hard jab to the ribs. With every jab and hit, some of the rage and frustration that's been boiling over inside me for a week eases.

I don't stop hitting him. Over and over, I pummel him until he lies there limply. "Stay the fuck away from Mira! Are we clear?"

"She doesn't love you. She loves me," he croaks.

I pick him up by his jacket. "You're delusional. If she loved you, she wouldn't be fucking me every chance she gets. And damn does her pussy feel good."

His eyes go manic and his hands claw at my gloves to release him.

"Soaking wet every damn time." I get a sick sense of satisfaction at the look of horror on his face.

"You don't deserve her," he says.

"Maybe not, but that doesn't make her any less mine." I toss him on the ground, and he whimpers in pain, going into the fetal position. "And if you say one word about who did this to you, I will make sure your entire family ends up with concrete boots. Don't think I won't. You don't want to test me, Lorenzo. Keep your mouth shut."

From his look of resigned anger, I know he won't be ratting me out to anyone.

CHAPTER TWENTY-NINE
MIRABELLA

Sofia's books land with a loud bang on the library table, causing everyone to give her dirty looks. "Oh my god, I have to tell you something."

"Shhh. Sofia, what the hell?" I whisper.

"Sorry, sorry. But I couldn't wait until I saw you at dinner to tell you."

"Tell me what?" My forehead creases.

"I just overheard some people talking about how Lorenzo was taken to the hospital last night. That's why he wasn't in class today." Both her eyebrows rise.

A sinking feeling weighs down my stomach and my pen slips out of my hand onto the table. "Why'd he go to the hospital?"

"That's just it. Apparently, he won't tell anyone what happened." She glances around quickly then leans in closer. "Do you think this is Marcelo's doing?"

I squeeze my eyes shut. "Of course it's Marcelo." I push my chair back and pack my books.

Sofia's eyes widen. "Where are you going?"

"To go figure out what the hell he's done." And how it's going to affect me, I don't add.

I swear, if he gets kicked out of the academy and expects me to follow him like a puppy with its tongue hanging out, he has another think coming.

"Are you mad?" Sofia swings her bag up over her shoulder.

"I don't know what I am right now. I'll see you at dinner."

She nods.

I knew it was too much to hope that Marcelo wouldn't exact retribution from Lorenzo. I mean, my ex has broken all the rules and shown Marcelo absolutely no respect as a made man and the head of his family. Marcelo had no choice but to make an example of him, otherwise people will think he's weak and come after him.

I push through the library doors and walk down the path that leads to Roma House, where I'm hoping to find Marcelo.

I don't have an issue with him teaching Lorenzo a lesson. I just don't want it to come at the expense of me having to leave the Sicuro Academy. I want to finish out my time here and learn all I can. It'll only make me more of an asset and get me closer to Marcelo seeing me as an equal.

When I reach the dorm, I go straight to Marcelo's room and knock on the door.

"He's not in there."

I whip around at the sound of Nicolo's voice. "Do you know where he is?"

"Not one-hundred-percent sure, but he did mention that he was going to work out before dinner tonight. You might find him at the gym."

"Great, thanks." I spin around and stalk back toward the elevator.

"Everything okay?" Nicolo calls.

"Peachy." I stab the elevator button and stand there waiting.

By the time I reach the gym, my thoughts are in overdrive. If he did attack Lorenzo, and I have no doubt he did, how can he possibly be sure Lorenzo won't rat him out? Then again, if Lorenzo were going to do that, I think he would have already. Unless he's in such bad shape that he can't even speak right now.

Once I'm inside the gym, I spot Marcelo. He's with Giovanni in the free weight section. Marcelo's shirtless and watching himself in the mirror while he lifts dumbbells overhead. The muscles in his back flex with his movements and I have to strip my eyes away from them to stay focused.

He notices me charging his way in the mirror and, with a sigh, bends to set down his weights.

"What did you do?" I snap as soon as I reach him.

"Hello, dolcezza. What seems to be the problem?" Marcelo looks up and down my body.

I narrow my eyes. "You know damn well what the problem is."

Marcelo looks over his shoulder at Giovanni, who's looking at me with distaste. "Make sure no one bothers us."

Then Marcelo drags me by the upper arm toward the room we usually use for sparring. Once we're inside and he's shut the door, I spin to face him.

"You beat the shit out of Lorenzo?"

"Why are you surprised?" Marcelo puts his hands on his hips. "He should be happy I didn't kill him."

"You said you wouldn't."

He steps forward and lets his hands drop. "No, I said I'd think about it. I did and decided he needed to learn a lesson. To stay the fuck away from what's mine."

My book bag slides off my shoulder and lands with a thud on the floor. "How do you not think this will come back on you? He's definitely going to rat you out, then you'll be expelled. I'm telling you now. I won't go with you." It's all I can do to stop myself from stomping my foot like a child.

"If he likes breathing, he'll keep his mouth shut. Trust me."

My hands fly up at my sides. "What about my father? If Lorenzo tells my family, he could make problems for you."

Marcelo's eyes narrow on me. "If your dad knew everything about the situation, including the fact that that stronzo stole his daughter's virginity, he'd have no problem with what I did. My retribution was earned and due."

I frown. He's not wrong. My dad would probably kill Lorenzo himself for sleeping with me. Add on the fact that he completely disrespected Marcelo, as well as my dad's decree that I would be wed to him, and yeah, my fiancé is right. My dad would have no issue with Marcelo meting out justice.

I consider what I would have done if the roles were reversed. Would I have wanted retribution? Absolutely. But if it were me, I would have waited until a school break and done it off campus where the school would have no say.

"You could still be caught. What if it's on camera? And you didn't even tell me you were going to do it. I thought we were going to discuss it."

Marcelo's face draws tight and he steps closer to me. "There's nothing to discuss, principessa. He tried to take something that is mine, something I care for. There's no scenario where he doesn't pay for that." He walks toward me and I instinctively back up until I hit the wall. "Understand this, there are no lengths I won't go to in order to keep you safe. You are mine now and I will always protect what's mine—with my life. Every punch I landed is part of that vow to you. Anything or anyone that threatens to take you from me will be dealt with swiftly and with force."

I picture him pummeling Lorenzo with rage, telling him to stay away from me, that I'm his, and I have to clench my thighs together. God, why is that so hot? Why is the idea of him defending me and my honor, of his physical brutality against another man on my behalf such a turn-on? Every feminist in the world would throw rocks at me right now if they knew how wet I am over his bullying actions.

"Well . . . next time, don't keep me in the dark." I hold on to my bravado, but my voice comes out too breathy.

Marcelo smirks and takes the last step toward me so that his body is pressed against mine. The heat of his skin seeps through my uniform shirt.

"I think someone likes the idea of me doling out justice on her behalf." He dips his hand underneath my skirt and runs his fingers across the wet fabric of my panties. "Oh yeah, she definitely likes it."

My head drops back against the wall, and I sigh. There's no use denying it. My body has already betrayed me.

He continues to coast his fingers between my legs. "So greedy."

I reach past the waistband of his shorts to grip his hard length. "I need you inside me." There's desperation in my voice that I don't bother to hide.

Without warning, he pushes down his shorts and boxer briefs then lifts me. I wrap my legs around his waist on instinct and use one hand to pull aside the fabric of my panties. Seconds later, he pushes into me and I let out a relieved sigh.

I still can't get used to the feeling of having him bare inside me. It's so much more intimate and blissful than when he wears a condom.

My fingers dig into his shoulders as he pummels into me, his hands simultaneously holding me up and spreading me. I use the wall for leverage so he doesn't have to hold so much of my weight, and it changes the angle in a way that quickly builds the intensity. Quickly, it feels like too much.

I call out, but he acts as if he doesn't hear me. He keeps up his powerful thrusts like a man possessed, dragging himself in and out of me at a rapid-fire pace.

Just when I think I can't take any more, the intensity morphs into heaven and my orgasm overtakes me like a tidal wave. It's so all-consuming that I have no idea whether I call out, scream, or what, but by the time I come to, Marcelo is spilling down the inside of my thighs as he pulls out.

"I'll never let anyone or anything hurt you." He kisses my forehead.

To my utter shock, I wholeheartedly believe him.

CHAPTER THIRTY
MARCELO

A few weeks go by and Lorenzo has returned to campus. Seems he doesn't have a complete death wish because he never mentions it was me who put him in the hospital. I've seen him only a handful of times since his return, and each time, he turns in another direction or goes to the other side of the path, pretending I'm not there. I've asked Mirabella if he's approached her at all and she says he hasn't.

Speaking of my fiancée, her silky-smooth body rolls over into my arms as the morning sun seeps in through the crack of the drapes. She presses her tits against my chest and my hand slides down her torso and grabs her ass. Last night might've been a record sex marathon for us.

"I'm exhausted." Her eyelids struggle to remain open.

"When is your first class?" I pick her up and put her completely on top of me.

"You're crazy. I told you last night I'm sore." She kisses my chest as though she can't help herself.

"I can think of something else you could do and you wouldn't even have to use your pussy." I raise my pelvis off the bed to press my hard dick against her stomach.

She sits up. "I told you I won't get on my knees for you."

My hands mold to her tits and I run my thumbs over her nipples. "Are you sure? You have such a beautiful mouth. Do you know how many times I've imagined it wrapped around my hard cock?" I run my finger along her bottom lip and inch it into her mouth.

She sucks for a long time as if it's my dick, and I grow even harder until she bites it.

"Ouch, now I can't trust you with my dick." I pick her up and move her off me.

She laughs and I have to say I love the fucking sound of it.

Jesus, I don't even recognize the man I'm becoming with thoughts like that.

"You should feed me before class. That's what a good fiancé would do." She lies naked in my bed as I climb out and go into the bathroom to turn on the shower.

I come back and enjoy the sight of her splayed out on my bed. "I just tried to feed you."

She playfully narrows her eyes, and I walk over, pick her up over my shoulder, and carry her fireman style to the shower.

"How about I clean you up first?"

"As long as you promise to clean all of me." Her voice is sultry and sweet at the same time.

"I'll make sure to do a very thorough job."

* * *

A HALF HOUR later, we're at breakfast. These days, Mirabella sits at the table with my group of guys. If Sofia happens to be here, she'll usually join us. But it would appear to all that Mirabella has finally realized where she belongs and that's beside me.

She barely eats anything, while my friends and I have plates filled with eggs, bacon, and hash browns.

"I don't know how you guys eat that much." She eyes our plates.

"We're growing boys and need a lot of energy." I wink at her.

"Marcelo, more than the rest of us, just to keep up with your nympho behavior." Giovanni laughs, but Mirabella doesn't.

Instead, she gives me a scathing look. "Are you telling them about us?"

"He doesn't have to. The entire dorm *hears* you guys. Marcelo just fills in the blanks for us." Giovanni and the rest of the guys laugh as if it's the funniest fucking thing in the world.

Mirabella's face turns beet red. "I have to get to class. Enjoy your weaponry class, boys. I'll be learning how to host a dinner party for twelve." She rolls her eyes.

I grab her wrist before she can get away. "Hey. No kiss?"

She bends down and I wait for her to kiss me, but she keeps her distance. "Snitches don't get kisses, Marcelo." She stands up straight and saunters away, giving me a smirk over her shoulder.

"Pussy whipped." Andrea pretends to snap a whip. "Never thought I'd see the day."

"She's my fiancée." I dig into the food on my plate.

"I hate to break it to you, but everyone around here sees it," Giovanni says.

I look at him, forehead creased. "What?"

"The two of you falling in love. Hell, man, when we're out of the academy, you gotta put on a better front. People will hurt her in order to get to you if they figure out how much you really care about your wife."

"Which is why I'll protect her. She'll have a bodyguard even when she's at home." I pile food into my mouth because we're gonna be late for class if we don't finish soon.

"Keep that girl on a leash? Good luck, man. She's like the mutt from the kennel that refuses to be trained." Giovanni claps me on the back and stands with his tray to dispose of it.

My other friends do the same, no one disagrees with him.

Though I don't like the blatant disrespect in his statement, Giovanni has a point. Will Mirabella obey me if her safety is at risk? I can't honestly answer yes to that.

P. RAYNE

As we make our way to weaponry class, my thoughts about Mirabella's safety spiral. Will whoever was after me turn their sights onto her now? I need to figure out who the threat is and fast.

Dante is still my number one suspect, and lucky me, he's in class with me. He has motive, plus his yacht was parked near my father's.

Mr. Smith welcomes us to class then opens up the gun case. I'm sure I'm not the only one drooling over the fact that we'll get to feel the cold steel of a gun in our hands today. It's been too long. It's been a staple of my attire since I was fourteen until I came to this place.

"Goddamn, look at that Glock," Giovanni whispers in my ear.

"You know I'm more of a Smith and Wesson guy."

We've long argued about our guns and the ones we prefer. It feels good to have some of our usual banter going, but Mr. Smith interrupts when he addresses the class.

"I'm going to break you up in pairs. Each of you will have a gun and will be sparring. No real fists when fighting, this is a sparring exercise only. The guns do not have real bullets, they have blanks. When we move on to the portion where we'll be using them, we will be firing them. Those of you who haven't been in close range to a gun when it goes off need to get used to the sound. You can't freeze or panic. It could cost you your life." He looks around the room with a stern expression I'm sure he hopes will stop everyone from beating the shit out of one another.

"Dante and Marcelo." Mr. Smith points at us and we glare at each other. "You can each pick a gun."

I pick up a Smith and Wesson and he picks up an H&K.

"Put the guns in your waistband behind your back. Shooting is going to be the last of your options. I'll call out when you can draw, and we'll see who's the quickest. Take off your shoes and get on the mat."

Dante and I walk over to the mat, but the fire alarm blares before either of us has our shoes off. Disappointment makes my shoulders sag.

"Okay, class, you know the drill. Marcelo and Dante, leave the guns here and everyone file out to the north doors." Mr. Smith points in the direction he wants us to go.

We do what he says and place the guns back in the case. We all file out and hang in the field, waiting to be let back in. Dante approaches me, and Giovanni, Nicolo, and Andrea block him from reaching me.

"What do you want, Accardi?" Giovanni asks.

"I just want to talk to Marcelo."

"Sorry, he's busy." Nicolo widens his legs and crosses his arms.

"What do you want, Dante?" I ask behind the guys.

"You seem to be on the warpath to find out who killed your father. Obviously, Lorenzo got what he deserved. I wanted to apologize again for the stunt I pulled with Mirabella."

I can't help the smirk that transforms my face. "Let him through."

My boys step aside.

"Would you like it if our roles were reversed?" I ask.

Even if Dante apologizes for Mirabella, it's just because he's fearful. Worried I'm going to find *him* in a dark corner. But we still have the problem of his yacht being docked at the same pier as my father's.

"No, and that's why I'm apologizing again. I was the first one her father called about marriage until your father stepped in. It would've been good for my family too, to run the whole lower half of the country."

"Which would be another good reason to off me, no?"

The fire alarms quiet and Mr. Smith announces that we should go back inside. "Must've been a drill," he says.

"Listen, I grew up in this world too and I know the way it works. No woman is worth my life."

All the other students file in. I linger because before we go in there, I want him to know what else I have on him.

"Then explain something to me, Dante. Why the hell was your yacht docked at the same pier as my father's the night he was murdered?"

Dante's face pales and he opens his mouth.

"Come on, boys, we're short on time now." Mr. Smith waits for us outside.

"Cat got your tongue?" I raise both eyebrows and walk ahead of him into the classroom.

"I can prove it wasn't me," he says, walking behind me.

"Sure you can." I slip out of my shoes and grab the gun I selected, sliding it into my waistband.

Dante seems hesitant to join me on the mat, but he knows he doesn't have a choice.

"Remember what I said, no landing with fists. Pretend you're in a brawl and there's no silencer on your gun. Only shoot if you have no other choice." Mr. Smith drones on and on as if neither one of us has ever fought before.

I don't give one shit if a witness hears my gun. I'd flee the scene before anyone saw me. And if they did? We have ways of keeping people quiet or making them disappear altogether.

Dante and I circle one another. I pretend to punch him in the ribs, he acts like he uppercuts me. This goes on for at least five minutes and I'm practically bored to death.

"Let's do a shoot-out," someone in class calls. "Or give them knives."

"Okay, settle down." Mr. Smith toes the mat. "Marcelo, you pull your gun first. Dante, let's see how you'd try to get it off him."

I do that and point it right to Dante. He winces as if there's a bullet in it and pulls his out right away. Our guns face one another.

"I don't need a gun to take you down." I toss my gun and run toward him, ready to kick the feet out from under him and claim his gun.

Dante fires his gun, and heat sears my side. I stumble back and fall to the mat. Shit, that hurts like a motherfucker.

"BLOOD!" someone screams.

CHAPTER THIRTY-ONE
MIRABELLA

I rush out of the building and almost run into Aurora. She gives me a dirty look as I push past her. I don't have time for any of her bullshit right now.

It wasn't until the end of my second class today that the news that Marcelo had been shot in weaponry class reached me. My stomach bottomed out and I had to swallow back the bile that erupted up my throat.

No one has any information about the extent of his injuries, or even if he's alive, so I rush to the medical building with the hope I can get some answers.

When I arrive, Dante and some of his guys are hanging around one corner of the waiting area. In another corner are Giovanni, Andrea, and Nicolo. They're all glaring at each other while the chancellor and some other staff members stand between them.

I rush over to Giovanni and grip his shirt. "Where is Marcelo?"

"Dante fucking shot him." He looks over my head in Dante's direction, but I don't give a shit about all their dick measuring. Right now, I just want to know whether Marcelo's okay.

"Is he alive?" I shout.

Giovanni's gaze meets mine and he nods. "He's back there with the—"

I don't wait for him to finish. I rush off to find my fiancé.

"Miss La Rosa, Miss La Rosa! You can't go back there," the chancellor yells, but I ignore him. Let him try to stop me.

"Marcelo? Marcelo?" I call, walking fast down the hall, past a bunch of open doorways with empty beds.

A nurse pops her head out of a room at the end of the hall. "Can I help you, miss?" It's obvious from her scowl that she wants to do anything but.

I rush toward the door. "I'm looking for Marcelo Costa."

She puts up her hand. "He's in here, but you can't—"

I push past her and stop. Marcelo is lying on the exam table, shirtless.

I hurry to him and reach out but think better of it, pulling my hands away. "Grazie Dio, you're okay." There's a big bandage on his right side.

A wry smile crosses his face. "Careful, dolcezza. I might think you care about me with the way you busted in here."

"How can you joke around right now?"

"Miss, you can't be in here," the nurse says behind me.

Marcelo looks past me at her. "This is my fiancée, she can be here. Besides, I was just leaving anyway."

I glance over my shoulder with a smug look for the nurse, but she's shaking her head.

"I told you I want to check on your wound in an hour. Make sure you're clotting okay and that you don't need stitches."

Marcelo gingerly eases down from the exam table. "My fiancée can check it for me." He reaches for his discarded shirt with a huge bloodstain.

The nurse huffs. "Have it your way, but come back if it's bleeding. And don't get it wet for a couple of days."

Marcelo winks at me. "You hear that, dolcezza? Sponge baths."

He cringes when he raises his hands to get his shirt on. I can tell he's trying not to make it obvious that he's in pain, but he can't completely hide it.

"C'mon. Let's get out of here." He takes my hand and leads me down the hall, offering me no explanation of what the hell happened, but I know now is not the time to discuss it.

When we walk into the waiting area, everyone rushes us—Marcelo's friends, the staff who are waiting for an update, and even Dante.

Marcelo's glare stops them all cold. "I'm going back to my room with my fiancée, and I don't want anyone bothering us." He looks at the chancellor. "I want a copy of the security footage from the weaponry room."

The chancellor shifts his weight and looks between the two of us. "It was the first thing I asked for after I heard what happened. It's been scrubbed. There's nothing at all from this morning."

Marcelo's chest heaves, but he doesn't say anything before pulling me out of there and leading me to the path that goes back to Roma House.

Once we're a couple minutes away from the medical building, I tug on his hand to release mine and look at him. "What the hell happened? Are you really okay?"

He sighs. "I'm fine, it's just a graze to my side. Good as new in a few days."

"Dante shot you?"

His jaw flexes. "Yep."

"I thought there were not supposed to be any real bullets in the guns?"

"There's not."

"Marcelo." I pull him to a stop and cringe when I realize I'm tugging on his right arm, which is the side where he's wounded. "Sorry, I didn't mean to hurt you. But you're not giving me anything here."

He shoves his left hand in his pocket. "We should talk in private."

He's right. I nod, and he slides his hand in mine and walks us toward the dorm again. We're both quiet the rest of the way.

I can't get over how different I felt this time around when I thought that he might be dead. Months ago, I was overjoyed when my father told me he'd been killed. Sure, I put on a sad front, but once I was alone, I couldn't stop smiling. This time, I was beside myself. If I had stepped into that medical center and someone had told me he was gone, I would have crumpled in a heap onto the floor.

The realization is jarring. I knew that he'd grown on me of course, but I could not have predicted my reaction.

Does it mean . . . no, I can't be . . . am I in *love* with Marcelo?

Holy shit, I think I am.

My legs wobble when my realization becomes clear. I love Marcelo Costa.

And now I see why he wanted to rush off and beat up Lorenzo, because I want to kill whoever put that bullet in that gun.

We arrive at Marcelo's room and I lock the door behind us, wary now that someone on campus clearly has it out for him, and perhaps for me too.

I start in immediately. "Now tell me what happened."

"Dante and I were going through an exercise in class. The guns were supposed to have blanks. His didn't. That's honestly all I know at this point."

My mouth drops open. "Do you think he was trying to kill you?"

He hems and haws. "No."

"But the bullet came from his gun?"

"If Dante's responsible, he had one of his guys do it during the fire drill because he was with us the entire time. The only thing I'm sure of is that the fire drill was the opportunity the person took to load that gun. And I want to know who it is."

"Yeah, me too."

He sits on the edge of his bed and undoes his shirt.

I step forward. "Here, let me."

"Thanks. The fabric is rubbing against the dressing and bugging the shit out of me."

I nod and undo the buttons, gently push the fabric off his muscled shoulders until it falls to his wrists, then take out one arm at a time. He looks up at me oddly while I stand there staring at him. It feels different now that I know my true feelings for him.

"What? You're looking at me like I'm weak. I'm fine, Mirabella."

I nod slowly. "I know."

In a split-second decision, I sink to my knees in front of him.

He knows what this means, understanding that I'm giving all of myself to him. I know he does by the way his eyes widen and his mouth drops open.

"Dolcezza?" He runs his left hand over the side of my face.

"Don't make me say it," I whisper, reaching for his belt.

I carefully undo his pants and he inches up to help me get his pants and boxer briefs down to his ankles. I remove them by each leg. He remains sitting on the bed.

"Why don't you lie back on the bed?" I offer, thinking it will be more comfortable.

"Not a fucking chance. I'm watching. I want this seared into my memory for eternity."

I roll my eyes playfully and grip the base of his shaft, then I lean in and run my tongue from just above my hand up to the tip and swirl my tongue around the tip. I've never done this before, but it's not like I've never watched porn. I know how it's done.

When I suck on the head and twist my hand up from the base, Marcelo groans. "Fuck . . ."

The possession and lust in his voice spur me on. I do more of the same until his hips thrust toward my mouth as though he can't get enough.

Thinking I've teased him too long, I take him all the way in my mouth and push my lips down as far as they'll go. Marcelo is so big I can't fit all of him in my mouth, but what my mouth can't handle, my hand makes up for. I bob up and down on the end of his cock until my saliva runs down over my hand.

Marcelo groans, moans and growls the entire time I work him. Hearing his noises makes my core tingle and I want so badly to slide my hand under my skirt and get myself off at the same time. But this is about him and showing him how I feel.

When it seems like he might be close, I come all the way up off of him.

His eyes snap open and he looks as if he's about to say something, but when I dip down farther and suck on one of his balls, his eyes roll back in his head and he moans. I work his dick with my hand, squeezing the tip when I reach the end, while I gently suck on his balls until he becomes a desperate version of himself.

"Fuck, Mira, I need my cock back in your mouth. I'm gonna come soon."

With a smirk, I bring my mouth back onto his dick and push him to the back of my throat, maintaining eye contact with him the entire time. He sucks in a breath and he doesn't release it until I'm twirling my tongue around the tip again.

With a growl, he threads one hand into my hair, pushing me back down onto his cock and thrusting up his hips. He's done letting me set the pace.

He bucks up into me a few times before holding my head down on his cock. I try to relax my throat even though I'm struggling to breathe. Tears stream down my face until finally, he pulls me back up off him by the hair. Then he does it again and again.

"Finish me off, dolcezza." His voice is gravelly, and I gladly do his bidding.

I work him some more. Seconds later, I can tell he's about to come just from the sounds he's making. But rather than keep himself at the back of my throat, he pulls out and jerks himself off so that he comes on my face.

His seed marks my cheek, my chin, and my neck, and when he's done, he looks at me with awe. "Never seen anything more beautiful."

The inflection of his voice makes me believe him.

It's then I notice red seeping through the bandage on the side of his rib cage.

"Oh no, you're bleeding." I look at him with concern, but he shrugs.

"This was worth the trip back to see the nurse."

CHAPTER THIRTY-TWO
MARCELO

The good thing about being shot is that I'm excused from classes this week with no repercussions. In fact, I told Chancellor Thompson this morning that those two strikes against me should be repealed since I was shot in a supposedly no-violence school. He happily obliged and told me that they were doing everything they could to find out how the bullet got onto campus, let alone in the gun.

The shitty thing about being shot is that Giovanni is in my room all the damn time, hovering over me like my nonna or something—except when I kick him out when Mirabella joins me.

"What about Mr. Smith?" Giovanni asks.

I shake my head. "Why would he jeopardize whatever he has here?"

"What olive-toned guy with thick dark hair and even thicker gold chains is named Mr. Smith?" He raises an eyebrow.

I laugh then grab my side. "I know there's something weird going on there, but my gut says it wasn't him."

The sound of a key being inserted into my door has Giovanni scrambling up, preparing for some ambush that isn't coming. Instead, a gorgeous woman in a plaid skirt saunters in with my lunch.

"You gave her a key?" Giovanni's head whips in my direction. "What the hell?"

Mirabella places the bag on the table beside me and I pat my leg for her to sit down.

She kisses my cheek when she does. "We need to find Giovanni a girl."

"I have lots of girls." Giovanni sits back down.

"Sure you do." Mirabella rolls her eyes. "Any word on who put the bullet in the gun yet?"

"No." My lips press into a firm line.

"Well, I have some interesting news. As I was getting my lunch, Dante approached me." I stiffen under her and she pats my thigh. "Relax. Nothing like that. He wants a meeting with you. Wants to plead his case."

"He's going through her now?" Giovanni throws up his hands. "I'm his second. Me!"

He storms out of my room and we both laugh when he slams the door.

"He's going to put a hit out on me," she says.

I place my hand on her neck and pull her toward me. "I'd kill him first." Then I pull her to my lips and slip my tongue in her mouth.

Our kiss grows frantic and my hand dips between her legs, teasing her over her panties.

Just when my finger grazes the elastic to slide over her panties, she strips her lips from mine. "Unlike some people, I have to get to class."

"Skip it. I have some clout with the chancellor now." I run my thumb over the wet spot on her silk panties.

"Uh-huh. I'll be back later. And what do you want me to tell Dante?"

I lean back and crack my neck, not wanting to talk business when all I want is for her to go down on me again. Goddamn, for someone with no experience, she's got me addicted to her mouth. "You like being the middle person?"

She shrugs, but it's clear from her smile she does.

"Tell Dante to meet me tonight at ten in my room. He better come by himself. My guys will be guarding the doors."

She kisses my cheek and bounces off my lap. "I'll deliver the message," she says as she walks toward the door.

"Get back here and give me a real kiss."

She breaks the distance and leans in to kiss me fully. I smack her ass and she yelps, pulling away.

"You're killing me." I groan, shifting the hard-on in my pants with my hand.

"I'll make it up to you tonight."

"Lingerie?"

"You'll have to wait to find out." She blows me a kiss, shakes her ass, and leaves the room, locking the door behind her.

After she leaves, I wonder how we got here. Only months ago, she hated me, didn't want this marriage. When she went down on me last night, I know it was her way of saying I love you. I haven't said anything back to her. There's no place for love in our life. Not to say I'm gonna do the shit to her that my dad did to my mom—I'm not gonna cheat on her or any of that shit—but love? It's a short word with a big meaning. Love will change the way you think. Mess with your head and make you sloppy. Move your eye off the prize.

A knock on my door pulls me from my thoughts.

"Is she gone?" Giovanni says through the door.

I shake my head, slowly stand, and open the door. "Yeah, she's gone. Don't you have classes?"

I open the brown paper bag Mira brought me and pull out a sandwich, chips, and a cookie.

"Ah, she brought you a cookie."

"Cut the shit," I say to Giovanni. "She's my fiancée. Deal with it."

"I just never thought—"

I hold up my hand to stop him. "We have more important things to talk about than your jealousy over my fiancée."

He deeply inhales. "The Dante situation?"

I give him a sharp nod. "I told Mira to tell him to meet me here at ten o'clock. He's to come alone, but we both know he'll have someone nearby. He's not an idiot. I want you three to guard the floor. One by the stairs, one by the elevator, and the other outside my room. Mirabella will be with Antonio."

"You told her that?" he asks, raising his eyebrows, knowing how stubborn she can be.

"Not yet. But he'll keep her safe in case this is an ambush to get to her while Dante distracts me."

"Okay, I'll fill in Andrea and Nicolo as soon as they return from class." He pauses for a beat. "Can I have your cookie?"

I scowl at him. "Hell no, Mira's cookie is only for me."

He rolls his eyes and I take a big bite of the cookie just to piss him off.

* * *

LATER THAT NIGHT, I send an angry Mirabella to her brother's room. I'm pretty sure that surprise she was going to give me isn't happening now. I filled Antonio in on everything and he promised she wouldn't leave his room until I went to get her myself. I'm perfectly prepared for the silent treatment, but her safety will always be my number one priority.

Andrea is at the elevators, Nicolo is at the stairway, and Giovanni is standing by my door.

A knock sounds at exactly ten o'clock. I'd bet my left nut that Dante's been about to shit his pants all day. Giovanni opens the door and Dante steps in.

"Marcelo," Dante says with a nod. "Thanks for seeing me."

I shake his hand and nod at Giovanni to shut the door. Once we're behind closed doors, I signal for Dante to sit.

"Listen, Marcelo, I know it looks bad. The yacht, the Mira thing, and now the bullet. I own the first two. Was I docked there? Yeah.

But I didn't have anything to do with your dad's murder. And the Mira thing . . . we'd control the whole south if she would've married me. My dad was on my case, and honestly, it didn't seem like she wanted to marry you."

I remain silent.

He moves his hand into his pocket.

"Dante," I warn though I'm sure he's not armed. There's no way Giovanni would have let him in here without patting him down first.

"It's just this." He holds out a jump drive. "This is the surveillance footage from our yacht that night. You'll see neither I nor any of my guys left my yacht all night. We ported, then all we did was party and sleep. I didn't even know what had happened until the next morning and I got out of Dodge quick. Knew it wouldn't look good if anyone knew we were around."

He hands it to me, and I say, "I don't have a computer here."

"I think you know someone pretty good with them."

I hold the drive in my palm. "I do. I'll check it out."

He's quiet.

"Is there something else?" I ask.

"The bullet. I would never. If I would've put bullets in that gun, they would've kicked me out and you would have a hit out on me. I want to be around when it's my time to take over for my father. I have no proof, but it wasn't me."

"Yeah, I know. I've been shot at before and no one's that pale and looks like they're going to pass out when they mean to shoot you. You're not that good of an actor."

He chuckles. "True enough." He looks at the floor for a beat then back up at me. "Have you considered another option? Someone else with something to gain?"

I tilt my head. "Who?"

"Gabe?"

I blink in rapid succession. "Gabriele Vitali?"

Gabriele Vitali's dad runs the Northwest quadrant of the country. He's a quiet guy and not really threatening in any physical way, at least not to me, but rumor has it he cuts the throats of his adversaries because he likes to watch as the life leaves his victims' bodies. Plus, Gabriele's one of those computer guys, so I have no doubt he can wire a bomb. But he's a bit of a mystery to everyone. No one really knows much about him.

"What do you think his motive would be?" There's only one reason that I can think of, but I want to hear where Dante's head is at.

"With you and your father gone, there's a chance he could marry your sister, Aria, and run the entire upper half of the country. Marrying Aria is beneficial to him."

"Interesting theory." I nod, but I'm not really sold on Gabriele— yet. "Well, thanks for that. Maybe I'll pay him a visit."

Between the little sister theory that doesn't hold much weight and the drone and how savvy Gabriele is supposed to be around computers, it's worth my time to question him.

"So, I don't have to watch my back?" he asks, a wry smile on his lips.

"Not from me, no. But you're such a dick I'm sure you have a lot of other enemies."

He holds up his hands. "As you and I both know."

I stand to walk him out. When I open the door, Giovanni's on the other side and he lets Dante pass to walk down the hall to the elevator.

"I'm going to get Mirabella."

I don't wait for him to respond before I walk to the stairs and head down to Antonio's room. I knock and Antonio opens the door, signaling with his finger that Mirabella's inside.

"I almost had to tie her up to keep her here," he grumbles.

I laugh, but when I enter and see my fiancée's pissed-off expression, I mourn the night of crazy sex that's now not going to happen.

I hold up the jump drive. "Still angry, or do you want to help me out with something?"

Her eyes light up and she stands, snagging it from my hand. "What's this?"

"That's what you're going to help me figure out."

She leans into me. "Say 'please, Mirabella, I need your help,'" she singsongs.

"Not a chance." I eye Antonio over her head.

He's acting as if he can't hear us, but we both know he can.

"Come on. Do it and maybe I'll get down on my knees again." She gives me a sultry smile that makes my dick twitch.

"Take your crazy sex games elsewhere, Mira, or I'll tell dad what you're up to," Antonio barks.

She sticks her tongue out at him and I take her hand and lead her out to the elevator.

"How are we going to get in the computer lab?" she asks.

"You let me worry about that."

As we make our way across campus to the computer lab, I already know whatever is on this drive will prove Dante's innocence. Now, instead of being closer to figuring out who my biggest threat is, I feel further than ever.

CHAPTER THIRTY-THREE

MIRABELLA

The computer lab is already open by the time we get there. I forgot that tonight is the one day it's open late for students to work on projects if they've fallen behind.

Marcelo frowns when he sees he won't be able to show off his breaking and entering skills. I can't help the smile that spreads across my face.

"Miss La Rosa. Mr. Costa," Professor Bowers says when we enter. "How are you, Mr. Costa? I heard about the incident." The line between her eyebrows deepens in concern.

"Doing okay, thanks."

I smile. "I'm just helping Marcelo stay up to speed in class."

She nods. "Take any seat you like." She motions toward the sea of computers.

I glance around the classroom. Only one other student is in here, and he's closer to the front. Since I have no idea what's on this jump drive, I opt for the desk in the back corner. The professor won't be able to see what's on the screen and I'll have plenty of notice if she heads our way.

Marcelo and I take a seat, then I turn to him. "So, what's on this thing?"

"I'm not exactly sure, but Dante says it's the recording from his yacht's security cameras the night the hit was executed on my dad and me. He says it proves he and his guys were on the boat all night."

I swallow hard. "I guess this will show us whether he had anything to do with it or not."

A flush rushes through my body. I'm guessing if Dante's offering it up, it'll prove his innocence though. Damn it. If that's the case, that could still mean that I helped kill Marcelo's father.

Marcelo's forehead wrinkles. "Are you okay? You look like you're sick or something."

I wave off his concern and swallow the bile making its way up my throat. "Sure . . . yeah . . . I just didn't eat a lot at dinner, that's all." Before he can question me further, I push the jump drive into the computer and open the folder.

"I need you to tell me if this file is legit. Has it been fucked with or spliced or anything like that? Are the date and time stamps unique?"

He hammers me with questions, and I don't even have an image up yet. I open the folder and find a bunch of different files named Camera 1, Camera 2, etc. When I click on the first one, it brings up a video of the side of a good-sized yacht. The time stamp says it's 17:00 hours and it's date-stamped the day of the incident.

I make the video run at two times speed since nothing is happening and eventually see one of Dante's guys come out onto the deck, then he disappears to the back.

"What do the other cameras show?" Marcelo asks, obviously thinking this one isn't offering what he wants.

I exit the file and click on a few different ones until we come to one that shows the inside of the yacht—the lounge and living area, more specifically. In it, we can clearly see Dante and his guys. They're partying with a few girls, drinking and carrying on.

"This is more like it," Marcelo says.

We watch in silence as the guys play cards while the women sit on their laps, fawning over them. Eventually some song the women like must come on because they all get up and dance together in a way that's clearly meant to divert the guys' attention from the card game and onto them.

It works because Dante motions for a pair of them to come over to him. They saunter over, and when they reach him, they both get onto their knees and undo his belt buckle.

I cringe. "Gross. Let's skip this part."

"Agreed." Marcelo's voice is hard.

I fast-forward past the part where the three of them get naked and have a threesome while everyone else in the room continues to play cards as though nothing is amiss. Once everyone's clothed again, I return the video to running at double time.

"What time is it now?" Marcelo asks after a few minutes.

"Midnight."

His mouth presses into a thin line. "The car had already blown up by this point."

My stomach sours and my breathing falters. "Um . . . okay, let me see if there's anything to indicate that the video has been altered."

I say a silent prayer that that's the case, then I glance up at the sound of heels clicking to see Professor Bowers walking over. I hit a few buttons to pull up a different program and smile right as she peeps her head in on us.

"The lab is closing in a few minutes," she says.

"Do you think we could stay? I could lock it up when we leave. Marcelo and I still have some more things to go over." I give her my best innocent smile and she returns it.

"Sure thing. The door will lock behind you, so make sure you have all your things when you leave." She yawns. "I'd stay with you guys, but it's so late. I hate these nights that the lab stays open."

"I don't blame you. We'll be sure everything is locked up when we leave."

"Thanks, Mirabella. I knew there was a reason I picked you to help me this semester."

That shovelful of guilt she just loaded on my shoulders makes the weight I'm already carrying feel almost overwhelming, but I smile through it.

A few minutes later, she's packed up her things and left.

Marcelo claps his hands in front of him. "All right, so how do we figure out if this has been doctored or not?"

I frown. "There isn't an exact way to tell if a video has been doctored. It's a combination of common sense while looking at it . . . are there obvious splices in it, checking the metadata from the various camera angles and making sure they match, checking the . . ." I can tell that he doesn't care one way or another how I figure it out, just that I do. "Let me get started. You can watch the other files of the rest of the boat to make sure no one else came or went during that time."

I airdrop the other files to Marcelo to watch and show him how to speed it up so he can get through them faster. While Marcelo grumbles about how boring the videos are, I do my thing, trying to figure out whether Dante messed with the videos.

After what feels like hours, I swallow down past the lump in my throat and turn to Marcelo. "I don't think these have been messed with. The time stamps match up perfectly with the metadata, even when you compare various camera angles."

Marcelo looks at me, studying me for a beat, and I've never felt more like I want to crawl out of my skin in my life. Can he tell I'm holding something back from him?

"Okay." He nods.

"That's it? Okay?"

He shrugs. "If you say they weren't doctored, I believe you."

The realization hits me with a truckload of guilt. He believes me, which is like trusting me. He said himself, you can't trust anyone in this life. Even though he didn't understand what I was checking in the metadata, he didn't even question me.

My hand flies to my stomach. I feel as if I'm going to be sick. The feeling of betrayal is like a thick sludge worming its way through my intestines.

"It's late. We should get out of here." I leave no trace of what we were doing on the computer, pocket the thumb drive, and stand, quickly making my way to the door.

"Where's the fire?" Marcelo asks from behind me.

I look over my shoulder with a wan smile. "Just tired. Looking forward to getting into bed."

He comes up behind me where I stand with my hand on the door handle, moving a little slower because of his injury. "You mean my bed, right?"

I stiffen. "I think I'm going to go back to my room tonight. I'm really tired. Besides, you should rest up with your injury." I push open the door and he follows.

"Mirabella?" He studies me.

I do my best to put on an unaffected air. "Yeah, just been a lot these last days. And now that Dante's off the list, I'm wondering who's next."

He places his hands on either side of my face. "Don't worry, dolcezza. We'll figure out whoever is responsible, and we'll make them pay."

While I like the notion of Marcelo thinking of me as a part of that "we," that's exactly what I'm afraid of, which is why I have to figure out how I'm going to tell my fiancé that I think I played a role in murdering his father.

CHAPTER THIRTY-FOUR
MARCELO

Since the video proves Dante's innocence, Giovanni and I knock on Gabriele Vitali's door the next morning. There wasn't much to keep me in bed since Mirabella went to her own room last night.

I figure we should keep our numbers low so Andrea and Nicolo aren't with us. I don't want Gabriele to think we're accusing him outright, but I need at least one guy at my back in case things go south. No one knows a lot about Gabriele, so he's harder to predict than most.

I knock on his dorm door on the fourth floor. He has his own room, similar to me.

"Open," he says.

I give Giovanni a look of confusion. He just lets people in?

I open the door a smidge and peer in to make sure it's safe to enter. Gabriele's sitting at his desk with a computer—how the hell did he score that in his dorm room?—his fingers flying over the keyboard. I can't help but see what Mirabella was talking about. With guys like Gabriele as my enemy, I need someone around me who's better than him at computers.

As we enter, Gabriele doesn't even turn to face us. When I see the small screen to his right, I know why. It must be hooked up to a camera outside his room. Actually, the screen changes to a different camera that covers the entire floor. No wonder he wasn't scared to let us come in.

"What do you want, Costa?" he asks, still doing something on his computer that almost looks like what you see in the movies when they're hacking. But what do I know?

Figuring I might as well get straight to it, I say, "I'm here to ask you where you were the night my dad got murdered."

He flicks off his computer screen, circles around on his chair, and stares at me for a minute, eyes assessing.

He's tall, olive-toned, with thick dark hair, and has the body of a runner—muscular and strong, but he's not spending his time lifting weights at the gym. Every girl I know who's ever met him or seen pictures of him carries on and on about his piercing blue eyes.

"You think I killed your father?" His tone is measured, somewhat unaffected.

I shake my head. "I'm not saying that, but someone brought up that you might have a motive."

"Which is?" His head tilts.

"Besides all your computer guru drone shit?"

He laughs and says nothing.

I clear my throat. "If my father and I are both dead, you could swoop in and marry my sister, then run half the country."

He laughs and stands, shaking his head as he walks over to a makeshift table with a . . . cappuccino maker? "Do you want a drink?"

"Why don't you just go to Café Ambrosia?" Giovanni asks, and I scold him with my eyes.

Gabriele shrugs. "I'm a night owl and I don't like people."

"Fair enough," Giovanni mumbles.

He makes himself a drink. "You can't honestly think I would start a war by trying to off you and your father?"

I shrug. "I'm running out of options here."

"I understand you wanting payback, but it wasn't me. I was in Italy with my father right before he brought me here. It was supposed to be a bonding trip, him telling me that after I graduate, he's stepping back."

"Shit, really?" Giovanni speaks up again.

Gabe glances at Giovanni, then me, narrowing his eyes slightly. "Yeah, but you know the drill. The only time they really step down is if they get too damn old, sick, or die."

I nod. My dad never would have relinquished his power. Even if he got sick, like my nonno.

"Maybe that was your motive to kill your father? After all, you did end up living through the attempt on your life." Gabriele arches a brow at me.

"I'll do you a favor and pretend I didn't hear you say that, Vitali." My hands clamp into fists at my sides.

"Not to mention, and no offense to Aria, but my understanding is that she's young and naive. Nowhere near being the kind of bride I need. Plus, we all know I'm going to be arranged with someone, just like you and Mirabella." He sips some of the foam off the top of his drink. "Speaking of, that looks like it's going well . . ."

I don't say anything. Thankfully, Giovanni keeps his mouth shut. Otherwise, I would've had to beat his ass after we left here.

"Who knows, maybe my sister is the person you'll be arranged to marry. That's my decision to make now." I arch an eyebrow.

He shakes his head before sipping his coffee. "Anything else? I'm right in the middle of something."

"If you hear anything—"

"You'll know. I'd like to know if I was you, so I'd tell you, but I haven't heard anything. But for it to follow you to campus . . . for someone to plant a bullet in that gun? I mean, imagine if Dante was a better shot. You could be dead in what is supposed to be the safest place in the country for guys like us." He sits in his chair.

His words sink in. I figured whoever put the bullet in the gun was the same person who planted the bomb, but I can't be sure. I've made some enemies here. I see Gabriele doing all his computer shit and the chancellor's words repeat in my head.

"Hey, funny thing is, the camera footage isn't on the tape for the time period of the fire drill. Not many people around here could get rid of evidence like that."

He swivels back around to face me. "I'll tell you what. I feel bad for you, what with being almost murdered, falling in love with your arranged bride, and now shot. I'll dig up that footage for you and you can see it wasn't me." He circles back to his computer and his fingers move over the keyboard, typing codes on a blank screen.

"If things had been the other way around—"

He holds up his hand. "No hard feelings, Costa."

Within ten minutes of him working, video footage comes up and shows someone sneaking into the weaponry room during the fire alarm. And the person is exactly who I should have known all along it would be—Lorenzo.

"Give me a copy of that," I demand.

"Sure, but make sure I'm not involved. If I get shut down in here, I won't be happy." He gives me a look that makes it clear there would be hell to pay. He digs in his drawer and grabs a jump drive, inserts it, and saves a copy before tossing it to me. "You can deliver that message in person."

"Thanks, Gabe. Shit, you've gone above and beyond," I say.

"And now you owe me one." He waves one hand, already typing away. "See yourself out."

Giovanni and I leave his room and take the elevator up to my room.

"What are you thinking?" he asks.

"I really want to kill him." My fists clench at my sides, but I can easily get Lorenzo expelled without blood on my hands.

"I think it's time we start a watch. I'll guard your room tonight. Nicolo can stand outside your classes."

I shake my head, although it's a good idea. "I need to talk to Antonio. Mirabella needs to be safe as well. I can handle myself."

"Marcelo, we think he's working alone, but what if he's not? What if other members of the La Rosas are helping him? We have no idea what we're dealing with. You have to put yourself first. Maybe you should leave school for a while. Hunker down at Nonno's until we figure it out."

I look at him with disgust. "I'm the leader of this family. I'm not going to go hide out in Nonno's basement like some scared little girl. I'm Marcelo Costa, leader of the Costa crime family. I just have to decide if I want the pleasure of strangling the life out of him right now or if I should get him off campus and take my time later."

I put the key in my door. When I swing it open, I'm relieved to see Mirabella. She was acting strange last night.

"Talk to you later," I say and slam the door in Giovanni's face, locking it.

"Pussy whipped," I'm pretty sure I hear him mumble on the other side of the door.

"I figured I owed you a little treat."

She's lying on the bed wearing a black see-through nightie. Her tits are spilling out and I don't waste any time kicking off my shoes, shedding all my clothes, and joining her on the bed.

For the rest of the night, I lose myself in Mirabella, forgetting the decision that keeps flipping around in my head.

CHAPTER THIRTY-FIVE
MARCELO

Sunday morning comes, and Mirabella goes downstairs for her phone call. She said her mom wanted to talk wedding details, and she did not look very excited.

The jump drive is burning a hole in the pocket of my jeans from last night. If I pass this on to the chancellor, I'll look like a fucking pussy. Any man in this academy would handle it himself if someone tried to kill him. There's no reason to rat Lorenzo out to the chancellor—except that if I get caught, which is doubtful, I'll be kicked out and that either means I allow Mirabella to stay and we live apart, or I rip away her dream and make her come with me. The fact that she's even a factor in the decision tells me I'm losing my edge.

I pick up my phone and dial Giovanni. He answers right away.

"Let's go," I say and hang up.

A second later, Giovanni knocks on my door and walks in, happy as shit because he's my second guy again. "Plan?"

I hold up my hands. "They're all I've got, and thankfully, they're all I need."

"Want the guys?"

I shake my head. "I need your help with the body, otherwise I would've done it by myself. Less people, the better."

He nods and I throw on a black sweatshirt before glancing at my watch. My injury is much better. Still a bit of an annoyance but healing nicely. An hour before my call to Nonno. Perfect.

We ride the elevator down to the main floor. After Lorenzo got beat up, they moved him down here, next to the security office and our house manager.

I peek in the window of the security room. The guard isn't in his office. The house manager is known for his love of brunches and heads off campus every Sunday morning. The opportunity couldn't be better.

Giovanni knocks on Lorenzo's door and I rest my back on the wall so he can't see me if he looks through the peephole. The door opens and Giovanni's eyebrows rise in my direction.

"Chancellor?" he says.

"Giovanni Costa, can I help you?" The chancellor pushes open the door and I turn toward the doorway. "Marcelo as well. Hmm, you boys just wanting to see Lorenzo?"

"Um . . . yeah, we had some business to talk about, but we'll come back later." Giovanni steps back.

"Actually . . ." I second-guess myself, but I need to be smart about this. The best way to get at this guy is to get him off the property, so I have free rein to kill him. And time to really make him suffer. I toss the jump drive at the chancellor and he catches it. "I trust you'll do what you should do with this information."

He holds it up and inspects it. "What is it?"

"You'll see for yourself. I'm not going to rat on the person who gave it to me, so don't bother asking. Just take care of the problem before I do." I give him a meaningful look.

The chancellor fiddles with it and stares at me for a long time. If he thinks he can intimidate me, he's severely wrong. "Okay. Thanks."

I've never felt like more of a fucking pussy as Giovanni and I leave. But I have to take my own advice that I gave to Mirabella. When you're in power, you cannot act irrationally. Everything needs to be planned and organized. Sometimes you forego the battle to win the war. Lorenzo Bruni will get his when he least expects it, and he'll be staring into my eyes when he takes his last breath.

An hour later, I go downstairs to the private room where no one can hear anything. I dial up Nonno and he answers but coughs right after.

"Are you okay?" I ask.

"I'm fine. Just this cough. Allergies." He coughs again. "I talked with Joey, and he told me that you're looking into Lorenzo Bruni as a suspect."

I inhale deeply. "I got a tape, Nonno. He's the one who put the bullet in the gun that shot me. He was trying to date Mirabella, been stalking her on campus, and even forged a note pretending to be me to get her alone."

He clears his throat. "To me, that sounds like if Mirabella goes missing, he'd be blamed. What does this have to do with you?"

"Guess he figures if I'm not in the picture, he can slide into my position."

Nonno laughs and laughs some more. "The man has nothing that would make Frank La Rosa want to hand his only daughter over to him. His father is capo and there's nothing wrong with that, but you're the head of your family."

"Maybe Lorenzo thinks he would. Did you get the phone records?" I'm growing annoyed and impatient.

"We did. There are very lengthy phone calls and text message strings between your fiancée and Lorenzo. In fact, I hate to tell you this, but I think they may have been involved."

Shit. I didn't want Nonno to know any of this. He's old school and definitely not going to approve of the fact that Mirabella slept with Lorenzo. Since I have no idea how explicit the texts were, I don't want to show my hand, so I say nothing on the subject. "Can you send them over?"

"I think you might find some quite disturbing and your temper isn't exactly—"

"There're no worries with Mirabella, she's been truthful with me." I decide to play it off. "It was just her trying to make me jealous. You know how insecure some women are."

He laughs. "All these messages are a ruse?"

"Until the ones where she asks him to leave her alone."

Nonno doesn't say anything for at least ten seconds, and an uneasy feeling creeps up my spine. "Besides the flirtatious text messages, there're a few talking about writing some computer code for him and giving him a copy. Lorenzo's asking Mirabella. 'Do you know how to do such a thing?'"

War Games comes to my mind. Her ability to put a bomb together.

"What does it say exactly?"

He coughs again. "'Hey babe, do you think you could write some computer code for me?' She replies, 'love to.'"

My teeth grind together and my stomach turns over. Did she have something to do with my father's murder? Was she trying to murder me too?

"The exchange was a few months before . . ." His voice is grave. "Then there are more sexual ones. There are no specifics on what he needed, but about a month before the bombing, he talks to her about how you'd rig a remote with the code she wrote. My gut tells me it was Lorenzo who planted the bomb, and sorry to break it to you, but Mirabella might have been the one who put the bomb that almost killed you in his hands."

My entire body blazes with the fact she had something to do with it. "Anything else?"

"Yes, I had my intel search for any text messages from Lorenzo the night of the murder. There's an unregistered number that sent him a text two minutes before it all went down. They're almost positive it was a burner phone though."

"And?"

"It said, 'Fight's over. They'll be out in a couple minutes, be ready.'"

I can't believe I gave him up to the chancellor. All my muscles tense and about a thousand ways to slowly kill the son of a bitch, torture him, make him admit what he did and who else was involved come to mind. I can't even process Mirabella right now. That she could have made the bomb to purposely have me killed. I know she didn't want to marry me, but to kill me seems ruthless even for her.

"The chancellor has the evidence from the shooting here and I'm sure he's being expelled," I admit to Nonno.

"So he won't be a threat to you."

I squeeze the phone so hard it creaks. "No. There's not much I can do on campus anyway, but once break hits . . ."

He coughs again. "I can arrange it to happen sooner than that."

"No." My voice is firm.

"You want to handle it yourself?" he asks.

"Definitely."

"You're the leader, this is your decision. But I'm proud of you for wanting to handle it yourself."

"Thanks." I have no idea how I'll sleep knowing Lorenzo's out there and not at the bottom of a large body of water.

"Marcelo?"

"Yes."

"What are your plans for Mirabella? We should alert Frank La Rosa about his daughter's actions."

I'm silent. "I don't know yet." I know how lovesick and stupid I sound.

"Be careful, Marcelo. Never underestimate your enemy."

"I won't, Nonno. Everyone involved will pay."

I hang up and head upstairs, envisioning Lorenzo on the ground under me, pleading for his life. I open my bedroom door, surprised to see Mirabella there. She looks uncomfortable, like she did the other night in the computer lab. She looks pale and has a sheen to her skin as though she's sweating.

"What's up? Are you sick?"

She shakes her head. "What did your nonno say?"

I sit on the edge of the bed and look at her. I want to see her reaction before I go off half-cocked. "It was Lorenzo who put the hit out on me and he planted the bullet that shot me too."

She rushes off the bed, leans over the trash can by my desk, and throws up.

CHAPTER THIRTY-SIX
MIRABELLA

I run to the garbage can and lose my breakfast from the pure venom in Marcelo's voice and cold certainty in his eyes.

I knew this day would come, though I prayed it wouldn't. I prayed he'd eventually stop searching and Sam's death would be one of the thousands of Mob kills that never get solved. The guilt that I unknowingly helped take out Marcelo's father has felt like a semi crushing me. Maybe it's a good thing I have no choice but to come clean now. I'd wanted to anyway. What the hell am I thinking? Marcelo is most likely going to kill me when he learns the truth.

"Are you okay?" Marcelo watches while I spit out bile.

I straighten and wipe the back of my hand over my mouth. "I'm fine. Probably just something I ate at breakfast." I walk over to the other side of the room, my back still to him, unable to face him.

But he comes behind me. "Are we expecting a little bambino?" His voice is void of emotion.

I whip around in horror. "Bite your tongue. We cannot have a baby right now."

He shrugs. "It would certainly complicate things." There's an edge to his voice.

I step back from him. "I can assure you I'm not pregnant, Marcelo. My stomach's just upset, that's all."

He frowns and I think maybe I see disappointment in his eyes and it's like a little pinprick to my heart. He hasn't told me he loves me, but it's clear to me now that he's all in on this arranged marriage, which only makes this whole thing harder.

I walk over to his mini-fridge, grab a water, and take a few swigs to clean my mouth. When I'm done, I look at him warily. "Why are you so sure it's Lorenzo?"

"My nonno had his phone records when I called. The night of the attack, he was texting someone with a burner phone and getting updates about when we'd be leaving the building."

"Maybe Lorenzo was talking about something completely unrelated."

Marcelo's forehead creases. "The timing on the texts fits. Not to mention he has a motive. He wants something of mine. What's this? You trying to cover for your former lover?"

His hands clench and unclench at his sides as if he's barely controlling himself from sending his fist through the wall.

"Of course not."

He steps forward. "Nonno mentioned a lot of back and forth between the two of you that he thought it better I don't see, but maybe I'll have him send me the transcripts anyway."

I narrow my eyes at him. "Don't you dare. Those are none of your business. How would you feel if someone were reading our text messages?" I cross my arms. "But . . ." I'm more nervous than ever to confess the truth.

Marcelo cocks his head, and it reminds me of a Doberman who's caught a whiff of a steak. "What aren't you telling me?"

This is the point of no return. I can drop it and let Marcelo kill Lorenzo and hope that Lorenzo doesn't implicate me—or I can tell him the truth and ruin everything we've built.

My stomach feels as though it's ready to revolt again and sweat dots the back of my neck. Maybe Marcelo's right and I don't have what it takes to be a real part of this life. Anyone else would probably lure him to bed right now and let this conversation fade into the past. Let Marcelo kill Lorenzo without thinking twice about it because at least it wasn't me.

But I can't. I can't live with this truth hanging over my head like a storm cloud, following me around the rest of our lives. I swallow hard, hands fidgeting in front of me. Marcelo clocks the movement and narrows his eyes.

"I have to tell you something. But please let me explain it all before you say anything."

He stills. So much so that it almost looks as if he's not breathing.

"I'm the one who made the computer code to set the bomb off that killed your father."

My words hang in the air like a grenade with the pin pulled. I'm counting down for the inevitable explosion.

When Marcelo says nothing, I decide to get it all out. "I didn't know that's what I was doing though, I swear. I just put two and two together after you mentioned how you knew the bomb was set off using computer code. That night by the pond with Lorenzo . . . he made some weird comment I didn't understand at first, wondering how you'd feel if you knew your fiancée was so good at computer programming. It didn't make any sense at the time, but later it came to me.

"Lorenzo had asked me if I'd show him how to write code to set off a bomb, then he wanted to know how to build one. My brother showed me after I begged him relentlessly, and I guess somehow Lorenzo knew. He told me he just wanted to make himself more useful to the family, that he wanted to work his way up the ranks, and I believed him. I didn't realize when I handed it all over to him what he was going to use it for." I stare at Marcelo with tears in my eyes and admit the most painful part. "I swear I had no idea what he was using it for. I didn't know how to tell you."

Marcelo's face is still blank and the air between us is thick with tension.

"I'm sorry." Tears drip down my face. "I was scared to tell you. I didn't want to lose this connection and—"

He takes two steps forward, sets his hands on my shoulders, and then backs me up against the wall. His blank stare is replaced with a mask of fury.

I was naive to think we'd get past this. I'll be lucky if he even lets me live.

CHAPTER THIRTY-SEVEN
MARCELO

Rage and disbelief course through my body. I tower over her, my hands clenching on her shoulders. If she were anyone else, they'd be around her neck.

"All this time you were playing a game?" I ask, not caring for her answer. "Were you going to have me fall in love with you and kill me in my sleep at some point?"

Her eyes widen and she shakes her head.

"I've been an idiot for months, letting you lead me around by the dick. But you know what?" I step back and she crumples to the floor. "Killing you would be a mercy."

I bend down and run my finger down her face, her chin, then her neck. I pop a button on her blouse.

"You'll be my bride soon enough, and I'm going to make your life a living hell. Your body is mine for the rest of your life. You can stay home and raise babies and throw parties. You'll be lucky if I let you see the outside world beyond church services and family events." I snicker at the venom in my voice, knowing this is exactly what she was trying to avoid with her deception.

I step back and turn away, unable to look at her anymore. Everything was a lie. All of it.

She whimpers and cries. "I swear I didn't know what it was for. I was—"

"I don't want to hear a fucking word out of your mouth!" I spin around and point at her, the blood pumping through my veins, throbbing in my neck. "You're just trying to cover your tracks now that the truth has come out. I'm not going to fall for your lies again!"

There's a loud knock on the door. "Marcelo!"

"Go the fuck away!" I yell back. She scrambles up to rush to the door, but I block her with my back to the door. "I don't remember saying you could go."

"Marcelo," she begs, eyes wide with fear.

I have to glance away. I remember when those wide eyes looked up at me with lov—no. It was all a lie. And somehow that feels like more of a betrayal than the fact that she had a hand in trying to kill me. And to think that she lied to me and all the while she was worried about her precious ex-lover . . .

"What did you think I would do when you decided to tell me the truth?" I grab her arm and drag her to the bed.

"I don't know. I wouldn't be able to live with myself knowing I was keeping a secret." Tears track down her face and I ignore the way the sight makes my stomach sour.

I laugh, a huge, exaggerated laugh designed to make her feel fucking stupid. "And that's exactly why this fairy tale of being some equal partner with me, having a real job in the family business, is never gonna happen."

She scrambles farther away from me so her back is against the wall and brings her knees up to her chest.

There's another bang on the door.

I shout over my shoulder, "Fuck off, Giovanni!"

"It's Antonio, and if that's my sister you're screaming at, you better fucking let me in!"

"Antonio!" Mirabella yells.

There's more pounding on the door, but it sounds more like kicking than hitting. I hear a fight erupt on the other side of the door and Giovanni telling Antonio to leave.

"Now you want your brother to save you, but here's the thing, dolcezza—if you want to play with the big boys, you should be able to save yourself. And this time, using your body is not an option."

She winces and I step back before I do something I told myself I would never do. I swore I'd never hurt a woman, no matter how mad I was.

"You know what?" I open the door.

Antonio falls in, landing on the floor on his shoulder. Word got around fast because a bunch of people are outside my door, all clamoring to see what's going on.

"What the fuck, you two?" Antonio shouts.

Mirabella slides off my bed and rushes to Antonio's side as he stands.

He looks at how fearful she is and his nostrils flare. "Go get Sofia and I'll meet you in my room." He ushers her out as Giovanni stares at us from the doorway. "I've been on your side."

"You want to stay out of this, Antonio, believe me."

"The hell I do." He throws a fist, but I duck then push him out into the hallway, slamming the door after him and flicking the lock.

Giovanni knocks. "Marcelo?"

"Get lost."

He sighs. "I'm just down the hall when you wanna talk."

I don't respond and instead pace the floor, scared of what I'll do if I leave this room.

* * *

SICK OF FEELING like the world's biggest chump and unable to continue with these thoughts of wanting to harm Mirabella, I leave my room and go bang on Giovanni's door. I have no idea what time it is, but it's long past dark and he answers the door in his boxers.

"What do you have here? I need something to drink and a pack of smokes," I say.

"What happened, man?"

I could be honest with Giovanni. I should be—he'd probably kill her for me. Although I meant what I said. I won't kill her because making her life miserable will garner more satisfaction. But I'm not ready to out her yet. I wish I had an explanation, but I want to handle this by myself.

"Just a shitty night. We got into a fight."

He hands me a new pack of cigarettes and a bottle of whiskey. I don't care how he got it. Giovanni always makes connections, and although they don't sell alcohol on campus, getting contraband in here is no different than getting it in jail. There are ways.

"Just make sure everyone leaves me alone tonight."

"You got it." Giovanni stares at me, concern etched on all his features, and I know he wants to ask me something.

"What?"

"What did she do?" he asks.

He knows it must be serious. One night, my dad came home drunk and pissed off and hit my mom for not saving him a plate. He continued to berate her and hit her. I told Giovanni that night that I would never hit a woman; it only shows weakness on the man's part.

"Just . . . I need to process all this before I talk about it."

He nods and lets me leave. Luckily, it's late and tomorrow is a school day, so no one is in the hallway.

I lock myself in my room, twist off the cap, and down a good portion of the whiskey before lighting a cigarette. I open my window, letting the chill of the outside air overtake my room. My body is running hot, so the breeze feels nice.

Every time I think about her face and how scared she was, I swig. How could I be so stupid? All these months, the guys have been calling me pussy whipped, and I thought I was the lucky one because I was gonna fall in love with my arranged wife. But all along, she was playing me.

She had a hand in *trying* to kill me.

She had a hand in *killing* my father.

This kind of shit is not taken lightly in our world. If I tell anyone, she's dead. Her hands have blood on them from killing the head of a family. Her father, Antonio, her mother, everyone in her family should suffer for this. What the hell was she thinking?

The part that angers me the most is how upset I am that none of it was real, that she played me. That pisses me off more than her playing a role in killing my father.

I chug back two solid gulps and it burns down to my stomach.

My head is swimming from the alcohol. Unable to deal with all the information swirling in my brain, I drink and smoke until, at some point, I stagger out of my room and down the hall to the elevator.

Pressing the down button, I wait for the doors to shut and my body sinks to the floor. I laugh and crawl out of the elevator once I hit the main floor. Then I stumble across campus until I reach the chancellor's office. He and his assistant have phones on their desks, and since the security for Roma House is right outside the rooms where we have our Sunday phone calls, those aren't an option.

When I reach the door that separates the chancellor's area from the hallway, the door is locked. Of course it is. I punch my fist through the glass and smile when an alarm doesn't go off. My stomach is queasy, so I put my hand over and reach in with the other to unlock the door.

A few seconds later, I stumble over to the assistant's desk. How come I haven't done this before? Easy peasy.

When I pick up the receiver, there's a dial tone. I squint at the ceiling in an effort to remember my nonno's number, then dial.

He answers.

"Nonno," I say.

"Marcelo? What's going on?"

"She admitted it to me."

And I spill it all to my nonno. He's the only one I trust. He's here to guide me and I have no one else with the expertise of all his years. He doesn't say much but does ask me to clarify again. He sounds sort of weird. Maybe he's on the mend.

"She made the bomb and programmed it for him, but she didn't know. She says she didn't know what it was for, but how can I believe her when she hated me?"

Nonno doesn't offer the advice he usually does. In fact, he quickly gets off the phone and tells me we'll talk soon. I'm not one to talk back to my nonno, but what the fuck?

I leave the office and make my way back to Roma House, managing to get in the elevator before everything goes black.

CHAPTER THIRTY-EIGHT
MIRABELLA

"You what?" Sofia practically shouts after I tell her what Marcelo and I were fighting about and why I dragged her to my brother's room.

My mind spins, and I massage my temples. "I didn't know, I swear! I didn't figure it out until recently. I was trying to figure out a way to tell him."

"Mira, this is going to cause a lot of problems." Her voice is grave.

I squeeze my eyes shut. "I know!"

I'm actually surprised that Marcelo didn't kill me on the spot. The monster inside him came out when I confessed my betrayal.

"What did Marcelo do when you told him?" she asks, sitting on the chair by my brother's desk.

I can't sit, so I pace in front of her while I tell her what he did, what he said, and about Antonio coming to my rescue. When I'm done, I stop and stare at her.

She's chewing her bottom lip. Tears fill her eyes. "Mira, do you think he'll kill you?"

The truth is, in the world we live in, it would be within his right to do so. "I don't think he will. I think he was serious when he said he'd rather make the rest of my life a living hell."

"But what if someone else finds out?"

Before I can answer, the door of the room slams open and Antonio rushes in a few minutes later. I'm sure he and Marcelo have been arguing.

"Are you okay?" He beelines over to me and places his hands on my shoulders, eyeing me from head to toe for any sign of injuries.

"I'm fine."

"I'm gonna kill that bastard if he hurt you."

"Maybe you should wait until I explain why he's so mad."

Confessing to my brother what I did is almost as hard as when I told Marcelo because it's only really now dawning on me the steaming pile of shit I've unknowingly dragged Antonio and my father into.

"Jesus Christ, Mira." He rakes his hands through his hair, glaring at me. "I'd almost be impressed if I wasn't so pissed right now."

"I'm sorry," I cry. "I thought I could trust Lorenzo. I had no idea he was using me. That's not an excuse, I know, but I didn't know. I was trying to figure out a way to tell Marcelo." I wipe the tears away with the back of my hand, ready to take whatever verbal lashing my brother dishes out.

"We'll figure it out." He pulls me into a hug, and I sink into the comfort of his arms. The only man who will have my back right now. "Family sticks together."

His wanting to protect me makes me sob harder.

"Shh, I'm not going to let him hurt you," Antonio whispers.

I draw back and glance between him and Sofia. "It's not that. It's just . . . I fell for him, you know? And now he thinks I can't be trusted, that what I feel for him isn't real."

"Mira, that's the least of your concerns right now," Antonio says, voice hard. "Right now, we need to keep you safe."

"I agree with Antonio," Sofia says.

They're crazy. Did they not hear what I just said? I love Marcelo and I want him to understand that more than anything.

"No! I need Marcelo to understand that I'm sorry and I'm telling the truth when I say that I didn't give Lorenzo that program so he could kill him. That my feelings for him aren't a part of some plan to get close to him so I can kill him."

"My first priority is your safety." Antonio's voice is hard, like he has no time for my bullshit about feelings. He sounds just like my dad.

"Maybe once things calm down, the two of you can discuss it," Sofia says, giving me a hopeful look.

My brother looks between us. "I want you two to stay here. I'm going to go make arrangements to get you out of the academy. I'll station a couple guys at the door, but you do not open it for anyone. Anyone, you hear me?" He bends down so we're eye level.

Leave? I can't leave Sicuro. This is where I've wanted to be for years and I'm finally here. It hasn't even been a semester yet. If I leave now, there's no coming back.

I clutch his shirt. "Please don't make me leave. Please, Antonio."

"I'm not making you do anything," he says, removing my hands from his shirt. "You've done this yourself."

My hands drop to my sides, and I sink to the floor in tears. Sofia wraps her arms around me, rocking me back and forth as the door of the room slams shut.

While I lie on the floor in despair, I realize that my life isn't my biggest concern. It's Marcelo knowing that everything between us was real.

* * *

SOFIA AND I don't say much once I collect myself off the floor. She tries to engage me, but I'm content to stare at the wall and rehash how I've fucked up my life. I always thought it would be my father or my fiancé who forced me out of Sicuro Academy, but in the end, I did it.

I don't know how much time passes before Antonio returns. Hours probably. But when he rushes in, slamming the door, I bolt up from the chair like a soldier caught napping.

He runs his fingers through his hair. "You're leaving at dawn."

I frown. "Where?"

"A car will meet you at the gates. Dad called and cleared it with the chancellor."

"I'm leaving tonight?" I look at Sofia as a life preserver, but she has no control here. I knew I was leaving, but I guess I thought I'd have a little more time to wrap my head around it.

"How did you get a hold of your dad?" Sofia asks.

My brother frowns and pushes a hand through his hair once more. "Gabriele Vitali. I'd heard that he hooked himself up with a computer in his room, so I used it to make a call to Dad."

"He just let you use his computer?" I ask. There's no way.

"No. I had to trade him a favor he can call in at any time." There's anger in his tone and I'm sure he's annoyed with me for causing all this. "I'm starting to think that guy is a bigger threat than any of us thought."

"I'm sorry." I force back my tears. I know my brother doesn't want to be in the position of owing anyone anything. Especially not someone from another family.

"It's fine," he says, his jaw clenched. "Just go lie down in my bed and I'll wake you when it's time."

"I'm not sure I can sleep."

My heart begs me to find Marcelo, to talk to him. The thought of never having his arms around me again . . . seeing that cocky smirk when he's about to undress me and fuck me . . . I could cry a million tears for the loss of Marcelo Costa.

I lie in the bed and Sofia positions my head in her lap as she runs her fingers through my hair, telling me it will all turn out. I hear light whispers between her and Antonio until, eventually, I succumb to sleep.

"Mira, it's time."

I wake to see Antonio dressed in black.

"I'm gonna walk you down," he says. "The car should be there by now. It'll drive you to the airfield where Dad's jet is waiting. It's not going to be the airfield nearby that we used when we arrived though. Dad thought it best that we choose another in case the Costas are lying in wait to ambush you. They've gotta figure that we're going to get you out of here and away from Marcelo."

Just the sound of his name feels like a sword slicing off a limb.

I nod numbly, still in disbelief at how much my life has changed in the past twelve hours. "What about my stuff?"

My brother scowls. "Forget your shit. Sofia will pack it up and ship it to you at home."

When I turn toward Sofia, tears are streaming down her cheeks. We embrace in a tight hug, crying. My brother sighs behind us.

When I pull away, I wipe my face with the back of my hand. "You'd better not forget about me."

"You're gonna be my phone call every Sunday," she says, and we cling to one another again.

"Mira, we have to go," my brother says, gripping my arm.

I allow him to pull me away from Sofia, giving her one last look before I'm in the hallway.

Leaving the building and walking across campus is all a blur. There aren't any people around because it's so early. Two of Antonio's guys are behind us. I doubt what I did is common knowledge—this isn't the type of thing either the Costas or my family want to get out.

We walk in silence down the long, winding road that leads to the gates. As we approach, I see a blacked-out SUV waiting on the other side. The guards must expect us because the large iron gates slowly open as we approach, but the guards remain in the guardhouse.

Antonio stops us as we reach the border between the school and the real world. "Try not to worry too much. Dad and I will sort this out."

I frown, knowing he's referring to somehow keeping me alive. I'm the only one concerned about the betrayal Marcelo is feeling right now. Neither Antonio nor my dad would understand how I could be concerned for someone else. Maybe Marcelo's right. Maybe I don't have what it takes to survive in our world.

"I'm sorry I dragged you into this." I struggle to get the words out around the tightness of my throat.

I can't believe this is it. I'm leaving the Sicuro Academy for good. I take one last look at the tall trees, the iron gate with Sicuro Academy welded in. Some of the taller buildings can be seen over the tops of the trees. I'm going to miss this place even though I only called it home for a few months.

"We'll discuss it later. Right now, the priority is getting you safe. Dad will be waiting for you when you land in Miami."

"Thanks for everything." I give him a hug that he tightly returns.

"That's what big brothers are for."

We pull apart and I walk to the SUV, head down. The sun hasn't come up yet, but it's teasing the bottom of the horizon. I stop and give my brother a little wave before I open the door and climb in the back seat, shutting the door behind me.

I blink, but my brain doesn't process the scene in front of me. There's a man in the driver's seat with a gun pointed at me, and the driver, one of my dad's guys, is slumped over in the passenger seat with an obvious bullet to his temple.

I open my mouth to scream, but before any sound comes out, he tsks. "Wouldn't do that. It'll take nothing for me to turn this gun on your brother and shoot him instead."

I snap my mouth shut and glance through the tinted window, seeing my brother still standing on the other side of the open gates.

It's then that the voice and the face registers. The man pointing the gun at me is Marcelo's uncle.

My chest caves in. I guess Marcelo changed his mind. He'd rather have me dead.

CHAPTER THIRTY-NINE
MARCELO

Everything is a haze. I squint and reach for my phone. Seven o'clock in the morning. I grab my pillow and roll over. I have no intention of getting up before noon, especially with this killer hangover.

Then the lingering scent of Mirabella's shampoo that's embedded into my pillow punishes me and brings the events of last night to the forefront of my mind. Just twenty-four hours ago, her petite body was pressed against mine. My hands were on her tits, my thumbs playing with her nipples. She was moaning and writhing under me. Now, there's absolutely no way I can ever trust her again.

I roll to my back and stare at the ceiling. I'm used to things happening quickly and having to react immediately, and if it was anyone but Mirabella who'd killed my father and tried to kill me, they'd already be dead.

A fist pounds on my door. "Open the fucking door!"

"Antonio, I swear to fucking God, you're on thin ice." I roll out of bed and whip open the door.

He stands with as much vengeance on his face as I imagine I must have on mine.

"My dad wants to talk to you."

I rock my head back and roll my eyes. "Tell him to relax. I haven't done shit and I'll talk to him before I do." I slam my door in his face.

"Mirabella didn't make it to Miami," he says from the other side. "She didn't even make it to the plane."

Fear ruptures through me like a sickness. "What?" I swing open the door.

"Did you—"

I shake my head. "I drank myself into a blackout. Where is your dad?"

"He's on the phone in Gabriele's room."

I narrow my eyes. Where the hell is she? Did someone take her to try to get to me? Does someone else know she's behind the bombing and they're going to take vengeance into their own hands? Either way, worry has my heart racing, which makes zero sense. The woman betrayed me in the worst way. She doesn't care for me, she was pretending the whole time. So why do I feel as if I'll rip whoever might have her limb from limb?

I grab my shoes and my sweatshirt, following Antonio to Gabe's room.

Gabe is waiting for us, standing in the doorway to his room with a pissed-off expression. "You guys are taking advantage. You'll both owe me."

"Yeah, yeah," I say, picking up the phone. "Frank."

"What did you do to her?" His voice is scathing. "I swear, if you put a hit out on her or did it yourself, you've started a war. I will avenge my daughter's death."

"I didn't touch her."

He carries on ranting and raving, threatening my life, which is reason enough for me to have him killed, but I let him go on until I get sick of listening to him.

"I didn't do anything! I got drunk and passed out last night. Now tell me what the hell is going on."

"One of my men was to have picked her up at the gates to the school and brought her to my private plane and flown her home. There was a lot of fog in the area, so my pilot didn't think much of it when they were delayed since they couldn't take off anyway, but they never showed up. From what I can tell, you've taken your shot first."

I shake my head and glare at Antonio. "One might say she took hers first," I say, referring to the car bomb. "I promise you, I had nothing to do with Mirabella's disappearance. I got piss drunk last night after our fight and passed out until Antonio woke me up. That's all I fucking know."

"Listen, Marcelo, I understand how betrayed you must feel, how blindsided you are, and I promise you, none of us had any idea of Mirabella's actions. I never would've allowed her to go through with it had she told me. Please, can we just hold off on others knowing until we find her? I haven't even told her mother yet, because I'm afraid I'll have to give her so much Xanax she'll sleep for a week."

I run my hand over my head. This is not how things are done in our business. But neither is not killing someone who admitted they tried to kill you. Male or female, the same rules apply. But Mirabella might be the one person on this earth I would never be able to kill. To see the life drain from her eyes would haunt me until my own death.

I might have wanted the opposite to be true last night, but it's apparent that she's under my skin like a tattoo and I'll never be able to remove her. I may never be able to trust her again, but I refuse to let someone take her from me—if it isn't already too late.

"I'll help you find her. We can discuss what happens from there."

"My best team is coming up there. I don't want to alarm my wife, so I'll be here."

"Understood. Antonio or I will keep you informed." I hang up.

Gabe stands from the bed. "Thank fuck. What's going on?"

Antonio and I stare at one another. We have no information on any leads at this point.

"My sister was supposed to be picked up by a car my dad ordered at dawn. I saw her get in and drive away, but they never made it to the plane."

"Shit. If you need anything from us, let us know. I'm sure my dad would be happy to help. I mean, the daughter of a leader going missing?" He shakes his head as if it's unheard of and it is.

I would do anything to avenge my sister. Hell, this sick feeling in my stomach suggests that maybe I'd do the same for Mirabella.

We say our thanks and Antonio follows me up to my floor. I'm guessing he's following me because he thinks I meant what I told his father. That we would work together and find her.

"I'm more of a one-man team," I tell Antonio on the elevator.

"Humor me," he says, continuing to follow me.

When I get to my door, Giovanni exits his room next door as if he has a radar track on me. He smirks. "I'm surprised to find you up and about. You were passed out cold."

I glance over my shoulder at Antonio. I'd prefer him not to hear whatever Giovanni knows, but I have no choice because he's my shadow today.

"What are you talking about?" I ask Giovanni.

"I knocked on your door and you didn't answer. I tried the knob and you never locked it. After not finding you there, I went to search for you. I found you in the elevator completely pale and passed out."

The hairs on my arms stand on end. "Where was I before that?" Panic sets in. Did I kill Mirabella in a drunken rage and not remember?

Antonio must see my expression because he shakes his head. "I took her to the vehicle at dawn." He looks at Giovanni. "When was this?"

He shrugs. "Probably closer to two or three a.m. It was completely dark outside."

I run my hand over my head and pull at the nape of my neck. Thank fuck. Not that it explains where I could've been during the hours before. I think back but don't remember where I went.

"Why do your knuckles have little cuts? This from last night?" Giovanni asks.

But I don't have to answer because the elevator dings and Chancellor Thompson comes walking out. He's clearly not happy. "Costa, you need to come with me."

Giovanni and Antonio follow me to the chancellor's office, and he tells me how they checked security footage from last night and they have me on camera, breaking into his office and using his assistant's phone.

"This would be your third strike, but after the shooting—"

"Do you know who I called?" He gives me a hard stare and I decide that now is not the time to get into a power struggle with this guy. It'll only take longer to get the information I need. "Please, it's important that I find out."

He shakes his head. "I can get that information if you'd like."

I nod. "I would."

We sit in his office as he gets on the phone with IT. After about fifteen minutes, he jots down a number and slides it across his desk to me.

I look at Giovanni and Antonio. "My nonno. That's who I called."

Antonio stares at me, jaw clenched. "Would he have put a hit on Mira?"

I shake my head, but can I be positive of that? I've seen him be ruthless many times and she did kill his son. The one he chose to take over after him. Shit. I don't know.

"Can I call him, sir?" I ask the chancellor and he turns the phone my way.

God, I hope drunk me was just as hell-bent on not telling anyone what she did as sober me. Otherwise, we're in a shit ton of trouble. Mirabella most of all.

CHAPTER FORTY
MIRABELLA

Marcelo's uncle Joey doesn't say a word as he drives, but he keeps his gun close should I try something. He's put the window and child locks on so I can't escape. I attempt to engage him a couple of times to figure out what his plan might be, but he doesn't respond.

At least he doesn't want me immediately dead, otherwise he would have pulled the trigger as soon as I got in the vehicle. Time is my best friend right now. It gives me a chance to turn this situation around. Though I'm not sure any number of seconds will make a difference.

I've witnessed too much in this world. If Marcelo wants me dead, it's as good as done. Even if I escape this attempt, there will be another until the job is finished.

The fog is so thick I have no idea where we are, but half an hour later, he pulls onto the tarmac of a small private airport. I'm pretty sure it's the same one we landed at when Antonio and I arrived at the beginning of the semester, but it's hard to tell when I can barely see a quarter mile in front of me.

After the vehicle comes to a stop, Joey turns around. "Try something and you'll regret it."

He climbs out of the driver's seat and rounds the front of the car. My door whips open and he points the gun at me while dragging me out of the back seat by my hair. I yelp, clawing at his hands.

"Shut up, bitch." Little pockets of spit land on my face.

I close my eyes before I throw up all over him. He'll punish me more if I do that.

He drags me from the SUV to the plane because I can't keep up with his speed while he has my hair wrapped around his fist. I trip on the first stair of the plane, and he just yanks harder, making my scalp burn, until I can get back on my feet.

"Sit down and don't say a word or move an inch unless you want to die." He tosses me onto one of the seats.

I scramble into the chair and notice someone sitting across from me.

Lorenzo.

What the hell?

My gaze darts between him and Joey, who has a sick smirk as realization dawns on me.

"You weren't supposed to hurt her," Lorenzo snaps at Joey. Then he gets off his seat and comes over to sit beside me, palming my thigh. "Are you okay?"

Before I can respond, the pilot emerges from the cockpit. He doesn't bat an eye at the gun pointed at me, which isn't surprising. He's the Costas' family pilot and has probably seen far worse.

"We have a problem, sir," he says to Joey.

Joey glances between me and him. "What kind of problem?"

"We can't take off in this weather. We have to wait until the fog clears." The pilot acts as though I'm not even on the plane.

I want to scream to the pilot that my father will kill him when he finds out he is part of this plan. Anyone who contributed to my death will be dead by the end of my father's wrath.

I bite my lip to keep from smiling because there might be hope for me yet. The moment my dad realizes I didn't make it to his plane at the other airport, he'll deploy his own resources to find me. And I'm sure that's going through Joey's head right now too. Not to mention Lorenzo is here and seems to want to keep me safe. That has to bode well for my life.

"How long's that gonna take?" Joey asks.

I suck in a sharp breath when the gun twitches in Joey's hand.

The pilot swallows hard, obviously not relishing the information he's going to impart. "At least a few hours, sir, if the weather reports are correct."

This is good news for me. All I need to do is stay alive long enough for my dad's guys to find me. There are no guarantees, but at least then I'll stand a chance of not being murdered. Although Joey doesn't seem too concerned about this development, which is worrying. Why wouldn't he want to take off right away?

No matter, I'm always telling Marcelo how I want to be a real part of the family business. Now is my time to prove that I'm worthy.

Joey swings his gaze to the pilot. "Keep me informed of when we can leave."

He nods. "I'm going to head into the airport to grab some food and talk to the agents. They might have better information than I do."

The pilot doesn't give me even a cursory glance when he walks past me, out of the plane, and down the stairs that lead to freedom.

When Joey turns his cruel gaze my way, I figure the best thing for me to do is to try to get these two talking. At least with some information, I can figure out how dire of a situation I'm in.

"What am I doing here?" I ask Lorenzo.

Joey barks out a laugh. "Really? Why don't you take a guess?"

I look at him and shrug. "You tell me."

Joey sits directly opposite me, keeping the gun trained on me. "Lorenzo and me. We make a good team, don't you think?"

A shiver runs down my spine from his sadistic grin, and I look at Lorenzo. "What is he talking about?"

Lorenzo reaches for my hand and I let him take it if only to keep him on my side so I can get the information I'm looking for. "Joey approached me about working together toward a common goal. He wanted Sam and Marcelo out of the way so he could be the leader of the Costas, and I didn't want you marrying Marcelo." He squeezes my hand. "I told you you're mine, Mira."

My eyes widen. This whole time they've been working together?

My head snaps in Joey's direction. "You killed your own brother?"

He shrugs as if it's nothing. "I did what I had to do. That's what a *real* leader does."

My mind whirls, trying to make the connections. I unknowingly provided the bomb, Lorenzo must have been the one to set it off, and I'd bet anything that Joey was using the burner phone those texts came from the night Sam Costa was murdered.

"How did you know Lorenzo and I were a thing?" I narrow my eyes at him.

Joey laughs as if I'm an idiot. "Are you kidding? It was so obvious the night both families were celebrating your upcoming marriage to Marcelo. Your boyfriend here looked like he wanted to kill my nephew and every time he looked at you, he was a lovesick puppy."

I look at Lorenzo and can tell he doesn't appreciate this description because his cheeks are red.

"None of that matters. What matters is that now we can be together like we should be," Lorenzo says.

My forehead wrinkles. "Marcelo is still alive." Maybe I can somehow negotiate my way out of this with him. I have to at least try. I don't even know if he's aware of the circumstances of why I'm leaving the academy.

"Not for long," Joey says. The certainty in his voice makes my stomach sink. "I've made it easy for him to find us—the old man has a tracker in here. Even though he's been crushed by your betrayal, I'm sure Marcelo's still going to come after you once he hears that you didn't make it to your father's plane."

Cold sweat breaks out on the back of my neck. Rather than showing him how afraid I am, I raise my chin. "Why do you think that?"

He smirks. "Because my drunken idiot of a nephew called me last night and told me. Poor thing. Marcelo was beside himself with your betrayal. You really did a number on him. He's not going to let you go that easy. It's just another example of why he doesn't deserve to be the leader." He chuckles as if there's some joke I'm not aware of.

If I can incapacitate Joey, maybe I could win Lorenzo over. I don't think he'd hurt me. Not after he's gone to these lengths to try to be with me. I look around for anything I can use to defend myself or to knock Joey out with, but unfortunately, there's nothing.

"You'll never get away with this," I say.

"We've got it all planned out," Lorenzo says, squeezing my hand again as though I'm a willing participant.

"Actually, there's been a change of plans." Joey shifts the gun a little to the right and pulls the trigger.

I yelp and my heart seizes. When I look to my left, Lorenzo is slumped against the seat with a bullet hole in the middle of his forehead, dripping blood. His hand is limp in mine now and his eyes stare up, unblinking.

I drop his hand and scurry back into the corner of the seat, breathing heavily and in shock. "Why did you do that?" I shout.

"Just tying up loose ends. That kid was a liability. First, he fucks up the bombing, then he doesn't make sure that bullet I gave him in the hospital hit its target. He serves a better purpose dead. Now we just need Marcelo to show up to finish this."

"What do you mean?" I glance at Lorenzo and squeeze my eyes shut for a second.

"Do you want to know? It's really such a tragic tale. Lorenzo kills you in a jealous rage when he realizes you'll never feel for him what you do for Marcelo, so Marcelo attacks him, but Lorenzo gets off a shot that kills my nephew. Then I have to kill Lorenzo as retribution. I'll be the last man standing and the hero. Pretty good, right?"

"You make me sick," I spit at him.

Joey leans in with his arm outstretched and points the gun directly at my chest. "What do you think happens to rude little girls, Mirabella?"

Thinking back to my sparring lessons with Marcelo, I run over the technique he taught me to get the gun from someone pointing it at you. I haven't mastered it, but it's my only chance at the moment.

Before I think better of my decision, I slowly draw my hands up, like a normal person does when they have a gun pointed at them. Then as fast as I can, I position my right hand on the outside of his right hand holding the gun while using my left hand to twist the gun, so it's not pointing at me.

To my surprise, the gun does fall from his hand, but I can't hold on to it and it bounces on the carpeted floor. I don't waste any time bolting toward the door. Hopefully the thick fog will be to my advantage and I'll lose him. Or if I'm lucky, other people will be around and can help me.

As I make it to the door, I'm tackled from behind. I hit the stairs with an "oomph," and my lungs scream as all the air is pushed from them because of Joey's weight on top of me. I flail underneath him, screaming and trying to get free, but he grips the hair at the back of my head and uses it as leverage to bash my head into the stair.

I'm dizzy and disoriented as he rolls me onto my back and straddles me, staring at me with crazed eyes. I open my mouth to scream again, but he smacks me in the face.

"Shut it, putana." He drags me back into the plane and slams me into one of the seats before putting the seat belt on me. He retrieves the gun from the floor and points it at me with a shaking hand. "I'm gonna make you regret that little stunt."

I squeeze my eyes shut, sure that he'll pull the trigger now. For some reason, the fact that he doesn't lights another fire inside me. "So, what's your plan? What are you going to say when your father wants to know why you took the plane in the first place?"

A sinister laugh falls from his lips. "I'm going to tell him I came out here to see my nephew, who called me distraught last night. Then when I arrived, I saw Lorenzo here with you, trying to charter a plane to run away together. Of course I confronted you both after what Marcelo told me. When Marcelo showed up, the shoot-out happened, and I was the lone survivor. And that, my dear, is how a leader takes control."

"You'll never be half the leader Marcelo would be."

He whips me across the face with the butt of the gun and the metallic taste of blood fills my mouth. I lean over and spit it onto the carpet.

He crouches low and gets his face right in front of mine until I can see the yellow of his teeth from years of cigarette smoking. "You should learn when to shut your mouth."

He sits across from me once again.

"How did you know I'd be leaving the school?" I ask. Someone had to have given him the information. There's no way he would have known otherwise.

He smiles. "How do you think? I had Lorenzo do some digging after the phone call from my nephew. Keep your friends close but your enemies closer, right?"

My hands clench into fists.

"Oh, someone's angry. It's a real pain in the ass when someone betrays you, isn't it? Soon enough, I'll be running this family and it will all be thanks to you."

"Over my dead body," I grate out.

He chuckles. "Yes, exactly. Good thing we're in agreement."

CHAPTER FORTY-ONE
MARCELO

I pick up the phone to dial my nonno, all the sets of eyes on me. "Can I have some privacy?"

The chancellor surprises me by standing and ushering the other two out. He's been very accommodating since I was shot on campus.

Once everyone is out of the room, I dial up Nonno. It rings for so long I fear he won't answer. He finally picks up at the same time a large bolt of lightning shines through the window. "Marcelo?"

"Nonno."

"You've made quite a shitstorm out of this entire thing. Frank La Rosa called me already."

"Oh."

He blows out a breath and I hear a door slam. "Tell me whatever Frank La Rosa didn't."

I explain the situation, and he patiently listens. He probably wants to make me tell him all this again while sober as punishment. "Shouldn't you know this already? I got drunk and called you last night."

"It wasn't me you talked to. It was your uncle. I assume he's decided to take her punishment into his own hands."

Every one of my muscles tenses.

"Since my plane is currently at an airport outside of Sicuro Academy, he's the one who's started a war with the La Rosa family. Frank has told me that if his daughter comes out of this without a scratch, they won't retaliate due to what she's done. But she tried to kill you, son. You're the leader of this family. It's your decision what happens to her."

I stare out into the courtyard where Mirabella and I walked hand in hand the other day. Except today there are puddles from the rainstorm and it's dreary and foggy instead of sunny. I might be a fool, but I can't let Mirabella die at the hands of my family.

What I need to know now is whether she really was telling the truth and didn't know what the bomb was for.

"I think it's a misunderstanding."

"A misunderstanding?" Nonno asks, disbelief lacing his tone. "Marcelo, she should be punished. I understand she didn't put the bomb there, but she helped make it and there is no way to know whether or not she knew who it was intended for. You know as well as me, punishments must be dealt out."

"By me. She is my fiancée, and I'm the one who should see her punishment through, not Uncle Joey. He's out of line for acting on his own. I had already decided that I was going to punish her for life by making her my wife, the one thing she doesn't want to be."

"But?" he asks, apparently all too aware that feelings have formed even if I've been trying to act as if they haven't.

"Nonno, you said it was my decision, and my decision is for her to spend her life by my side as my wife."

There's a long pause and I exhale, waiting for him to tell me if it's okay or not.

"Fine, but Marcelo—"

"I understand the repercussions. I have this handled, but I have to find her. Tell me what airport they're at."

"From what I can gather, all the airports near you are closed because of the weather. First, it was the fog, and now it's the wind with the storm. If they're still on the plane, they're at the small airport you flew into when you first went to the academy. I'm sending some other guys, but they won't be able to land until the weather clears. You'll most likely get there first. You, Giovanni, Nicolo, and Andrea all need to go."

"I'm going by myself." The rain slashes against the windowpane and everything outside feels darker and more ominous than it did moments ago. "I'm going to be the one to deal with that bastard, no one else."

"Marcelo!"

"I'll let you know what happens." My eyes catch on the chancellor's keys on the desk. I pick them up and pocket them.

"Marcelo!"

I hang up, praying Nonno understands that I don't want anyone else involved in this. There're already too many people who know something.

I walk out of the chancellor's office and Antonio pushes off the wall first. "What'd he say?"

I ignore Antonio and look at my cousin. "Giovanni, I need you to go back and watch Mirabella's room in case she comes back. I want to be the first to talk to her."

He stuffs his hands in his pockets and rocks back on his heels. He's suspicious and I can't blame him. He'd usually be my right-hand guy for a thing like this. Since I'm in charge though, he nods and walks away.

"Chancellor, thank you for letting me use the phone. My nonno is working with Mr. La Rosa, and as soon as we find Mirabella, we'll let you know."

He nods then reaches into his pocket and pulls out a business card. It's black with only a phone number on it.

"This is a direct line to my cell phone. All of the student's families have it in case of emergency. Use it if you need to reach anyone inside the school to achieve your end."

I should probably feel guilty that I just stole the man's car keys and he's now offering assistance, but I don't. I nod and walk away and Antonio quickly falls into line with me. Right before we walk outside into the thunderstorm, we put up our hoods, then we run until we reach the overhang outside the main building.

"I'm leaving campus and I need you to be my distraction." I dig out the keys to the chancellor's car. "Pay the guards. I'll pay you back when I return."

"I'm going with you," he says. "Where is she?"

I stop us right inside the dorm as we shake the water off us. "I have to go by myself. My uncle Joey has her—at least, we're pretty sure. I'm going to break into the weaponry room to steal a gun and go find them. I promise I'll bring her back alive."

"I said I'm going with you." He steps toward me.

I hold up my hand. "My uncle will only listen to me. I'm the one in charge of the Costas. You're the enemy."

His jaw tightens and his hands fist, but eventually he heads back out into the storm toward the gates while I jog toward the weaponry class. God knows what weapons my uncle has on him. Although I'm stronger than him in hand-to-hand combat, if he has a gun, I'm a dead man if I go in there without any heat.

Mr. Smith is in the classroom when I arrive a wet mess, and I have no time to make an excuse.

"Mr. Costa, how are you today?"

"Good. I was just checking in on something."

He stands and rounds his desk. "I heard there have been some developments in your dorm?"

I narrow my eyes.

He moves to the case with the guns in it and uses his key to unlock it. He sets two guns on the table. "You were asking about the difference between these two guns the other day if I recall?"

Anyone who knows me knows I know every gun imaginable.

He locks the case and uses another key to open a drawer in the bottom I hadn't noticed before and pulls out four magazines, two for each gun, on top of the magazines already attached. "Take these two for example."

I walk farther into the room since he's playing some kind of game I don't really understand, but I know I need to play along to get what I want.

The storm siren on campus begins its eerie wailing, and a small smile tugs up one corner of his mouth. "The storms must be setting off the alarms. We should really get going, Mr. Costa. There might be a tornado. We should take shelter."

I frown. "Mr. Smith?"

"Be careful, Mr. Costa. Storms like this are unpredictable and can take brutal turns." He grabs his coat from his chair and walks toward the exit. "If someone was looking to leave campus, right now would be the time, with all the alarms going off and everyone scrambling to take cover." He gives me a half smile and walks out of the classroom.

I knew there was something shady about that guy, but whatever. All the better for me right now.

I stare at the guns for a second before grabbing them, removing the empty magazines, adding full ones, then pocketing the rest of the ammunition. When I step out of the building, I see everyone scrambling and seeking shelter, so I race toward the chancellor's residence, break into his garage, and steal his car.

Luckily, most of the security staff is concerned with getting the students somewhere safe, so I take the road that leads to the gated entrance. As I approach the iron gates, they open for me, the guards not even coming out of the guardhouse.

Thank you, Antonio.

Once I'm outside of the Sicuro campus, I slam on the gas. The back wheels slide on the wet pavement, trying to find their grip. I put the windshield wipers on high and ignore the flashes of lightning and booming thunder. My mind is only on Mirabella and having her safe in my arms again.

Time will tell whether that makes me a goddamn idiot or not.

CHAPTER FORTY-TWO

MARCELO

The good thing about a small airport is that I can get close to the plane. I drive around until I find my nonno's plane sitting outside one of the hangars. Although I don't see any signs of life, the stairs are down, so I imagine they're inside. I park along the side of the hangar and stuff one gun into the back of my pants, move the extra magazines to my jacket pockets, and keep one gun in my hand.

I carefully close the car door but don't shut it all the way to avoid giving my uncle the heads-up that I'm here. I pull up my hood, but it's worthless because I'm soaked through in seconds. But it'll keep me from being able to be identified on camera. If this all goes to shit, we'll still have to scrub any tapes, but it's extra insurance, nonetheless. I stalk to the edge of the hangar and look around the corner, but I see no movement on the plane.

I step forward but quickly back up when someone walks out of the door of the hangar. It's our pilot, so I race up behind him, stick my gun to his temple, and walk him back into the hangar.

"What the fuck?" he says and reaches for his gun, but I knock it out of his hand. I walk around in front of him, gun raised, and his eyes widen. "Mr. Costa?"

I look out the small window on the door. "Have you talked to my grandfather?"

He shakes his head. "I was awoken by Joey and was told to fly down here. I thought maybe we were getting you, but then . . . well, it's not my job to ask questions."

"Is there a woman with him? Is he holding her hostage?"

"Yes, sir. A woman and another man." He nods gravely.

"That's my fiancée," I seethe.

"I had no idea. If I had . . . I've had no communication with anyone. Cell service is sketchy because of this weather."

"Who's the other guy on the plane?"

"I heard Joey call him Lorenzo."

I'm surprised my teeth aren't dust with how hard my jaw is clenched. What the hell is Lorenzo doing with my uncle? He was supposed to be mine to kill.

I put the gun away, knowing our family pilot isn't a threat, but my eyes remain on the plane. "Where was he having you fly him to?"

"A remote place in Upstate New York."

"Our cabin," I say.

He shakes his head. "Nowhere I've ever been before."

I blow out a breath. If he wanted Mirabella and Lorenzo dead, he would've done it the minute he had his hands on her. There's a reason he's keeping her alive.

I swallow back vomit when the idea that maybe he plans to have his way with her before offing her comes to mind. "Has he . . . were her clothes . . ."

He looks at the ground. "Everything was intact as far as I could see, but I've been in the airport getting updates on the weather, so I'll have an idea when we can get out of here."

Since my uncle didn't involve me in this decision, I have reason to believe this is some kind of punishment he is inflicting upon me. Or is he out for blood because Mirabella and Lorenzo had a hand in his brother's murder and he wants revenge?

I know he spoke his displeasure to my nonno the day I was declared the new leader of our family, but that's the way the hierarchy usually works unless the first son is too young or can't be trusted. I was brought up knowing I would lead this family someday. Could Joey be holding her, knowing I'll come after her, so he can kill me and become the new head of the family? But he was so happy when Nonno revealed I'd survived the bomb.

"Fuck!" I can't stop thinking I'm correct that Joey wants to be the leader and he kidnapped her so I would follow her here. But if that's the case, why is Lorenzo here? What part does he play in all of this?

"What?" The pilot moves to look out the window, but his quick movement causes me to draw my gun on him. He backsteps with his hands in the air.

"Sorry." I shake my head, pointing the gun away. "Stay here. We're going to have a mess to clean up when I finish. Tell me the airport is opening soon."

Just then, my uncle peeks his head out of the airplane and looks around. He's growing antsy and anxious. People in that mindset make stupid decisions.

"Sky's supposed to open up soon."

"Whatever happens, I need you to fly this plane back to my nonno."

He nods and I'm sure he understands. He's been our pilot for years and has seen worse than what is about to go down.

I crack open the door, slide out of the sliver, and duck down until I reach the staircase of the plane. I try to listen from the bottom of the stairs, but I can't hear anything over the rain, so I tiptoe up each step and peek in the plane.

Oh shit, Lorenzo is slumped over, dead from a bullet in his head. Mirabella is seated with her hands tied behind her back while my uncle playfully runs the gun along her temple. At least I have the advantage that his back is to me.

"You must have one magical pussy to be able to capture and keep my nephew's undivided attention. Seems he can't get enough of you, which couldn't be better for me. When he called last night, he was so heartbroken by what you'd done." A caustic laugh leaves his lips.

Mirabella seems surprised, her eyes widening for a beat, but she lifts her chin when he brings the gun down the center of her chest, letting the gun pull down the fabric of her shirt. My hand fists my gun, but my timing has to be right.

"Which is why he's not going to come for me. Your plan isn't going to work." Her voice is full of venom.

"Maybe I should get a taste of what that mouth feels like on my cock before I kill you."

She stiffens as he runs the barrel over her nipple. "I bet you have a pencil dick. It would be more like flossing for me."

Seriously, Mira? He's got a gun on you.

"Fuck you!" He spits in her face, but she doesn't give him the pleasure of a reaction.

"You might as well kill me because you'll never get that from me."

He plunges the barrel of the gun between her legs. "Believe me, if I wanted you, I'd already have had you, you filthy whore. Yes, my nephew told me how you aren't a virgin on his little phone call last night. What would Daddy think about that?"

She rises up in the seat, but she can't go too far. I need that gun pointed anywhere but on her for me to tackle him to the ground.

"My dad's gone soft, letting Marcelo go against rules, always listening to his woes and guiding him. But I'm not sure even my dad would accept a woman into the family a Costa didn't claim for her first time."

"Just kill me," she spits out. "Marcelo hates me. He isn't going to come looking for me."

He laughs. "Oh, the man I talked to last night would go to the ends of the earth for you. Fool." A sinister laugh escapes him again. "He'll show up. Then I can say Lorenzo killed you both and I had to kill Lorenzo as retribution. If Marcelo doesn't come for you because he's seen the light of day, I'll still kill you and show my family that I'm the one who took out both the people who killed my brother. It's a win-win."

"I saw it in his eyes last night. He wants me dead. I'm telling you, he's not coming." She almost sounds hopeful.

"Just shut up! How can he handle how much you talk?" He shakes the gun at her, and I tense.

Joey stands to his full height and looks over his shoulder. Out of time and not willing to risk shooting Mirabella by accident, I shove the gun in my waistband and I rush into the plane, tackling him to the floor.

"You son of a bitch!" I hold his hand with the gun above his head. It goes off, the bullet flying somewhere toward the cockpit. With both hands, I squeeze the life out of his wrist until he eventually drops the gun, and I slide it as far away as possible.

We roll around on the floor of the plane. He hammers my head into one of the arms of the chairs, and I smash a bottle of vodka over his head. Scrambling, we both get to our feet, but he's still disoriented from the hit to the head. I grab his shirt, walk him backward to the bathroom, and slam him against the door.

"Who the fuck do you think you are? I'm the leader of this family! You take my fiancée without my say so? How do you think I should deal with you?"

"You little piece of shit. You should have heard how pathetic your whining was last night. Moaning on and on about some girl and how you thought you would have it all. It's *bullshit*! You think the organization needs someone like you to be their leader? You're too young and too fucking dumb. It took you forever to figure out who killed your dad and who got you shot in class. You're not meant to be a leader. So, I put a plan into action to make sure I would reign over this family."

I pull him away from the wall and slam him back again. His head hits the corner of the exit sign, blood trickling down immediately. I drop him and he falls to the floor.

Pulling out my gun, I point it right at his head. "What plan?"

"Marcelo," Mirabella says next to me, and I point the gun at my uncle as I undo her seat belt with one hand.

"You're pathetic. Didn't even realize that I'd planted an accomplice at your school. I got your father to that underground fighting ring, planted the bomb, but Lorenzo fucked up because he didn't wait for you to get in the car. Fucking idiot," my uncle says.

"You were working with Lorenzo?"

"The promise of him getting to be with Mirabella once you were out of the way was enough to get him on board. He was perfect to defile your little princess and I did need that bomb from someone who wasn't in the family. I'll give you props, little girl, it was a great bomb."

Mirabella groans.

"He loved her and hated you as much as I did," Joey says. "It was a win-win, except he was too anxious and detonated it too fucking early."

"All done now?" I keep the gun pointed at him.

"You'd never kill your uncle. You were born into this life, you know the rules. Nonno will have no choice but to have you killed if you shoot me."

"Bullshit. You know as well as I do that Nonno hates you." I fire the gun, sick and tired of hearing his bullshit.

My uncle's body jolts back and blood seeps from his chest. His body slithers to the floor and his head slumps forward.

I kneel, put the gun on the floor next to me, and quickly undo Mirabella's restraints. "You just couldn't keep your mouth shut.

You're lucky he didn't kill you when you were egging him on like that."

"I knew I had until you came. He told me his whole plan."

Once she's free, she propels herself toward me, and I lose my balance, falling onto my back.

"You came for me." She looks down at me in awe.

"You're welcome," I say dryly.

Tension fills the air. There's a lot that's still unsaid between us.

"I'm so sorry, Marcelo. I swear I never . . . I would never . . ."

I put my finger to her lips. "We have some shit to sort out, but we'll figure it out."

And it is crazy. And unheard of. But Mirabella just fits in my life. She's the kind of strong woman I want by my side.

"Really?" Her eyes fill with tears.

"We can't tell anyone the part you played though. We'll blame it all on my uncle and Lorenzo."

She plasters her lips to mine, but I participate, as hard as it is.

When we pull apart, I ask, "You're okay? He didn't touch you?"

She shakes her head. "Just roughed me up."

My teeth gnash together so hard I'm surprised they don't shatter. I push back her long hair and stare into her beautiful eyes. "God, it's so good to have you in my arms. I was terrified I'd be too late the whole way here. Let's collect all the guns and make sure my uncle is really dead."

"You both make me sick."

We both turn to find my uncle pointing a gun at us.

CHAPTER FORTY-THREE

MIRABELLA

Joey is lying in a pool of blood, pointing a gun at us.

We're idiots, thinking we had our happy ending when Joey had another gun on him. Of course he did. We were naive to think otherwise.

I slowly roll off Marcelo, eyes wide, nonverbally asking him what we should do. He's had way more experience having a gun pointed at him than I have.

"Neither of you has any idea what it takes to run this family," Joey says with more venom than I would have thought possible, given the amount of blood he's lost. It's amazing he's still conscious, much less coherent.

Marcelo stumbles to sit up. "It's over, Uncle. Put the gun down."

Joey shakes the gun at us. "You don't get to tell me what to do, kid. Get your hands up! It's over when I say it is."

We both raise our hands and I search the area, desperate to find us a way out. The gun that Marcelo got off Joey is behind me. By the time I roll over and reach it, he'll have the opportunity to shoot one, maybe both of us.

Our only chance is to keep him talking, and maybe he'll lose enough blood that he'll pass out again. We'll have to tread carefully though, because if one of us says something that pisses him off, he'll just kill us.

"Joey, what if Marcelo doesn't want to run the family?" I ask.

Marcelo's gaze shifts my way, clearly wondering what the hell I'm saying and where I'm going with this.

"He knows I don't want to be a kept woman and that's all I'd ever be as the don's wife. Like you said, he loves me. He wants me to be happy. Maybe he wants to step down."

Marcelo makes a sound now, realizing my intentions. He picks up where I left off. "She's right. Mirabella could never be happy living the way my mother did. What if I step down and the two of us leave to go live our lives far away?"

Joey scowls. "Do you two think I'm stupid? What kind of idiot would step down from the most powerful position in our organization? Stop playing me for a fool."

"Like you said, I love Mirabella and I'll do it if you let us walk out of here alive. She's worth it to me."

Joey is silent for a moment, but any hope I have that he was pondering the decision sinks when he shakes his head. "You're lying. No man with the amount of power you hold would walk away from it for some whore." He continues to shake his head. "No pussy is that good."

Marcelo's jaw flexes. He's clearly trying not to come back at his uncle for that comment.

"Mirabella's is," he says, holding his hands in the air. "Let's make a deal that gets us all out of here alive. You're about to bleed out on this plane if we don't get you medical attention. And if you die here, you can't run the family."

"I can do whatever I want!" He waves the gun around, then points it directly at me.

Marcelo raises his hands higher and his movement pulls up the back of his sweatshirt. Light reflects off the metal of a gun tucked into his waistband.

All I have to do is get closer to Marcelo, grab the gun, and I might be able to shoot Joey before he kills either of us. Talking isn't working. He's not buying that Marcelo would leave the family. He's only getting more erratic and not showing any signs of passing out.

I need to act fast. I've never shot a real gun before, but thankfully, some of Marcelo's training will come in use. But I need Joey's attention on Marcelo, not on me, in order for this to stand a chance.

"Marcelo already told me how much he hated his dad. How sick he is of this life." I look at my fiancé. "Tell him."

Our gaze holds, him questioning where I'm going with this. Then there's a sparkle of recognition in his eyes. He may not know exactly what I'm about to do, but he knows I have a plan.

He turns and looks at his uncle. "It's true."

While Marcelo keeps trying to convince Joey that he'd willingly step away from this life, I wait for my opportunity. Joey's gaze continues to flicker from Marcelo to me. He has to be completely engaged in what Marcelo is saying before I act. Then Marcelo tells Joey all the shitty things his dad said about him, and I see the rage building in Joey, causing him to focus solely on Marcelo.

I lower my right hand, slide it around Marcelo, and grab the gun. I point it at Joey, but he's faster than me and straightens his arm toward Marcelo. Our guns fire at the same time.

Everything around us moves in slow motion. I scream and leap in front of Marcelo, blocking the bullet from hitting him. The burn as the bullet pierces the side of my abdomen is excruciating.

I collapse on the floor as searing pain explodes through my body and everything goes black.

CHAPTER FORTY-FOUR

MARCELO

"Mirabella!" I hear her name off my lips as if I were in a tunnel.

Her body collapses in front of me on the floor of the plane and she moans, curling her legs up into a fetal position. She stares at me, mouth open to say something before her body goes lax.

"*No!*" I scream.

I pick up the gun Mirabella used to shoot my uncle, ready to avenge my fiancée. He's slung back on the floor, blood smeared on the wall behind him. Mirabella shot him right in the heart. I check for a pulse to be sure he's really dead this time, and when I feel nothing, I stand and shoot him in the head just to appease some sick part of me that needs to make him pay for what he did to Mirabella.

Mira.

I rip Joey's cell phone off him as the pilot pokes his head in the cabin.

"What's going on?"

"You need to help me bring her to the car."

He takes the top half of Mirabella's body and I take the lower half. "I need to find help. After you help me with this, you need to fly that plane back to my grandfather. He'll be expecting you and will meet you at the airport."

We get Mirabella into the front of the vehicle because I'll have to put pressure on her wound until I find a doctor.

"Closest city?" I ask the pilot once I've closed the passenger door.

"Just outside of Kansas City."

"Dante." I sigh and pull the card the chancellor gave me from my pocket and dial the number. As it's ringing, I walk around the car to the driver's side. "Make sure there're no bullet holes in the plane before you take off."

His eyes widen and I get in the driver's seat of the vehicle while he runs to the plane. The skies have cleared, so hopefully he can take off and get back to New York to clean up that mess.

"You stole my car?" the chancellor answers in a bellowing voice. Guess he was expecting my call.

"I had no choice. I need you to get Dante for me. Now!" I rip off my sweatshirt and use it to apply pressure to Mirabella's wound.

"If you think—"

"Get me Dante *now*!" I yell.

"Fine, but we'll discuss this later."

I hear his heavy breath as he runs for a few minutes and then the sounds of an elevator and then I hear Giovanni say in the background, "What's wrong? Is that Marcelo?"

There are some sounds I think might indicate a scuffle and then Giovanni's on the line. "What happened?"

"I need Dante right away!"

He doesn't ask any questions for once and a minute later, I hear a knock and another knock and another knock.

"Dante!" he shouts.

"Fuck!" I slam the fist holding the phone on the wheel and look at Mirabella. She's pale and lifeless looking.

"He's in there, I can hear the moaning." Giovanni pounds with his fist again.

"What the fuck?" I hear Dante say.

"Jesus, you could've wrapped a towel around yourself, I don't need to see your dick."

"Give the phone to Dante," I say with barely restrained fury.

"It's boss man and sounds urgent," he says.

"Marcelo?" Dante's voice comes on the line.

"I need a favor. I'm outside of the small airport by the school. I don't know its name, but I'm in your territory. I need a doctor."

"For you?" he asks, and I hear some noises behind him. "Sorry, business," he says to someone else.

"We had business, but whatever," a girl says, then a door slams.

"You owe me for this," Dante snipes. "She was a hot piece of ass."

"It's not for me, it's Mirabella. She's been shot—"

"Fuck, man, why didn't you say so? I gotta call my dad, hold on, I'm going up to Gabe's room."

Gabe is gonna turn us down at one point and I cannot afford for that day to be today.

"Are you telling me if I was shot, you wouldn't have helped, but since it's my fiancée, you're willing?"

He laughs, but I don't. After hearing Dante run down the stairwell, he bangs on Gabe's door.

"I need to use the computer to get a hold of my dad." Dante sounds almost out of breath.

"Fuck you. All of you. You owe me. What's the problem now?" Gabe asks.

"It's Costa. He's got Mirabella and she's been shot. He's in my territory, so I have to get our doctor to see to her. They can't go to the hospital."

"No shit," Gabriele says. "Go ahead."

"Tell him thanks," I say.

Not a minute later, Dante has his dad on the phone. He explains the situation and his dad agrees to send one of their doctors. He asks where we are, and after I tell him, he tells me where to go to.

I put the location into my uncle's phone. "Thanks, Dante."

"I heard you stole the chancellor's car. You really don't want to stay here, do you?"

"Fuck off, Accardi." I end the call.

I follow the directions until I get to a small farmhouse in the middle of a field. I drive up the gravel driveway, kicking up dirt, and a man comes out, motioning for me to drive into the barn. After he shuts the doors behind me and I turn off the car, I race around to the passenger side, saying a small prayer that Mirabella is still warm in my arms.

He turns on a light. There's a bed in the middle of the barn and it's set up like a hospital operating room, white sheet and all. "Lay her here. Where was she shot?"

"Her stomach," I say, staring at Mirabella.

He checks her vitals. "She's breathing and there's a weak pulse. My wife will be out in a second to assist. I'm not sure how long this will take, but you can go for a walk around the property if you'd like."

"I'm good here." I look around for a chair.

"It wasn't an option, son."

I run my hand over her forehead and kiss it. "Damn you for having to save my life." I cover her lips with mine, unprepared for how lifeless they are.

The wife comes in and washes her hands in their makeshift operating room. They resemble any regular middle-aged couple, not people who would want anything to do with the Mob.

"I'll find you when we're done," the doctor says, not bothering to look my way.

The wife offers me a gentle smile. "She's in good hands, son. Don't worry."

I nod and back away. They put an IV in Mirabella's arm and a mask over her face.

Outside the barn, I collapse to the ground, saying a small prayer that she pulls through. Then I heave out the contents of my stomach. Seeing Mirabella like that . . . I don't ever want to witness my fiery fiancée so lifeless again.

After I wipe my mouth, I stand to call my nonno.

"What the hell are you doing?" he yells into the phone.

"It's me, Nonno."

"Marcelo?"

"Yes."

He sighs. "I'm too old for this shit."

"Well, I have worse news." I run my hand over my head and stare at the ground.

"What?"

"The plane is on its way back to you. Uncle's on it."

"Oh?"

I nod as if he could see me.

"And where are you?" he asks.

"I'm helping a friend." I'm trying to not give anything away. This is a cell phone, not a secure line.

"Is your friend okay?"

"Not sure yet." My voice catches.

"And how are you?"

"I'm good. Just a little shook."

"Looks like you're one of the lucky ones then." His voice is grave.

I chuckle because I might not be if she doesn't come out of this. "Let's hope."

"We need to settle some things, so once the plane returns and I've handled them, I'm coming to the academy. We need to set a new plan for this family. In the meantime, stay put and only worry about your friend. Let me know the outcome."

"Sure thing, Nonno."

He's silent and I'm sure he's figured out his second son is dead. "Ti voglio bene, Marcelo."

"Ti voglio bene, Nonno."

We hang up and I sit on a giant rock protruding from the ground. It's only then that I realize I'm covered in her blood. My hands, my shirt, some on my pants. All my time with Mirabella flashes through my memory as if we won't have any more. She's more than proved her worth to be my equal in our world, but she has to live before I can make that happen.

Eventually, the sun falls behind the horizon, leaving me with only dark thoughts to keep me company. Shortly after, the wife comes out of the barn, then the husband. I search their faces for any idea of whether Mirabella made it or not.

"She's lost a lot of blood, but I gave her some and operated. She's lucky the bullet missed anything vital. An inch to either side and it would be a different outcome. She should be waking up soon. I'm sure she'd like to see you waiting for her." He holds out his hand and pulls me up to my feet. "I'll be back to check on her."

"Thank you." I squeeze his hand. "Your payment is coming."

He waves me off. "Mr. Accardi took care of it already."

Huh, Dante's playing nice. Interesting. But I can't worry about what that means now.

I walk through the barn doors, hoping my Mirabella wakes up soon. I just want her back.

CHAPTER FORTY-FIVE

MIRABELLA

My eyes flutter open and the first thing that comes into view is the top of a barn. I try to move my arm, but something tugs on my skin. Alarmed, I try again, and a stabbing pain assaults my hand.

"Mirabella, baby? Are you awake?"

I relax when I hear his voice, knowing I'm safe wherever I am. Marcelo's face comes into focus above me. His eyes are wide and full of concern, deep grooves underneath. He looks as exhausted as I feel.

"Where am I?" My voice is scratchy, my throat dry and sore.

He gently brushes my hair back from my forehead as he chuckles. "Good question. I don't really know to be honest." I must give him a look because he adds, "You were shot."

I blink a few times, then the whole thing comes back to me. His uncle, Lorenzo, the plane, me grabbing Marcelo's gun. "Did I kill him?"

He nods, snickers, and kisses my forehead. "Shot him right through the heart."

I smile. Bastard. He deserved it.

"You also saved my life." Marcelo looks down at me, his dark eyes intense. "If I had any doubts about how you really felt about me, consider them gone."

I try to raise my hand to touch his face and wince when the skin tugs at what I'm assuming is an IV.

"Just relax," Marcelo says, touching his fingertips to my own. "I'm so sorry I reacted the way I did when you told me the truth." His eyes glisten. Or maybe I'm imagining it from all the painkillers I'm probably on.

"It was a shock. I understand why you questioned my loyalty, whether you could trust me."

"No!" His words come out harsh. "No, I reacted poorly, and I swear to you on my life that I will never do anything like that again."

I nod slowly. It's clear he means what he says.

"I love you, Mirabella. I love you and I want you to be my wife. Most of all, I want you to be my equal."

The air rushes from my lungs and it must register on some machine I'm hooked up to because a beeping sound comes from one of them. Marcelo's eyes widen, panic setting in, but then I inhale and the machine settles.

"I love you too."

He sighs with what I think is relief and places a lingering kiss on my temple.

"What does that mean . . . equals?" I ask.

He sits on the edge of the bed and takes my hand. "It means that I don't want to hide you away in some mansion. I want you to be as involved or uninvolved as you want in our business. The choice is yours."

A tear tracks down my face. That's all I ever wanted—a choice. "Are you sure?"

He nods. "More than I've ever been about anything. You're just as capable as, maybe even more than, any man in our organization."

Pride swells in my chest. "Kiss me?"

He chuckles and leans in, bringing his lips to mine, pulling away far too soon.

"I love you," I whisper.

"Remember that the next time I piss you off." He winks.

It's then I know that everything will be fine. We may have started as adversaries, but now we're equals.

* * *

A FEW WEEKS later, I'm well enough to return to the academy, though it was a hard sell to get my father to let me go. He didn't want me out of his sight after what happened. I returned home to recuperate, and my parents allowed Marcelo to stay to help after my dad spoke to Marcelo and they both agreed to keep my unwitting involvement in the bomb out of it. According to everyone, the slate was wiped clean when I took a bullet for Marcelo.

I still have to take it easy because my wound is still healing inside, but I don't want to wait any longer before returning to campus. The truth is, I don't want my fiancé getting too used to the idea of us both being out of school.

When I asked him what would happen with school now that he no longer needed to search the campus for who was plotting to take his life, he told me we'd talk about it once I was feeling better. So far, he hasn't brought up leaving school this year, so I'm content to let it ride. Though next year is still up in the air.

I stand hand in hand with him to enter Roma House.

"You ready for this?" he asks.

"As ever," I say.

We step through the doors to a round of applause and cheers. I blink a few times, surprised by the number of people here—even people who aren't members of mine or Marcelo's crime families.

"You scared me so much!" Sofia flies toward me, but Marcelo puts a hand on her shoulder, forbidding her. Her arms continue to reach out for me, and everyone laughs.

"Take it easy. She's still recuperating," he says.

Sofia winces. "Sorry." Then she envelops me in a gentle hug I return. It's so good to see her. "Don't you dare do anything like that again," she whispers into my hair.

"Promise."

She pulls away and we maintain eye contact, conveying so much without saying a word.

"My turn." Antonio pushes Sofia out of the way in order to give me a hug. "You scared us, sis."

"I scared myself."

He laughs as he pulls away, then looks at Marcelo. "Thanks for making sure she saw a doctor right away."

Marcelo nods and they shake hands.

Next, Giovanni steps up in front of me. I've never really been sure whether he actually likes me or not. He's made it clear that he's not a huge fan of Marcelo's feelings for me, so I'm not sure what to expect when he opens his mouth to speak. "I'm glad you're okay. Sorry if I was an ass at times. I'm over it if you are."

I don't give him what he wants immediately, preferring to make him squirm for a bit before I smile. "I'm over it."

He gives me a hug before giving Marcelo one.

"You look better than ever." Dante approaches with a grin and pulls me in for a hug that lasts longer than any of the others.

Marcelo clears his throat, and when Dante doesn't back up, he clamps Dante on the shoulder.

Dante laughs and winks at me. "Relax, Costa. We were just catching up."

Marcelo looks as though he wants to say something, but Dante is the guy who helped to make sure I'm alive, there's not much he can say.

I make the rounds and chat with people for an hour. Marcelo never leaves my side. Eventually, I can't keep a yawn at bay and my eyes water as I cover my mouth to hide it.

Marcelo frowns. "All right. That's enough for you. Let's get you to bed."

Though it's my natural instinct to fight him on it, I don't. He's right. My side is aching, and this is as much activity as I've had in weeks. "Okay, let's go."

We slip away and when we get in the elevator, Marcelo presses the button for his floor.

"I want to sleep in my bed tonight," I say to him.

He shrugs, looking nonplussed. "Okay."

I lean in to press the button for my floor, but he stops me. "What are you doing?"

"Trust me?" He raises an eyebrow, so I nod. "Good."

I have no idea what's up as we make our way down the hall. He pulls out his key to unlock his dorm door then walks inside. I follow, and it takes me a minute to realize why everything looks a little different. It's because my things are in here too.

"I had Sofia and Giovanni move all your stuff in here. I hope that's okay with you."

A slow smile spreads across my face. "The chancellor is okay with this?"

Marcelo looks smug. "Let's say the chancellor and I have come to an understanding."

The chancellor wasn't happy that Marcelo stole his car, but he didn't do anything about it because not only had Marcelo been shot on school property, but I'd also essentially been abducted. Seems we have a little bit of wiggle room with the rules now.

I wrap my arms around his neck.

"You okay with this? Seems I can't get enough of you now." He kisses my forehead.

"The feeling is entirely mutual, Mr. Costa."

He nips my ear. "Good to know, Mrs. Costa."

I laugh. "Soon enough."

He shakes his head. "Not soon enough for me."

MIRABELLA

It's Christmas break and we're spending the first half with my family in Miami, then we're flying up to New York to spend the rest of our time off with Marcelo's nonno and nonna.

I'm still recovering from the gunshot wound, but I'm making progress every day and I'm almost as good as new, except for the scar on my abdomen. But Marcelo spends a lot of time running his tongue over it and he seems to think it's pretty cool—says that none of the other wives will have one, which I guess is true.

On Christmas Eve morning, there's a soft knock on my door while I'm finishing getting ready. I open it to Marcelo standing there with gift bags in his hand.

"Hey." I smile and dip in for a quick kiss. "I'm almost ready to head down for breakfast."

He glances left then right. "Can I come in for a minute?"

"My dad will shoot you if he finds us in here fooling around, fiancé or not."

He chuckles. "I have something I want to give you in private."

I glance at his dick. "I'll bet."

He shakes his head and pushes past me. I quickly close the door so no one will spot him in there.

"We can save that until we get to my nonno's. He already knows everything, so I doubt we'll have to sleep in separate rooms." He heads over to the couch on the far side of my room. "Now, come over here and sit."

Curious what's up, I do what he asks without arguing about him bossing me around. I take a seat beside him.

"I have something to give you in front of everyone tomorrow morning, but I wanted to give you these in private." He hands me the first of the three gift bags in his hand. This is the biggest of the three.

"Is it stuff for the bedroom?" I joke as I pull tissue paper out of the bag. Then I set the bag at my feet, pull out a black case, and set it on my lap. When I undo the latch and open the case, I gasp. Inside is a black-and-gold handgun. "It's so pretty."

"I thought you'd like that." He smiles at me. "I figured if we're going to be equal partners, you're gonna need your own gun."

A warm feeling spreads throughout my chest.

"But you won't be able to sneak it on campus, so you'll have to leave it here for the next few years," he says.

"What?" I gasp.

Marcelo knows I want to finish our time at Sicuro Academy, but we agreed that we'd discuss it in the latter half of the year. He's eager to take over operations and, in fact, already has to some degree while on campus. The first thing he did at my behest was put a stop to the human trafficking his father got rolling. I couldn't stomach the idea of my husband forcing unwilling women into a life of abuse and servitude, and he agreed with me. A lot of people weren't happy, but the plan is to replace that income with some online ventures I gave him ideas for.

"Does this mean . . ."

He nods. "We'll finish up at Sicuro. My nonno has agreed to deal with the day-to-day stuff, and I'll use my Sunday call to check in on anything I need to."

I lunge up off the couch and hug him tightly.

He chuckles and pulls me off him. "You've still got more to open, and I don't want your parents to catch me in here. Your father threatened to shoot my nuts off if he found me in here and I'd like to keep them right where they are."

I smile and sit back down to open the rest of the gifts. The next bag contains a switchblade and a hunting knife, and the last one contains a burner phone. I look at all the items on the couch cushion beside me, then up at my fiancé. "Thank you for all of this."

"Think you're all set to hold your own at the top of the Costa pyramid now?" He arches an eyebrow.

"With your help, yes."

"Good thing we're a team then." Before I can say anything, he holds up his hand. "I have one last thing for you."

"Does this have to do with wherever you went last night?" I ask, tilting my head since he doesn't have any more packages with him.

"It might." He grins.

Marcelo went out with my brother last night, but he wouldn't tell me where, no matter how much I bugged him about it. I was already sleeping when he came home.

"Well, what is it?" I impatiently ask.

He lifts the hem of his T-shirt and there's a fresh tattoo, swollen and raised and red around the edges. It's an exact replica of the scar I have from my bullet wound in the exact same spot on his body.

"Now we match," he says in a soft voice. "Plus, I figure yours is basically a symbol of your love for me. Now I have one of my love for you. I didn't take a bullet for you—but I would. Without hesitation."

I launch up off the couch and wrap my arms around his neck, pulling him down for a kiss. When he pulls away, he rests his forehead on mine.

"How did you show the tattoo artist what to ink you with?" I ask.

"I took a picture of your scar when you were sleeping." He places a chaste kiss on my temple. "I love you, Mirabella. More than I thought I could ever love anyone."

"Me too. We're going to have a great life together." I place my hand on his cheek and he pulls back to gaze into my eyes. "I can't wait to marry you."

"Bet you never thought you'd say those words." He laughs.

"Not ever." I grin.

"A king and his queen." He tucks a piece of hair behind my ear.

"Or a queen and her king," I say, laughing.

"And they lived happily ever after."

"Forever and ever."

We seal our promise with a kiss.

Can't get enough of Marcelo and Mirabella?
Turn the page for an exclusive bonus scene
from *Vow of Revenge*

MARCELO

Christmas Break – Eight Hours After the Epilogue

For the first time in my life, I'm having Christmas dinner with a different Mafia family than my own. Although, the La Rosa's dining room is much like my own, except for the palm trees instead of evergreen trees outside the window. My mom and sister flew in this afternoon and Aurora Salucci's family is here to celebrate her engagement to Antonio. The dinner was a long, drawn-out affair as it usually is with big Italian families. Now that dinner has concluded, some prominent members of the La Rosa crime family join us for cocktails and the official announcement of Antonio's engagement. Since my fiancée is miserable about having Aurora as her soon-to-be sister-in-law, I'm currently a prick.

I'd be on edge anyway because this isn't my house. I'm growing more comfortable around Mirabella's family, but being surrounded by a bunch of members from another Mafia family isn't something I'll ever get used to. I'll never be one of them and I'm sure the majority still see me as their enemy. Which means we all have eyes on every move with our hands on our holsters.

"Can you believe her? Was she raised by wolves? She just takes out her mirror and applies lipstick in the middle of cocktail hour. Ever heard of a bathroom mirror?" Mirabella whispers as if I noticed or care.

All I can really think about is next week when Mirabella comes up to New York with me. One whole week in my condo alone before we have to return to the Sicuro Academy.

"Hey, guys." Aria, my seventeen-year-old sister, walks up with what better be a club soda and lime that she wants everyone to think is a mixed drink. She's always trying to act older than she is even though she's about as sheltered and innocent as they come.

"Hi, Aria." Mirabella smiles at her. "I love your dress."

Aria beams at Mirabella's compliment. "Thank you. Mom and I bought it especially for this dinner. Tomorrow we're going out on your dad's yacht, right?"

Mirabella nods. The only good thing about that is that I'll get to see Mirabella in a bikini. I'm crossing my fingers that it's a thong.

"I can't believe you two are willingly coming to New York City for the rest of your break. It's so cold and snowy right now," Aria says.

"I love the snow. I've only ever seen it a few times." Mirabella looks at me, then rests her head on my shoulder. I dip down and kiss the top of her head, then lift my drink to my lips.

"It's not the newly fallen pretty kind, it's slush and dirty snow." Aria sips her drink. "I wish I could be the one marrying Antonio so I could live down here where it's warm all the time."

I choke on my scotch, barely swallowing it. "He's way too old for you."

Mirabella bites her lip, but her smile still betrays her. She thinks this is funny. "He's only a few years older than her."

"Doesn't matter. Aria's way too young and way too innocent for any talk of marriage or . . ." I can't even think about the other things.

Both Mirabella and Aria roll their eyes in unison, and I take another swig of my drink.

"For what it's worth, I'd rather have you marry Antonio, too." Mirabella looks in Aurora's direction. Her arm is linked with Antonio's and she's snug against his side. She even takes one hand and smooths his shirt down. "Disgusting." Mirabella sticks her pointer finger in her mouth and gags.

"Aria, can you please excuse us for a moment? I need to speak to my fiancée in private." I give my sister a "beat it" look and she looks down at the ground and turns and leaves.

Mirabella whips around to face me. "Why did you scare her away like that?"

I lean down and whisper into her ear, "Meet me in the powder room on the far side of the house in two minutes."

Her eyes sparkle with intrigue when I pull away and she simply nods.

I escape the room without drawing any attention to myself and a minute after I arrive, there's a soft knock on the powder room door. I swing the door open, and Mirabella wastes no time stepping inside. Once the door is closed again, I lock it and face her.

"So . . . why are we in here?" Mirabella drapes her arms around my neck, her eyes already brimming with lust.

"For exactly the reason you think." My hands slide down over the silk of her dress until they rest on her ass, and I pull her flush against my body.

"I like how your mind works."

"You'll like how my tongue works better." I lean in and kiss her deeply, our tongues meeting and, as always, she fights me for control for a beat before she acquiesces.

When I pull away, I lift the hem of her dress up to her waist, slowly, drawing it out for the both of us. Her red fitted dress rests on her waist, leaving her in a matching red silk thong.

"I thought you could use a stress reliever. You seem like you're wound pretty tight tonight." I trace the knuckle of my middle finger over the center of her mound and her eyes flutter closed.

"I could." Her voice is low and breathy, just how I love it.

"Good, now lose the underwear." My voice is strong and commanding.

She wastes no time pushing the small piece of fabric down her legs and stepping out of them, kicking them to the side with the toe of her four inch heel.

"Now turn around and face the sink." She does as I say and I stare at her through the mirror. "Put your hands on either side and stick your ass out."

Mirabella bites her plump bottom lip and does exactly as I say. When she's splayed wide, I see how wet she is for me and my cock hardens in my pants, straining painfully against the fabric.

I drop to my knees behind her and with one hand on each of her ass cheeks, spread her further. "I want you to watch in the mirror while I devour this pussy."

A small whimper leaves her mouth and then another when I lick her from one end of her pussy to the other.

I work her hard and fast, knowing we can't be missing from the party for too long, and within minutes she comes on my tongue, trying her best to hide her cries in her throat.

I lap up every drop of her desire before I help her back into her panties and pull her dress back into place while she's still catching her breath.

The moment she turns around her lips crash to mine and her tongue is in my mouth. It's all I can do not to open my slacks and satisfy us both.

"What about you?" She takes a small step back and looks down at my bulging erection.

"You can pay me back for my generosity later. We need to get back to the party before the announcement."

"Okay." She smiles. The grin says she can't wait to make good on that promise.

My Mirabella is so much more agreeable right after an orgasm.

I nod toward the door. "You go. I'll meet you out there in a few minutes."

She nods, and after a quick peck on the lips, she exits out into the hallway and slips away. After waiting a few minutes for my erection to subside, I return to the party and find her talking with Sofia.

Sofia's dad is an underboss, so her parents are here tonight, too. Though if my instincts are right, I'm sure she'd rather be anywhere but watching Antonio be promised to someone else.

"Hello, ladies." I nod at Sofia and share a knowing glance with my fiancée over what just went down in the bathroom.

The sound of clinking glasses rings throughout the room and we all turn in the direction of the sound to see Frank, Mira's dad, motioning for all of us to quiet down. "I have an announcement to make," he says, chest puffed out with pride.

Antonio wanders over to his dad's side, ready for it, while Aurora ventures over to her family as if the entire room doesn't already know.

"I want to scream," Mira murmurs to Sofia, who looks stricken with grief.

"I'll give you plenty to scream about later," I say.

Mirabella looks at me and I wink.

"With my daughter already secure in her upcoming nuptials to Marcelo Costa"—he nods in our direction, and I tip my drink to him while everyone else peers at us across the room—"Livia and I are happy to announce that our son, Antonio, is engaged to our very own Oronato Salucci's daughter, Aurora."

A ring of applause and tapping glasses ensues. People wait for Aurora to walk toward Antonio, where he puts his arm around her waist and leans in to kiss her, but she turns her head to offer him her cheek. Antonio acts like nothing is amiss when he pulls away and smiles out at the crowd.

"She's a bitch and a prude?" Mira rolls her eyes. "Sofia, how am I ever going to deal with this?"

"Just be thankful that you'll be in New York most of the time. You won't have to see them together as much as I will." She frowns.

"True story. I need another drink." Mirabella stalks off to the bar without a backward glance and I concentrate back on Sofia.

Oh yeah, I think my fiancée's best friend definitely has something for Antonio, but Mirabella's none the wiser and I won't be the one to tell her. I know she doesn't want Antonio to marry Aurora, but now that the announcement has been made, that's basically a done deal barring death. I'm not sure that she'd be any happier that her best friend is pining away for her brother.

Best not to rock the boat when it won't matter anyway. Crime family arrangements are never renegotiated and, if they are, it's usually a result of death.

When Mirabella returns with a new drink, I persuade her that we should go and congratulate the happy couple along with everyone else. She eventually agrees, but only after I promise to reenact our powder room activities later that night when I sneak into her room.

A vita è dolce. Life is sweet.

ACKNOWLEDGMENTS

No lie—this one was a beast to write. We didn't use our usual process and it took way longer to draft and revise than it normally takes us, so we can safely say we will not be doing that again. LOL

All that said, we LOVE this story! It's been fun writing books that are a departure from our usual M.O. with our Piper Rayne stories.

This book really started with the academy and Mira. We knew we wanted to set a Mafia story in an academy, and we wanted a strong heroine to kick off the series. One who wanted to be a real part of the family business and wasn't content to sit on the sidelines. She's willing to fight for what she wants even when everyone around her is telling her to sit down and shut up and we love her for it! Now, that's not to say that all our heroines at the Sicuro Academy will feel the same, but exploring that dynamic in this book was fun.

Of course, we needed a made man and preferably one who was leader of his family to kick off the series. Marcelo Costa was perfect. Especially since he came to the academy believing what he's been told his entire life. He's the man and his arranged wife will cater to him in every way possible. Boy, did Mira turn his head around on that assumption. It's always a blast to read an antihero who prides himself on his control lose it over the woman he's falling for, in and out of bed. ;)

We always have many people to thank for helping us get a book ready for release, and while we're grateful for the part everyone plays, this release deserves a special shout out to someone in particular.

Jen Prokop—your insight was invaluable to making this story what it is. We had a lot of "why the hell didn't we think of that?" moments and second-guessed this endeavor a few times, but it all came together in the end and that would not have happened without you. This story and its characters are stronger because of you. Thank you! Hopefully you weren't thinking "what the hell did I get myself into?" after your first read-through (though we're pretty sure you were). LOL

Big thanks also goes to . . .

Nina and the entire Valentine PR team.

Cassie from Joy Editing for the original line edits.

My Brother's Editor for the original proofreading.

All the bloggers who read, review, share, and/or promote us.

Every reader who gave this one a chance! Thank you so much! We're so grateful!

A huge thank you to May Chen, for loving this series enough to bring it in under the Avon publishing umbrella. We are thrilled to work with the team on this series.

Lastly, but certainly not least, we need to thank Kimberly Brower, our agent, for championing the Mafia Academy series to Avon. She's literally given us our dream of seeing one of our books in a bookstore.

Up next is Antonio and Sofia! This best friend's brother/love triangle will have some angst, a little bit of mystery, and lots of sexy times just like this one did. We hope you're up for it!

xo,
Piper & Rayne

ABOUT THE AUTHOR

P. RAYNE is the pen name for *USA Today* bestselling author duo Piper Rayne. Under P. Rayne, they write dark, dangerous, and forbidden romance.

DELVE INTO P. RAYNE'S
MAFIA ACADEMY
SERIES

A dark romance series set at a boarding school for the sons and daughters of the most powerful Mafia lords, now with new bonus content exclusive to the print editions.

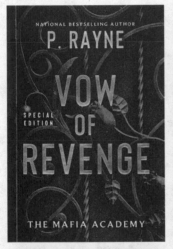

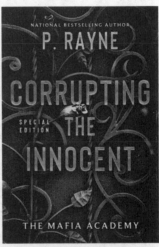

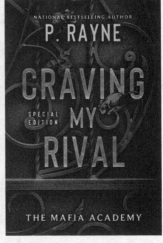